DEBBY LEE

THE CAREGIVER AT WOUNDED KNEE

ENDURING HOPE
BOOK FOUR

YOU are the reason we do what we do here at Barbour Publishing. We promise that we will always use our God-given talents to produce content with you in mind—and that we will remain biblically faithful, no matter what.

Thank you for being the heart of our business.

Print ISBN 979-8-89151-290-0
Adobe Digital Edition (.epub) 979-8-89151-291-7

All scripture quotations, unless otherwise noted, are taken from the King James Version of the Bible.

Published by Barbour Publishing, Inc., 1810 Barbour Drive, Uhrichsville, Ohio 44683, www.barbourbooks.com

Our mission is to inspire the world with the life-changing message of the Bible.

Printed in the United States of America.

Praise for *The Caregiver at Wounded Knee*

Debby's words captured my attention from the beginning of this story. Although I knew of the history of the massacre at Wounded Knee, she wove a tale so real I felt like I was living in Rose's shadow. I felt the deep love she had for her people and her family and her fierce defense against injustice. If you like a love story that is filled with historical details, you won't want to miss this one.

–Karen Kinney, author of *Before the Sun Sets,*
third place finalist/winner of the 2024 Faith Hope
and Love Readers Choice Awards

Debby Lee pours her heart onto the page in this vivid telling of a strong and brave woman determined to right injustices for her people, despite battling personal and family demons. Does God work things for our good during even the greatest pain, tragedy, or grave injustice? Her characters' honest response to that question is particularly poignant. Mercy, faith, and hope ring true in this tragic yet tender historical.

–Naomi Musch, award winning author of
Courting the Country Preacher, Season of My Enemy,
and more historical Christian fiction.

The Caregiver at Wounded Knee is a beautifully crafted, heartfelt story of resilience and hope. You will be inspired by Rose Rushing Water, a compassionate nurse from the Lakota tribe, as she faces prejudice and a devastating tragedy that upends her beliefs. Her tender romance with Nathaniel Gray Cloud adds warmth and depth to her journey toward faith, illustrating that even in the darkest moments, love and understanding can lead to hope.

–Darlene Panzera, ACFW Carol Award-winning author
of *The Groom She Thought She'd Left Behind*
(The Runaway Brides Collection)

DEDICATION

To those who have endured the heartache of betrayal, injustice, and wounds inflicted so deep you thought your heart would never be whole again: God sees you. He hears your cries and He saves all your tears. Do not let the horrid actions of selfish, unscrupulous people keep you from experiencing His love. I like to hope—believe—that with time, patience, and proper support, healing is possible.

ACKNOWLEDGMENTS

Many thanks to those who helped bring this book to fruition. I owe a debt of gratitude to those on the Pine Ridge Reservation for showing me around the site of the massacre and answering my questions.

To the Inklings critique group: Kyle Pratt, James Pratt, Heather Alexander, Barbara Blakey, Julie Zander, Joyce Scott, and Tammy Clark: Your input, critiques, and suggestions are appreciated so very much.

To my prayer group at Crossroads Foursquare Church: Thank you for your support, your encouragement, and as always, the prayers.

Thank you to my fabulous agent, Tamela Hancock Murray.

Many thanks to the team at Barbour Publishing for giving me the honor of writing this story, and for all the hard work you've done to bring this book to publication.

AUTHOR'S NOTE

This book presents a particular interpretation of a historical event, namely the Wounded Knee Massacre. Other interpretations exist, and this book is not intended to be a definitive or exhaustive account. While this story is based on historical research, some interpretations of events or motivations may be speculative. While I did my best to be as historically accurate as possible, any mistakes within the narrative are purely my own.

And we know that all things work together for good to them that love God, to them who are the called according to his purpose.
Romans 8:28

CHAPTER 1

Pine Ridge Reservation, South Dakota
Home to the Oglala Lakota People
October 1890

An overturned wagon lay sprawled along the road ahead. The splintered axles faced the heavens like gnarled fingers reaching into the cloudless blue sky. The sight marred the tranquil sea of short wild grasses swaying in the gentle breeze.

Even at a distance, Rose Rushing Water heard children wailing. A prayer escaped her lips for the victims of the terrible crash and that the wagon she rode in wouldn't suffer the same tragic fate.

She clutched the seat and reached for her medical bag next to her trunk. Children in peril. It always spurred her into action. Even more so, since Boston.

"Whoa," her driver hollered.

Before the wheels ceased to roll, she leaped from the conveyance, quickly tied on her Red Cross apron, hiked up her skirts, and sprinted to the carnage.

Two gunshots, in rapid succession, pierced the air.

Rose flinched at the sight of the wagon driver, who held a revolver in the midst of the wreckage. Trickles of blood flowed from the heads of two dead mules still hitched to the overturned wagon. For a half second she wondered why the man would shoot not one but two expensive commodities. Then she saw the beasts' mangled legs.

Such a costly tragedy, but perhaps the meat could be salvaged. The residents of this community couldn't afford to waste food.

Shoving the thoughts aside, Rose assessed the injured.

A man and woman sat leaning against the broken sideboards. Rose stepped over three torn burlap bags and hundreds of smashed potatoes and carrots to reach them. This family had lost not only their precious animals but the load of vegetables too.

"Help," the woman cried. Two children, one hardly more than a toddler, clung to each other next to her. Tears streamed down their thin cheeks.

"I'm coming." Rose ducked under one of the broken axles, likely the cause of the accident.

"There now, little ones. I'm a nurse, and I'll do everything I can to make your papa and mama better." She scanned the sobbing boy and girl, saw no obvious injuries, and turned her attention to the wounded.

The man's forehead oozed blood. Rose placed her fingers to his carotid artery. Feeling a steady pulse, she exhaled a grateful sigh. "Sir, can you hear me?"

His lack of response troubled her. Long measures of unconsciousness could signal a serious head wound. "Can you tell me your name, sir?"

She pulled a bandage from her bag and wrapped it around his head over the bleeding gash. "Sir, please respond if you can hear me," she said, noting his leg, twisted at an odd sideways angle.

Broken.

She hollered to her driver. "Find me two long, stout sticks, then ride to Pine Ridge as fast as you can. Bring back Dr. Eastman. Tell him to bring back a wagon or buckboard to transport patients."

The man scowled. He probably wasn't used to taking orders from a woman. Like that mattered when the parents of two small children were suffering! Stifling her exasperation, she infused more kindness into her tone. "Please."

The driver grumbled as he spun to the left then the right. "I don't see any sticks," he said, before hopping onto the wagon seat she'd just vacated. He drove off, thankfully at a good speed. The Pine Ridge Agency was only five miles away, but there and back could take close to an hour, especially if Dr. Eastman wasn't readily available.

Rose tied off the bandage. "I hope the driver hastens his journey to town," she mumbled to herself before turning to the woman.

"My children." Large dark eyes were filled with worry, and fear laced her tone.

"Mama." The little ones hugged her.

The woman wrapped her arm around them and winced in pain as she clutched them to her side.

"Ma'am, I'm Rose Rushing Water. Let me help you, please."

"My husband, is he all right?"

"I'll do everything I can to see he recovers." She reached to take the woman's pulse.

"Aah." The woman pulled from Rose's grasp.

"I'm sorry. I didn't mean to hurt you." The swollen appendage had turned a deep bluish-purple hue. "Can you wiggle your fingers for me, please? I need to assess if your wrist is broken or merely sprained."

The woman clasped and unclasped her fingers. "My name is Sarah White Bird. This is my husband, Joshua, and these are our children."

"Nice to meet you," Rose said.

Sarah continued. "We heard the first axle break. Joshua told me to grab the children and jump. We did, and then the other axle broke." A sob shook poor Sarah. "Joshua jumped just as the wagon overturned. A wheel rolled over his leg."

"Mama." The boy patted his mother's shoulder. Sarah smiled at her son and tousled his hair.

Such little dears, but weren't they all? The sheer helplessness of not being able to do more tore through her.

Rose prayed their father's head wound wasn't too serious. Poverty ran rampant through so many reservations, and without Joshua, the family would be mired deeper in it.

Sarah ran her fingers along her daughter's long braid, attempting to smooth it.

"I'm glad you can move your fingers all right. It's likely just sprained." Still, she hoped to splint Sarah's arm as a precaution.

Rose glanced about and huffed. The driver had neglected to locate two stout sticks to stabilize Joshua's broken leg. But there wasn't much he could have done anyway. Trees weren't in ample supply on the rolling hills around them. She scanned the horizon for something suitable to form a splint.

She didn't see anything, so she stood and eyed the disabled wagon. She circled it and pulled hard on a broken but stubborn sideboard. It popped loose with a fierce snap. The force sent her back two steps and lodged a painful sliver into her palm.

She dropped the board and pulled out the inch-long splinter. There was a small gush of blood. This would definitely need iodine.

Her stomach rolled. It was one thing to care for others' wounds, but something else altogether to treat herself. She grabbed another bandage from her medical bag and wrapped it around her hand; then she gritted her teeth, sucked in a breath, and tilted her face to the heavens.

Sarah began singing a lullaby to her family. The gentle melody comforted them. Or so Rose hoped.

Joshua moaned and reached for his head.

The air flew from Rose in a whoosh, and she hurried to his side. He blinked a few times and opened his eyes. They seemed to focus, and relief flooded through Rose. The man was coherent. It meant that he'd be all right, eventually.

Joshua emitted a croaky groan. "Sarah? Children?"

Sarah stopped singing and grasped her husband's hand. "Joshua." Tears choked her voice. Joshua nuzzled his head against his wife's shoulder. The children snuggled between them.

The scene was so tender, so poignant, Rose felt like an intruder. What a delight it would be to have a family, a sense of belonging, love. The thought pierced deep into her soul, as fierce and painful as the splinter in her palm only a few minutes ago. But love and family would have to wait. The Indians, like the White Birds, needed her. She pushed her secrets deeper into the recesses of her mind, fearing they would someday fester. But they would serve no purpose here and now.

She splinted Joshua's leg with the boards from the wagon and bandaged his head while thinking of how she'd graduated from nursing school, in spite of everything. Now, she was determined to serve her people. Her chin inched up a notch. And she would, no matter what the stodgy folks in the East thought of her.

The sound of pounding horses' hooves snapped her back to the vast, empty, wind-whipped prairie. She shaded her eyes with her hand.

Two horses pulling a buckboard galloped toward the scene. Another horse and rider approached as well. The men pulled the reins and the animals lurched to a stop. The single rider's horse reared, its hooves clawing the air. The riders quickly dismounted and looped the reins around a broken axle.

She recognized Dr. Eastman, and not just by his medical bag. The man was legendary back East among the Friends of the Indian groups, though in Rose's eyes those stuffy snoots were anything but friends.

The other fellow with Dr. Eastman was tall, sported a deputy's uniform, and moved with confidence.

"Uncle Nathaniel!" The children raced to him. He swept them into his arms, stood, and strode to the injured. His eyebrows scrunched together, his mouth a thin line, as he hovered over Dr. Eastman. How strong he must be to hold his niece and nephew as though they weighed no more than feathers.

Try as she might, she couldn't pull her gaze away from him. Was he Sarah's or Joshua's brother, or was he an uncle by marriage?

Did it matter?

Rose cleared her throat, but she was still finding it hard to breathe. Sometimes children made her uneasy, for reasons she didn't care to ponder at the moment. That secret threatened to bubble to the surface. She had to go, now!

She lifted her hems and proceeded down the road.

"Wait!"

A strong hand gripped her elbow. She turned and tilted her head up to see Nathaniel's face. His prominent cheekbones and thick black hair held her attention captive.

"I want to thank you for caring for my little sister and her family."

So, he was Sarah's older brother.

He pulled off his cap and clutched it between his fingers. "You won't have to walk into town. If you wait a few moments, I can take you."

He possessed strength *and* compassion. She noted the absence of a wedding ring and then struggled to steer her thoughts to more practical matters as he returned to assist the doctor. She didn't want anything to distract her from everything she'd worked so hard for.

How was she to keep whimsical hints of romance from taking root in her heart?

Nathaniel Gray Cloud struggled under the weight as he loaded his brother-in-law onto the buckboard bound for Dr. Eastman's clinic.

Joshua wouldn't die of his head injury, but that didn't stop Nathaniel from worrying about him. Or about Sarah and their children.

The loss of the wagon and the load of produce meant that there would be no money to purchase the goods to see them through the harsh winter months. Joshua wouldn't be able to work for a while at least. And the added doctor bills?

How would they survive?

Anxiety stampeded over him, and he chased it away.

If anxiety haunted him, he'd be no use to Sarah and the children, Chaske and Winuna. Every chance he had, their birthdays, Christmas, he lavished presents on them. New shoes, clothes, toys, and sweets, when he could find them at Dawson's store in town.

Just last week he'd given Sarah a new shawl and blanket in exchange for her mending his trousers. He'd given them to her in secret, hoping he wouldn't wound Joshua's pride. It was a lot for such a small task, but Nathaniel didn't mind. Because that's what family did for one another.

He stepped to Sarah's side and draped an arm over her shoulder. "Don't worry, he'll be fine. When you're done at the clinic, I'll drive you and the children home. I'll chop firewood for you while I'm there."

"Thank you," Sarah replied. He helped her onto the buckboard's seat, mindful of her splinted arm, then deposited the children in the rear of the wagon. Dr. Eastman chirruped to the horses, and the buckboard rolled down the road.

"Would you mind dropping me off at the clinic?"

He jumped at the voice behind him and pivoted.

The woman held out her hand. "By the way, I'm Rose Rushing Water." Miss Rushing Water raised her eyebrows at him. A smile lit her eyes.

So this was his best friend's sister. Peter hadn't mentioned how pretty she was.

"We're the only ones left," she said. "I appreciate your offer of a ride."

Nathaniel glanced north, south, east, and west. She was right. How could he have forgotten she was there? What a chump he'd been. So riddled with worry about his sister and her family, he'd neglected the woman who'd found and tended to them.

Had he even said thank you?

"My apologies, Miss Rushing Water. I'm Nathaniel Gray Cloud."

Her eyes twinkled. "You must be the Nathaniel my brother wrote to me about."

"Probably. By the way, thank you for caring for my sister and her family. I shudder to think what might have happened if you hadn't come along."

Her smile grew. "You're welcome."

"Certainly I'll give you a ride to the clinic. Do you mind riding astride?"

She shook her head and chuckled. "I don't mind if you don't. It's a good thing I have wide skirts."

He added, "And my horse can easily carry two."

Not only was she beautiful and funny, but she was smart too. She had informed Dr. Eastman of Sarah's and Joshua's injuries using words he'd never heard before. Compassion had flowed from her as she had spoken with his nephew and niece.

Nathaniel placed a foot in the stirrup and hoisted himself up. He extended his arm to Miss Rushing Water. "We're not so formal out here like in some places."

She guffawed. "Not like in Boston."

He hoisted her up, and she landed with a thud behind him. There she sat, unmoving, quiet and still for a moment.

Finally, he said, "You'll have to scoot closer and hang on so you don't fall off."

She inched forward a bit and placed her hands on his sides. "I won't fall off."

Was that a note of curt edginess in her tone? What happened to the adventurous spirit he'd seen only moments ago? Had he offended her in some way? How could he have? They had just met!

Ladies could sure be fickle sometimes.

He blew out a sigh, reached behind him, grabbed hold of her, and pulled her so close the buttons of her overcoat pressed into his back.

"Oh!" she cried.

"Hang on." Nathaniel kicked his horse's flanks, and the animal took off.

CHAPTER 2

Nathaniel clenched his jaw as he strode to his horse from Dr. Eastman's medical clinic. He dreaded leaving his brother-in-law. But if the man was to fully recover, he must remain in the care of medical professionals.

He thought of his sister and ached even more at the unfortunate predicament. At least the entire family had survived the accident. He'd asked a fellow tribal officer, Coyote Who Sneaks, to salvage the meat from the dead mules in exchange for keeping a portion of it. Though the man was unmarried and had no family, he demanded half of the meat. That left half for his sister and her family but did little to assuage the financial loss.

Miss Rushing Water exited the clinic and handed him a heavy burlap bag. "Miss Goodale and I packed this for your sister and her children."

"Thank you, ma'am. Elaine Goodale is a kind woman. She's allowing me the use of her wagon so I can drive Sarah and the children home. We're leaving as soon as we get loaded. Please tell Miss Goodale I'll return her wagon later tonight."

Miss Rushing Water tucked a strand of flyaway hair into the knot at the nape of her neck. "I'll do that. She does seem kind, and she's a good teacher too."

"Yes." Nathaniel rummaged through the bag and saw a wheel of cheese, a fresh loaf of bread, and a small sack of beans. Sarah and the children would eat well that night and for the next few days. Then he spotted two small toys, and his eyes misted.

"I hope your niece will like the rag doll and your nephew the carved buffalo. I picked them up at Dawson's General Store. I thought the toys would be a comfort to them while their father is recuperating here at the clinic."

In spite of the frigid temperatures, his heart warmed at her gesture.

"They will." His voice choked with emotion. Ever grateful, he tipped his cap at her, tucked the burlap sack into the rear of the wagon, and climbed onto the seat.

"You're welcome. Your brother-in-law is in good hands. I plan on staying at the clinic, sleeping in one of the exam rooms, until my house across the street is ready."

"It's nice to know Joshua will have someone nearby if he needs anything."

"Dr. Eastman and Miss Goodale, of course, will also help. We'll watch your brother-in-law closely. If any change occurs, I'll send someone for you right away."

"Thank you. I have a bed in the tack room in the barn down the street from here, where the deputies keep their horses. That's where I'll be after I'm done at Sarah's." He turned his gaze to his sister. "All ready?"

She nodded.

"It was nice to meet you, Miss Rushing Water."

She stepped away from the wagon and waved. "It was nice to meet you too, Mr. Gray Cloud. I'm sure we'll be seeing each other in town from time to time."

He tipped his hat, chirruped to the horses, and steered them toward Sarah's homestead. Chaske and Winuna were snuggled under an army-issued woolen blanket in the wagon bed.

His thoughts vacillated between worry for Sarah and admiration for the beautiful and educated Miss Rushing Water. It had been thoughtful of her to purchase toys for the children.

The Oglala people were fortunate to have this new nurse at the agency. She seemed professional and dedicated to her work. She could help the tribe in so many ways, especially with the elders and children. They suffered terribly from whooping cough, measles, and numerous other ailments. And they died at an alarming rate.

He hoped Miss Rushing Water could change that. In the short time he'd been with her, he had noticed how she'd allayed her patients' anxiety and earned their trust. He wished he could earn his people's trust as easily, but that wasn't likely, not with the tribal police uniform he wore. So many Lakota were mistrustful of anyone aligned with the government.

The horses whinnied and stomped.

"Brother?" Sarah said.

With a smidgen of embarrassment, he realized he'd steered his animals off the rutted trail. Nathaniel shook his head. Had his thoughts been that lost in the clouds?

Yes.

He blew a sigh into the early evening air. Wisps of fog momentarily obscured his vision, and then he guided the team back onto the proper path.

His sister was strong and capable. She and her children would be all right until Joshua could return to work. The children, though young, were no strangers to hard work. Such was life for all those who called the Pine Ridge Reservation their home. That wouldn't stop Nathaniel from helping around the small farm until Sarah's sprained wrist healed though.

If the stories he'd heard were true, Miss Rushing Water had to be a strong woman to survive school back East. He wondered how she'd found the resources to fund her education. And what persuaded her to travel to such a place to study medicine? Many of the Oglala women knew about healing without attending fancy universities.

Where had Miss Rushing Water said she'd studied?

Boston. That was it.

Sarah's children let out a whoop when the little cabin on the homestead appeared on the horizon.

Lord above. He'd been dreaming of Miss Rushing Water again.

The sun was halfway over the western horizon. Just enough daylight left for him to complete Joshua's nightly chores. Milking the cow and chopping wood wouldn't take long.

He stopped the horses in front of the cabin and jumped from the seat to lift the tots from the back of the wagon. They scampered inside, likely hungry by now. He handed his sister the burlap bag of food then tied the reins to the hitching post near the water trough.

"You feed the children. I'll take care of the chores."

Sarah nodded and ducked inside.

Nathaniel drew a bucket of water from the well and poured it into the water trough. The horses could drink while he did the chores.

The cow mooed when he entered the warm sod barn. Roughly thirty minutes later he'd finished the milking and taken the tin pail inside to Sarah. He snuggled Chaske and Winuna a moment, then stepped outside. He chopped wood until his shoulders ached, and with each swing of the ax, his anxiety dissipated. Not only did the chores help alleviate his worries, they would also keep Sarah and the children from freezing that night.

Would Miss Rushing Water be warm enough in the tiny room at the clinic until her home across the street was ready? Would she need firewood as well? If so, he'd be pleased to chop some for her.

What was he doing, thinking of her again? He steered his thoughts to more practical matters.

The potbellied stove in the clinic quarters emitted a fair amount of heat, but not nearly enough considering how cold the Dakota nights could be. He logged a mental note to check on Joshua and Miss Rushing Water when he got back to town.

Later, when he'd stacked a sizable amount of wood by the front door, he filled his arms with enough to keep the family warm for the night. Then he strode into the dimly lit one-room cabin and dropped it by the fireplace.

"Thank you." Sarah handed him a rounded piece of fried bread with wonderful-smelling cheese melted on top.

Famished, he bit into it and chewed briefly before swallowing. "What kind of brother would I be if I left my sister and her family to freeze?"

She smiled and rubbed his shoulder with her good hand. Nathaniel moved to the small bed where his nephew and niece slept hugging their new toys. He patted their heads, careful not to wake them, and moved toward the door. "I'll come back at first light and let you know how Joshua is doing."

"I'd appreciate that." She dropped onto a chair, cradled her wounded arm in her lap, and stared up at him. Dark half-moons showed under her eyes, and weariness shrouded her face.

Nathaniel shoved the last bite of bread into his mouth and donned his cap. "I gotta get Miss Goodale's wagon back to town and check on Miss Rushing Water, uh, I mean Joshua."

Sarah arched her eyebrows, a hint of a smile on her lips.

The need to justify his actions climbed up his windpipe and tumbled out of his mouth. "Don't give me that look. Our people need someone besides Dr. Eastman with knowledge of modern medicine. For the sake of our tribe, I don't want to see anything happen to her."

A grin dimpled his sister's cheeks. Did she think he was sweet on the woman?

He cleared his throat. "I'll see you in the morning."

Rose said goodbye to Miss Goodale and was about to close the clinic's door when a tall man with a bushy mustache entered.

He removed his cap. "Good evening. I'm Agent Daniel Royer. I take it you're the new nurse, Miss Rose Rushing Water?"

"Yes, I'm pleased to meet you." She closed the door, and they made small talk for a few minutes before he excused himself to speak with Dr. Eastman in the part of the clinic that served as a kitchen.

The front room was darkening. Rose lit the lamp and dropped into the rocking chair by the potbellied cookstove. She opened her newest medical book but hadn't read more than three pages when whooping and hollering echoed outside.

Agent Royer stormed into the room, tugging at his collar. Even in the dim light, she noted sweat beading on his forehead.

Rose asked, "Are you all right, sir?"

"As long as those dancers don't get all riled up, I will be. Are *you* all right?"

A scoffing sound flew from her lips. "Of course. Dancers you say?" Could he be referring to the Ghost Dance? She'd read newspaper articles from her younger brother Kaneenawup about Wovoka, the shaman from out West who'd invented the Ghost Dance. This man, whom many people revered, was attempting to bring back traditions that her people had lost. How exciting. Oh, how she wished to be part of it. She'd missed so much while she'd been away.

Practicing her native customs and speaking her language had been forbidden at the university. That hadn't stopped her, though, leading to more than one altercation with the stiff-necked dowager in charge. Rose had tried several times to teach the headmistress about natural herbs that helped reduce fevers and cure coughs, but the woman only scoffed and stuck her pointy nose in the air.

And then there was the unfortunate incident with Mr. Leon that had sent Rose packing for home sooner than she'd liked. Her chest constricted at the memory of those poor children. Drawing in a deep breath, she willed her hands to stop shaking.

"Miss Rushing Water?" The agent tugged at his mustache.

"Um, yes?" She'd been woolgathering again.

"You may think the dancers mean no harm, but it frightens the settlers. Dr. Eastman says it's nonthreatening, but for all we know, it's a war dance. The sooner the army puts a stop to it, the better for all of us."

Rose sucked in a breath. She chomped on her lower lip to keep from spouting that it most certainly would not be better for her people to forsake dancing. They had sacrificed far too much already, and still, it didn't seem to be enough to please the settlers. Would anything, other than their extermination, ever be enough to please them?

An icy chill ran the length of her spine as an unwelcome memory invaded her mind. The university requested that the students attend Mass every Sunday. There, Rose heard a mean-spirited nun whispering to Mr. Leon that the sooner the Indians were exterminated, the better it would be for the country. Rose had bitten her tongue to keep from lashing out at the woman.

She leaned back in the chair and hid her face behind her book. When the agent opened the door and stepped outside, Rose listened for the sounds of the Ghost Dance.

Moments later, the jangling of bridles and harnesses drew her attention. She stood, set her book on a crate, and reached for her shawl.

Could that be Mr. Gray Cloud returning with Miss Goodale's wagon? What would he have to say about the Ghost Dance? She stepped outside, intending to find out.

The night air contained a chill, and she shivered under her thin crocheted garment.

Mr. Gray Cloud drove past the clinic, his shoulders hunched, his face drawn and weary looking. She watched him climb from the seat and lead the team toward the barn at the end of the street, where he stayed.

Rose poked her head into the clinic. The sleeping powders she'd fed Joshua earlier were doing their job. He snored like a bear in hibernation.

She removed her shawl, yanked her coat from the hook, and slid it on. She hurried to the barn, hoping to speak with Mr. Gray Cloud. The moment she entered the structure, the earthy aromas of leather, horse tack, and wild grasses rose to greet her.

His back was to her. For a moment she watched him as he wielded a pitchfork to feed the stock. He moved with fluid, graceful motions. She imagined their forefathers using bows and arrows with as much ease when they hunted buffalo.

She swallowed hard, as if a piece of dry bread had lodged in her throat. "Excuse me, Mr. Gray Cloud. May I speak with you a moment?"

He turned and faced her. Strands of his coal-black hair had worked loose from his braid and clung to his sweat-streaked forehead. He gripped the pitchfork like a spear, resembling a warrior going into battle, and perhaps he was.

"What is it, Miss Rushing Water?" His soft tone belied his powerful stance.

She swallowed again, struggling for words, but the stubborn lump in her throat refused to move. "Wh–what can you tell me about the Ghost Dance? Can you help me be a part of it?"

He rammed the pitchfork tines into the earthen floor, creating a twang. His eyes widened, and his chest heaved.

Startled, Rose gasped in shock. The poor man looked terrified, but why? Shouldn't he be proud that their people had found a way to express themselves? Her thoughts whirled as she tried to make sense of his reaction.

In the space of her next breath, he was at her side, gently placing a hand at the small of her back. His dark eyes locked with hers.

"Mr. Gray Cloud. I'm sorry—" She gulped, unsure what exactly she was sorry for.

"Miss Rushing Water," he replied. His voice faltered for a moment. "Promise me, for your safety, you will have *nothing* to do with this Ghost Dance, and never mention it again."

CHAPTER 3

A good night's sleep hadn't abated Rose's frustration. As the morning sun peeked over the eastern horizon, warming the chilly air, she exited the clinic and stepped out into the street, wishing she could slam the door behind her. The fact that her patient needed rest kept her from doing so. No nurse worth her salt allowed her personal feelings to interfere with her duties to those in her care.

But how could Mr. Gray Cloud have done that? He'd threatened her to keep away from the ghost dancers or he'd speak to her older brother Peter about the matter. She huffed.

Nathaniel Gray Cloud had been lucky, in her opinion. Raised on the reservation among his family with plenty of opportunities to learn the Lakota language and traditions. He hadn't been taken away to live in a residential school as she had after the deaths of her parents. And from there she'd been sent to live in a city full of white people. Her brown skin had drawn stares and whispers.

Boston had often been so noisy she wanted to plug her ears with cotton to ease her headaches. The shops and buildings and people lived crammed together in the smallest of spaces. It had been like living in a stuffy wardrobe.

A melancholy sigh escaped her lungs, snatched away by the wind and carried across the rolling plains. Though she was grateful for her college education, feelings of missing out on a traditional upbringing in this beautiful place left a hollow ache in her middle.

The cold wind whipped circles around her, swirling her skirt around her legs. If Mr. Gray Cloud refused to teach her about the Ghost Dance, she'd seek the information elsewhere. Her brothers would help her. At least Kaneenawup would.

Kaneenawup. He was named after the Saulteaux chief from Canada, and his name meant He Who Sits like an Eagle. He clung to his Indian name rather than accept the white one his teachers had insisted he answer to. His rebellion against learning the white man's ways often landed him in trouble with teachers and school boards alike.

The letters she'd received from him most recently contained vivid descriptions of the ceremonies he'd attended. She could hardly wait to see him again. If anyone could teach her about the Ghost Dance, it would be him.

Kaneenawup had been only ten years old when their parents died from the measles. Peter had been sixteen; and she, just twelve. How terrible it had been for the three of them to be separated. She'd heard that Kaneenawup had been a handful. It was no wonder!

Shoving aside the painful memories, she strode toward the agency's administration building, intending to speak with Peter or Agent Royer. She hoped, at the very least, they'd have information about Sitting Bull. She'd had the pleasure of meeting the respected chief when Buffalo Bill's Wild West show had come to Boston. The man had a persistent cough that needed to be checked, and Rose had eagerly volunteered for the task. She thought him wise beyond his years as she tended him and he regaled her with stories of buffalo hunts and wild horses that had once roamed the reservations.

The Great Chief was a controversial figure, lauded by some, despised by others. Her plan to locate him might take a bit of detective work. If he wasn't out touring with Buffalo Bill, he'd be at his home on the Standing Rock Reservation. That was north of Pine Ridge, but if she wrote to him, she hoped that someone would read the letter to him and he'd remember her. Perhaps they'd write a reply to her on his behalf. She'd love the opportunity to see him again, if her duties at the clinic allowed her time to travel to his reservation.

By the time she stepped into the Pine Ridge Agency administration building, the wind had chilled her to the bone. She rubbed her hands together, then over her arms. In the years she'd been gone, she'd forgotten that the strong winds had such a bite to them. Next time she'd remember to wrap her shawl around her head.

"Excuse me," she addressed the clerk seated at the front desk. "I'd like to see Peter Rushing Water or Agent Royer, please."

The clerk pushed a pair of wire-rimmed glasses up the bridge of his nose. "Your name and the nature of your business?"

She straightened her spine. "I'm Rose, Peter's sister. I arrived from Boston last night. I'm a trained nurse. I'd like to speak with either of them and become better acquainted with the goings-on here on the reservation."

The clerk shuffled a handful of papers on his desk. "Peter's out. Royer's busy."

"When will my brother return? May I at least schedule an appointment with the agent?"

"Don't know. I'll tell Royer you stopped by." The clerk rolled a piece of paper into a dilapidated typewriter without so much as glancing at her.

Rose bristled at his curtness and indifference. "Should I stop by later this afternoon? Perhaps then Peter will have returned and Mr. Royer won't be as busy."

The clerk pounded on the typewriter keys.

"Fine." She huffed and turned to leave. Before she reached the door, shouts resounded from outside. The desk clerk leaped from his chair and stomped past Rose, muttering under his breath. He yanked the door open and bolted outside.

Rose followed and nearly bumped into him. He simply stood as if rooted in place. She sidestepped around him to see what caused the commotion.

Peter and Nathaniel Gray Cloud, in their deputy uniforms, sat atop their spooked horses. Her older brother had been diligent about sending her extra money for books and clothes while she attended the university. She wanted to run to him and give him a big hug and say thank you, but this was obviously not the time for that.

Their animals bucked and shook their heads from side to side. The men clutched the reins and clung to the saddle pommels.

She didn't recognize the other deputy standing near them. A scowl marred the man's face. He spit a stream of tobacco juice onto the dirt and folded his burly arms over his chest. His stance indicated he was spoiling for a fight.

She focused her attention on another man standing with his back to her. Dressed in buckskin, he wore a long dark braid that hung to his waist. Three feathers graced the beaded band around his head. He must be a warrior. His fists were clenched.

Two additional men, also dressed in feathers and buckskin, stood close to his side. Most noticeable were their shirts. Fashioned from white leather, they had fringe along the sleeves, and fancy blue embroidery covered the back.

More shouting filled the air, this time in the Lakota language. The three men spoke fast and with such venom, she hardly grasped their words.

The fine hairs on her neck prickled.

The desk clerk hustled inside. She hoped he sought Mr. Royer. The agent wouldn't stand for any brawling in the town's streets. He'd put a stop to any nonsense brewing.

The scowling deputy pulled a pistol from his holster.

"Coyote, holster your weapon!" Peter shouted. He brandished his own weapon. He turned to her. "Rose, get inside."

She couldn't. The soles of her feet were frozen to the ground.

The man in buckskin whipped around.

"Kaneenawup!" she shouted. Her baby brother. Why had he shouted at Peter? Why did Peter look ready to arrest his own brother?

Stories she'd heard back East about the Civil War flooded into her mind. Family had fought against family until the blood of both sides soaked the battlefields, scarred land that was pockmarked by cannonballs, wagon wheels, and horse hooves. Her two brothers were the only family she had left. They had no cause to slay each other.

Or did they?

"Stop!" she screamed.

Hiking her skirts, she bolted into the street and stood between them. "Peter, Kaneenawup, please, you can't kill each other."

Her younger brother moved closer. "Sister? Rose?"

"Yes, it's me. My, how you've grown." And how his voice had deepened over the years. She studied him from his moccasin-covered feet to the feathers in his headband. Seeing him clearly proved difficult through the sheen of tears.

He hugged her to him, squeezing her tight. When had this young boy become so strong and tall? She wanted to scream at the white social workers who had torn them from each other.

"What's going on out here?" Mr. Royer bellowed.

Rose startled and jumped, her feet momentarily leaving the dirt.

Kaneenawup leaned closer and whispered, "I just want to dance."

Dance? Merriment bubbled deep in her middle and escaped from her lips. "Do you mean the Ghost Dance? Oh, Kaneenawup, please show me how."

Agent Royer's eyebrows formed an angry V. His boots thumped the boardwalk as he paced. He roared, "There'll be no ghost dancing in town, or you'll all suffer the consequences."

Kaneenawup pulled away from her.

The scowling deputy, the one Peter had called Coyote, cocked his weapon.

"Holster your weapon." Mr. Gray Cloud dismounted and yanked the pistol from the deputy.

Fire filled her younger brother's eyes. He glared at Mr. Royer.

Then in a lightning-quick series of moves, Kaneenawup scooped up a handful of dirt, blew it into the air, and let out a loud yell.

He stomped the ground with one foot, then the other. An even louder yell pierced the air. Excitement hummed through Rose's veins, and she moved to join him.

"Stop right now!" Agent Royer yelled.

Confusion rolled through Rose. She halted mid-step. Why weren't her people allowed to dance? Everyone back East danced at parties and such. It was the very definition of refined behavior. Why would it be so different out here in the West? She strode back to the administration building but stopped before entering, hoping for a private word with the agent.

Before she could speak, Agent Royer's face turned a shade of red that matched the color of the ripe strawberries she'd picked in Boston. He pointed at Kaneenawup. "Arrest that man!"

"O–on what charge?" Rose sputtered.

Agent Royer stepped so close she smelled the musty stench of cigars on his clothing. She stepped back, her shoulder blades pressing against the building's rough exterior.

He wagged his finger in her face. "I expected to see better manners from a Boston-educated girl. You'll do good to forget all Indian nonsense and tend to your own knitting."

Rose gasped and watched him storm into the agency. She looked at her brothers, wondering if they'd defend her or at least explain what had just happened.

Instead she witnessed a scene of heartbreak.

Peter pulled a pair of handcuffs from his pocket and scowled at Kaneenawup. "Sorry, brother, but you were warned."

The scene unfolded before Nathaniel. He sucked in a breath. His stomach twisted at the stricken expression covering Miss Rushing Water's face. How it must distress her to see her two brothers raging against each other. The tragedy was that they both had good reason to spar with the other. One couldn't bear to let go of tradition; the other feared for the tribe's survival if they didn't assimilate.

And some said the Civil War had ended.

"Miss Rushing Water, wait!" He hopped over a frozen puddle and hurried to her side. Her emotions were likely in a tangle, and how could they not be? Perhaps he could help her unravel her feelings.

Every day he warred with himself. He'd been raised on this reservation, spoke the language, and worked hard to care for those mired in poverty and utter despair. But white folks marched across the prairie like soldiers on a military mission of vital importance. If his people didn't adapt, they would be lost.

She turned, her features etched with anguish. "Yes, Mr. Gray Cloud?"

The breeze picked up a lock of her hair and carried it across her forehead. Those dark tresses of hers were a sharp contrast to the white nursing apron she wore. She grasped the stray hair and tucked it behind her ear.

Why did his heart have to hammer in his chest every time she was near? He blew out a breath. "I'd like to see you tomorrow night. I can bring a few eggs from my sister's farm and a pouch of dried berries. It'd be my way of saying thank you for caring for Sarah and her family."

Her lips curved into a smile. "That's very kind of you. I have a stew planned for my supper tomorrow. I'm happy to share it with you."

"I'd like that." Why was he suddenly so tongue-tied?

Her eyes shone like polished onyx stones he'd seen at the Porcupine River. "Tomorrow I'll be moving into the small house near the clinic. You're welcome to stop by and say hello anytime."

"I'm happy to help you move, if you need it."

"Thank you for the offer, but I don't have much, and Peter said he'd help me."

Nathaniel twisted his hat in his hands. If he was to help his people adjust, and thereby survive, he'd need to know more about how the whites lived. What were their customs and traditions? Why were so many of them determined to exterminate his people?

He steeled himself. "I'd like to learn about the white customs you learned while away at college. If you have a few books you could loan me, I promise to return them."

Her smile brightened, and her cheeks turned a healthy shade of pink. "You like books? I read a great many of them while in Boston. The most popular one was *Little Women*, but that's understandable, considering that's where Louisa May Alcott was from."

Nathaniel had never heard of this Alcott woman. She must have been a great medicine woman to have earned the respect of Miss Rose Rushing Water.

She fiddled with the straps of her white apron and ran her hands down the front of the garment to smooth the wrinkles. Her chin lifted a notch as a radiant smile curved across her face. "I got this apron at a lecture I attended, one taught by Clara Barton herself."

He noticed a large red cross on the front, and the sense of pride in her tone. Even on the reservation, he'd heard of Clara Barton and the organization she'd founded, the Red Cross. Thankfulness for her and her medical skills seeped deeper into his soul.

He stammered, unsure of what to say next. Miss Rushing Water was a college-educated woman, and he'd hardly made it through eight years of school here on the reservation. His manly pride soured his stomach. He didn't want her pitying him for his lack of formal education.

"Mr. Gray Cloud?'" She placed her hand on his sleeve. "I need to check on my brothers. I've heard that Kaneenawup can be difficult, but I don't want Peter to make an example of him. If you can be at the clinic at six tomorrow night, I'll show you to my house. I'm happy to share a hot meal with you and any books you want to borrow."

"Six is good." He felt himself blush and stammered, "M–maybe you could call me Nathaniel, since we're going to be seeing more of each other?"

She smiled. "I'd like that. And you can call me Rose."

He straightened his spine. "I need to go too. I must check on my sister. May I tell her how her husband is doing?"

"He's much better, but you can stop by the clinic and see for yourself." She waved over her shoulder and disappeared into the agency's administration building.

He donned his hat. Little good it did to ward off the icy temperatures as he strode from the clinic with a full mind. Miss Rushing Water—Rose—had the ability to mediate between tribal members and white people. There was much he could learn from her.

And she was pretty.

Nathaniel shuddered and shook his head with such vigor his hat slid to one side.

No matter how cute and smart Rose was, he couldn't allow himself to become intoxicated with her. Yes, they had some things in common, but they had more things they disagreed about. She seemed determined to learn and practice the old ways, but the old ways wouldn't ensure the survival of their tribe.

Nathaniel ducked into the clinic. "How's the patient?"

Dr. Eastman yawned. "Just fine. He's still sleeping, but when he wakes, I'll see if Miss Rushing Water can serve him a meal."

Nathaniel's cheeks heated at the thought of her. Not knowing what to say, he cleared his throat, masking his lack of words with a cough.

A sly smile slid across the doctor's face.

"Speaking of Miss Rushing Water," Dr. Eastman said, "you just missed her. She went to the agency's administration building."

"Yes, I saw her outside a moment ago." Nathaniel blew out a breath.

The doctor laced his fingers together and placed them behind his head. He reclined in his chair and grinned as if he knew how Nathaniel felt about Rose.

Nathaniel spun on his heel and hurried from the clinic. He untied his horse from the hitching post and rode toward his sister's farm. He'd tell her about Joshua's condition, and if she so much as mentioned Rose, well, he'd do everything he could to keep her from thinking he was sweet on the woman.

Which he wasn't. Or was he? Dinner with her would be nothing more than a time to discuss an arrangement.

Tomorrow night he would ask her if she'd be willing to speak with

Agent Royer on behalf of the tribe if any sensitive matters arose. He believed she'd say yes and hoped the agent would listen.

With God's grace, maybe the two sides could reach a compromise, one where the Ghost Dance and the practice of their customs could be respected. The Ghost Dance was a harmless dance, after all, not one that was preparation for war. But how to practice it without frightening the Indian agents and settlers and having them believe their lives were in danger? That was a question he had no answer to.

But he prayed it was one they could resolve without bloodshed.

CHAPTER 4

The next evening, after Nathaniel had worked a double shift so Peter could help his sister move into her house, he stood at the front door to Rose's modest home. In one hand, he clutched a pitiful bouquet of wildflowers, the last blooms that would grace the prairie until next spring. In his other hand, he held a cloth sack containing two eggs, which was all his sister could spare, a small pouch of dried berries, and pieces of fry bread. He hadn't wanted to arrive for dinner empty-handed, so he'd asked his sister to prepare what had become a staple in the natives' diet.

Not having a free hand to knock, he paused, contemplating his actions. Half the town could see him standing at her door, holding flowers and a gift, and they likely wouldn't care. But Rose had spent years in the East, where propriety was much stricter. She shouldn't have to worry about propriety on the reservation, but maybe she did. He didn't want to cause her distress.

He inhaled deeply and blew out a breath that left wisps of vapor in the chilly, late-afternoon air. Mindful of her reputation, he had no intention of besmirching it. His stomach fluttered with excitement. Or perhaps hunger? Truthfully, he was hungry.

Did he care too much? Too soon? But he hardly knew her. How *could* he care too much?

Before he could form answers to the questions tumbling in his head, the door popped open and a gust of warmth drifted from the house's interior. Delicious smells wafted through the air and greeted him. He'd been so busy chopping firewood for his sister and doing the milking, he hadn't taken the time to eat lunch. Now his mouth watered in anticipation.

Rose filled his vision. Her white ruffled apron hugged her petite form. Tendrils of ebony hair escaped from their pins and framed her face. A smile graced her lips, and her cheeks turned a delightful shade of pink.

Should he be noticing these things?

His heart thumped in his chest. He wanted to tell her she looked radiant, but his tongue refused to cooperate. So he merely offered her the items he'd brought. "These are for you."

"Thank you." Rose took the bag and peeked inside. "Dried berries. What kind are they?"

Nathaniel liked seeing her happy. His stomach turned topsy-turvy like an upended turtle, and for a moment, he couldn't remember what kind of berries they were. His brain finally tugged itself from the fog. "Buffalo berries. They grow wild where I found them. Sadly, they are done for the season."

She popped one into her mouth. Her eyes widened, and her lips puckered. "They're good. Tart, but good. I'll add these to a cake I'm baking tomorrow and maybe share a piece with you, if you want."

"I'd like that." He hooked his thumbs into his belt, and a blast of cold wind blew over him. His hat flew off his head, and he caught it before it sailed across the prairie.

She stepped aside. "Please, come in out of the cold. Would you like a cup of coffee?"

He entered the home, grateful for the warm and cozy interior. "Yes, thank you."

A sitting room of modest size occupied the front of the house. The small potbellied stove did a good job of heating the space. She ushered him into a small dining area to the left, where he peered through a doorway that led into a kitchen. He noted a large cookstove. A pot of something that smelled heavenly sat on it. As they returned to the sitting room, he noticed a short hallway, which led to what he presumed was the bedroom.

"If you'll excuse me, I need to check on dinner." Rose hurried into the kitchen.

He strode toward the small stove and stretched his stiff, chapped hands close to it. A tall bookcase sat against one wall, a rocking chair not far away.

The coffeepot and tin cups rattled as Rose prattled on about how the brew was prepared in Boston. He could be imagining things, but he sensed she was nervous. Understandably so. The prairie was a different world compared to a big city.

He needed to tread carefully when speaking with her. Conflicts brewed on the reservation like coffee percolating on a hot stove. Every morning, he prayed his emotions wouldn't boil over and leave everyone around him scalded. Fears of serious conflict occurring between his people and the government officials kept him awake at night.

Rose padded into the sitting room and handed him a cup. "Here you are."

"Thank you." Nathaniel took a sip. The steaming brew slid down his throat, a comfort compared to the cold, wind-whipped outdoors. If only he could remain in her snug home for hours and speak with her at length about white customs in Boston. But that would be highly improper, especially at night.

"I hope you don't mind beef stew. I thought it would be a nice warm meal. This place is just as cold as the East Coast."

"I've never been there." Though he stood beside a hot stove, he still shivered. He was tempted to guzzle his coffee but refrained from doing so. The habit of conserving had become necessary due to the ever-shrinking government rations.

Rose glided into the dining area and placed their meal on the small square table. She stirred a crock of stew. Steaming pieces of fry bread sat beside a jar of jam. The aromas wafted into the air, tantalizing Nathaniel.

They sat, and with her clearly reluctant permission, he blessed the food.

"I have questions about the rations, Nathaniel. Why isn't there enough food allotted to everyone, especially the elders and children?" she asked.

"The government keeps cutting our rations. They were only meant to tide us over until we could farm and grow our own food, but this land isn't meant for farming. It's meant for grazing." Though it saddened him, he explained that the buffalo were mostly gone and the Indians had no other way of feeding themselves.

Her eyes seemed to lose their sparkle at this reality. "So how are we to feed everyone? If this land won't produce food, we'll starve. What does the government expect us to do?"

Nathaniel chewed slowly. "I don't know."

They finished the meal in silence. Afterward, she cleared the dishes and they retired to the sitting room.

"So," she said, "you would like to borrow several books that would teach you about white customs. In exchange, I would like to learn the Oglala Sioux language and more about the Ghost Dance. I believe that's a fair trade."

"Rose," he said, "many of our people don't like being called Sioux. It's a name the French gave us, and it means *snake people*, or *snake in the grass*."

She bit her lower lip. How could she have forgotten that? It was the one memory she associated with her grandmother, who had said as much.

"I hate to say it," Nathaniel said, "but Agent Royer and most of the settlers around here don't like us dancing and praying. They believe we're preparing to attack when we do those things."

An unladylike gasp flew from her lips. "But that's not true. It's just a dance. It's not unreasonable for our people to want to hold on to our customs and traditions."

Nathaniel tilted his head back and gazed at the ceiling. "I know that, and you know that, but because of the government's opinion of us, the settlers don't. As misguided as their fears are, they are still afraid. Which means we need to watch our step, literally."

She huffed. "You're referring to the Ghost Dance. From everything I've heard and read about it, it isn't a war dance."

"Be that as it may, they mean to assimilate us into white society, no matter the cost." He squirmed in his seat at the expression on her face.

Her tone increased in volume. "The Irish immigrants still celebrate Saint Patrick's Day and feast on soda bread. The Italians are allowed to speak Italian and practice Catholicism. And they weren't born here. We were!"

"Yes, but the Irish and the Italians don't parade about in loincloths and use tomahawks to scalp women and chil—" He dropped his head into his hands and groaned.

In a husky whisper, she said, "So that's why you don't want me learning any of our traditional dances or customs? To placate the land-grabbers squatting on the land we once called our home?"

Frustration swept over him. His chest heaved with deep breaths. "You don't understand. People remember what happened to Custer and his men."

"They never should have been on *Lakota* land." She scoffed and shook her head.

"Rose, you're not being fair. The settlers don't want the same thing to happen to them or their families."

"I know very well what it's like to lose one's family. I lost mine to diseases spread by settlers and the government officials. I was taken away and missed so much. You don't know what it's like to lose your family, your heritage, pieces of who you are. I do."

He grumbled and scrubbed his hand down his face. "We don't have to obliterate every custom and tradition. We just need to be careful."

She placed her palms on the table, as if to steady herself. "I had hoped you'd teach me about everything I missed out on while I was gone. Now, I'm not so sure I want you to."

"I can tell you all about our history and anything else you want to know. We just can't Ghost Dance down Main Street like it's a powwow after a plentiful buffalo hunt. I'm sorry, but if we're to survive, we need to learn to adapt. Your brother Peter agrees with me."

The hurt emanating from her eyes drove arrows into his heart.

"'Kill the Indian, save the man,' or in my case, woman?"

This wasn't the first time he'd heard those words. Because the government agents believed they had to wipe out the Indian customs and ways in a man in order for him to live in "civilized" society, there was a grain of truth to the saying. They must assimilate or be wiped out, or at the very least, forever feared. That fact slapped his heart once again with a force that left him reeling.

"I—I think you need to leave now," she stammered.

He remembered the books he wanted to borrow. Though it frustrated him, he thought it would be best to ask for them tomorrow or the next day.

"Very well. Thank you for the meal. It was tasty." He donned his coat and hat and left, doubting he'd receive a piece of cake with buffalo berries—tomorrow or ever.

Rose snuggled deeper under her covers, hoping to savor the warmth, but shivers continued to rack her. She should be used to the cold, but a niggling thought convinced her the shivers weren't from frigid temperatures.

People who had just stepped "fresh off the boat" could still practice the customs and traditions of their homeland, but the Indians, who'd been born and lived their whole lives here, couldn't. It wasn't fair!

She rolled over and fluffed her pillow with more force than necessary. For years she'd dreamed of coming home and basking in the culture she'd been denied. Instead, she'd returned to find those traditions seeping away like the ocean's water at low tide. Her throat thickened. Tears threatened to wet her pillow.

Any hope for a few more minutes of sleep dissipated. She emitted a mournful sigh and popped her eyes open. The charcoal-gray sky allowed little light to filter into her small bedroom window.

Rose threw off the covers and shivered as the icy air cut through her flannel nightclothes. She sat up and placed her bare feet on the chilly pine floor. Her feet absorbed the cold, and she gasped in response. Then she hurried to stoke the embers in the potbellied stove in the sitting room and added kindling. The flames grew, and she rubbed her hands together, allowing her body to soak in the heat.

Though this place was as brisk as Boston, the land had a wild, rugged beauty that captivated her imagination. There was so much structure and orderliness in being a nurse, it felt good to take in the uninhabited landscape, unmarred by stone and brick buildings, and breathe in fresh air.

As her hands warmed, she thought of Nathaniel. He'd stood in this very spot last night, warming his own hands. That was before their joyous night went horribly awry. She certainly didn't wish to drive a wedge between Nathaniel and her brother by asking Nathaniel to do something Peter would disapprove of. There must be a way to work out their differences. How could they find common ground?

When the front room was heated, she stepped into the kitchen and reached for the coffeepot. Part of her believed what Nathaniel had said about the settlers and government officials who feared Indian uprisings, but another part hoped the restrictions on native dancing and praying would end.

She'd speak with Agent Royer today and see what he thought about the matter. Hopefully, he would be sympathetic to her relearning the Lakota language. She could secure the agent's blessing for Nathaniel to teach her the parts of it that she'd forgotten so she could communicate better with her patients who didn't speak English. There had been several of them who'd stopped by the clinic. She must tread carefully though.

She'd been chastised for speaking Lakota in Boston. She wasn't sure if the same rule applied on the reservation, but she thought it prudent to find out first.

She hadn't given Nathaniel the books he'd asked for the previous night. If she offered him two or three, she was sure she could persuade him to help her. Once he understood her predicament, she believed he'd teach her.

Unless he decided to be stubborn about the matter.

She sighed, and the empty coffeepot slipped from her fingers. The lid popped off as it clanked onto the floor, and she flinched at the sudden noise.

Nathaniel was kind and cared about their people. He was also exasperating to a point that frustrated her. Granted, he was a tribal police officer, but why must he feel as if he should tell her how to behave? She'd taken care of herself in Boston. She could very well do the same on her own reservation.

She stooped and retrieved the coffeepot, added water and the grounds, and placed it on the cookstove. While waiting for the brew to heat, she closed her eyes and pictured Nathaniel.

Her traitorous heart thrummed at the possibility of seeing him again. If only she hadn't allowed her emotions to seize control of her tongue last night. What could she give him as a peace offering? The pouch of berries on the counter caught her attention. She *had* promised him a piece of cake.

She pulled a bowl from the shelf and was soon mixing the ingredients.

Hours later, she entered the administration building carrying the cake, the pan still warm through the heavy dish towel used to protect her hands. The desk clerk was out, and she breathed a prayer of thanks. There seemed to be animosity between her and the man.

Agent Royer strode into the front lobby, and Rose offered him a slice of the freshly baked dessert. With luck, he wouldn't be like many agents and schoolteachers who forbade the Indians from speaking their native tongue. She hoped to persuade him to grant his blessing for her to learn the Lakota language. Excitement bubbled in her as she dreamed of the endeavor.

The bell over the door jangled. Nathaniel strode into the room and pulled off his hat.

"Hello." Rose used the sweetest tone she could muster. "Would you like a piece of cake?"

The agent faced Nathaniel. "It's really good. She's quite the cook."

"Yes, she is." Nathaniel fidgeted with his hat. "Agent Royer, I'd like to speak with you first chance you have. There are rumors that rations are being cut yet again."

"I'm in the middle of ordering supplies right now, but I can read through the latest reports from the BIA in Washington. I'll see what I can find out. Can you come back in an hour?"

"Sure," Nathaniel replied. "Thank you." His tone told Rose that he didn't put much faith in the Bureau of Indian Affairs.

Rose watched the agent walk away, disappointed that she hadn't had a chance to ask him the questions she wanted. Then she turned to Nathaniel.

He leaned over the pan she held and eyed the cake. "So you don't mind if I have a piece?"

"No, of course not. I'm sorry for my behavior last night." She held up the pan. "Consider this my apology for being so curt with you."

He reached for a piece and bit into it. His eyes brightened, and he nodded, indicating he enjoyed the flavor.

Her pulse raced like a steaming locomotive at his reaction. He seemed to have forgiven her. There was hope for reconciliation.

"This is good," he said, and stuffed the rest into his mouth.

"Thank you," she replied, rather pleased with herself. She had heard the way to a man's heart was through his stomach. Perhaps she should bake for him more often. "So, if Agent Royer agrees, will you teach me the Lakota language in exchange for a few books?"

"Sure, if the agent is all right with it." His eyes shimmered. "Look, I gotta go. I'll stop by the clinic and check on Joshua. Then I have that meeting with Agent Royer. Can you meet me in the barn after your meeting with Agent Royer? And bring a few books then? We can talk about the Lakota language."

"Yes, I can do that." In the meantime she would try to obtain permission from Agent Royer. She couldn't imagine the man denying her the request.

Nathaniel donned his hat and left the clinic.

The desk clerk entered and seated himself in front of his typewriter.

Hoping to take advantage of her time at the administration building, she placed the cake on the clerk's desk. "Help yourself, sir."

The man grunted his thanks but plunked on the typewriter keys so hard she was sure he'd injure his fingers.

Rose strode down the hall with confidence in her steps and entered the agent's office. "I'm terribly sorry to bother you, sir, but I have just one quick question. You don't mind if Nathaniel teaches me the Lakota language, do you? I've been away for so long that I can't seem to remember all the words."

Agent Royer looked up from the papers on his desk, his eyebrows scrunched together, the hard lines of his jaw evident. He sat straighter in his chair, threw his shoulders back, and pointed a finger at her. "That's a bad idea, Miss Rushing Water."

"But, sir," she sputtered, "not all my patients speak English."

"Still, I don't like it. If you insist on ignoring my warning, I better not hear from anyone else that they've heard you speaking anything but English." He frowned even deeper. "I won't answer for what happens if I do."

Rose gulped. Her hands trembled, and she struggled to hold her tongue. What can of worms had she just opened? And how would this affect her and Nathaniel's lesson plans?

CHAPTER 5

Rose stumbled from the agency's administration building, thankful to have escaped what could have been a terrible confrontation with Agent Royer.

She stopped at the post office and delighted in a letter from Bridget, her friend from the university. She stuffed her hands, along with the letter, into her pockets to keep them warm as she hurried home, careful not to step on the frozen puddles. Despite the frigid temperatures, she warmed at the thought of meeting Nathaniel in the barn later. Her lips curved into a smile as she anticipated hearing the Lakota words again and also the legends of her ancestors, provided Nathaniel agreed to teach her. Excitement to hear more about her people hummed through her. She wanted to believe that was the only reason for her joy, but her heart suggested otherwise.

Nathaniel was a strong, handsome man. She had witnessed his compassion for others and his powerful determination to do what he thought was right. Land sakes, could she be sweet on him? She snorted. Of course not. They had only met a short time ago.

She reached her house and hustled inside before a woman passing by could notice the blush creeping into her cheeks. She leaned against the door and placed her hands on her face, hoping to cool the heat gathering there. After years in Boston without any decent male company, she supposed it was natural to desire the attention of someone of noble character.

She sat at the table and pulled the letter from her pocket. Bridget Walsh had been her best confidant and ally from the university and was good about writing to her. Bridget was her only friend during those dark and humiliating days when she'd tangled with the cruel nun and Mr. Leon.

Rose opened the envelope and began to read.

Hello Rose,

Though I'm loath to dredge up painful memories, I must write and tell you that Mr. Leon has once again been accused of terrible deeds, which lends credibility to your story of the events that occurred on that terrible night. I don't know if anything will come of it, but as a friend who loves you dearly, I wanted to let you know. Will keep you posted.

Love always,
Your friend, B

Rose finished reading the missive, folded it, and placed it back into the envelope. She blinked to clear the tears in her eyes and swallowed the lump in her throat. Later, she would spend the evening writing a reply to her friend.

For now, her mind was focused on reacquainting herself with her heritage. That meant she'd be spending long periods of time with Nathaniel.

What would her brothers say about Nathaniel teaching her Lakota? She imagined Kaneenawup would have strong words for her. He'd speak harshly if she spent time with *anyone* he thought was too assimilated.

If Peter found out, he'd likely be angry because he was so protective. She'd have to remember to bring it up with Nathaniel when she saw him.

Dread washed over her at the thought of conflict between her two brothers. To her relief, Peter had released Kaneenawup after the fiasco in town the other day. Using the threat of holding him in jail, Peter had convinced their brother to stop breaking Agent Royer's rules about ghost dancing.

Peter had been good about looking after her and Kaneenawup after their parents died. They had both changed so much while she'd been gone. At least they'd exchanged a few letters. Many times she'd wished for a family picture of her and her brothers, but pictures were expensive, and social workers didn't care to waste money on pictures of Indians.

Rose's pulse skipped faster at the thought of having an ally in her older brother. After all, he and Nathaniel were friends. If Peter trusted Nathaniel, how could he object if the two of them spent time together speaking the Lakota language?

She blew out a breath. Gathering wool wouldn't help one bit to accomplish her goals. Without putting on her coat, she rushed to the lean-to behind her kitchen, grabbed the kettle of last night's leftover stew, then flew out the front door to the medical clinic.

"Hello, Dr. Eastman." She placed the kettle on the potbellied stove. "I brought dinner for you and our patient."

"Thank you. Nathaniel said you were a fine cook. Miss Goodale is going to stop by later. You don't mind if I share it with her?"

"Of course not." Was that a grin on his face? Come to think of it, he always grinned when he spoke of Miss Goodale. An awkward moment stretched between them. Rose turned her gaze to the man sleeping on the cot, his leg still heavily bandaged. "I have only a minute, but I wanted to check on him."

"He's doing well. I'm careful to give him opium sparingly. Just enough to ease the worst of the pain. I don't want him becoming dependent on it. Besides, I have a very limited amount." The doctor folded his arms over his chest, his features drawn into a scowl.

Rose sensed his frustration. More than once, she'd heard him express his annoyance at the lack of medical supplies. She'd have to remember to ask Agent Royer to order more. Rather than stay at the clinic, she decided to wait for Nathaniel in the barn.

"I have to go." She hurried outside and down the road. She stepped inside the deputy's barn and noted the aromas of wild grasses, leather, and horses. Stalls lined one side of the building. In the far corner, reins, bridles, and stirrups hung on nails. Saddles rested on racks, and several folded blankets sat on a table nearby, beside a clock and a kerosene lamp turned low.

"Hello."

Rose jumped, startled at his voice.

Nathaniel stepped from the shadows. His hair hung loose, the tendrils on one side pulled behind his ear. A lopsided grin lifted one corner of his mouth. His eyes seemed to gaze into the depths of her soul.

She blurted, "Are you ready to teach me the Lakota words I've forgotten and more about our native traditions?"

He was by her side in an instant. In a hushed tone he said, "Did Agent Royer say it was all right? If not, we could be in a heap of trouble. Some agents send Indians to jail for speaking their language."

She gulped. "I know that. The agent didn't outright forbid it, as long as we're careful no one else finds out. If you're willing to teach me, I'm willing to take the risk."

Heaven help her. Was she up for this?

Hidden in the barn that housed the tribal police's horses, Nathaniel sat with Rose. His bed and a small chest of drawers provided in exchange for caring for the animals were in the tack room, but that was too intimate of a setting. So they sat side by side on hay bales in the middle of the structure.

He said, "The Lakota word for fever is *sikpasikpa*, which means 'hot' or 'burning.' If someone is injured, they might say *paniya*, which means 'ache.'"

She repeated the words, slowly at first, but with more ease as their lesson continued. It wasn't a prime location for lessons, with no schoolbooks, slates, or desks, but it offered privacy, something he feared they wouldn't receive in her home or the agency's administration building.

He leaned back and listened with a keen ear. He was happy she'd retained so much knowledge of their language, though her pronunciation was wrong in a few places. Pride in her accomplishments swelled in his heart. He almost thought he must be a grand teacher. Their native tongue wasn't an easy one to master.

"Thank you for helping me familiarize myself with our native vocabulary."

"It's been my pleasure." Truly, it was. "I hope to teach you more soon. As you spend time around the elders, more words and phrases will come back to you."

Though the lamp had been turned low, he noted the flush on her cheeks.

"Thank you. You'd be surprised how many elders who come to the clinic don't speak English." Gratitude filled her tone. Her lips curved into a smile, and she ducked her head.

"As long as Agent Royer or other military personnel aren't around, we can converse in our language. No honorable Lakota will complain about us speaking it." At least he hoped they wouldn't. His heart pounded against his rib cage. He leaned closer, admiring the wisps of her ebony hair that had a habit of working themselves loose from her bun and framing her face. He imagined how her hair would look if it were braided. Had she forgotten how to style it that way? If so, perhaps he could ask Sarah to teach her. He swallowed. What was he doing, thinking of how her hair was styled?

"I hadn't realized just how much I missed hearing it while I was away." Her eyes, filled with unshed tears, glistened in the light from the kerosene lamp on a nearby table.

Sensing her pain, his heart lurched, and he put his arm around her. The top of her head fit so perfectly under his chin. He wished he could assure her that she'd never have to leave the reservation again, but he couldn't promise her that. At least she hadn't pulled away from his embrace. That kicked his pulse up a notch.

Silently, he chafed against the policies that told Indians where they had to go and where they had to live. He shuddered, knowing that he and Sarah could have been sent away when they were children. If they had, what would have become of them, or their mother? God rest her soul.

He'd grown up hearing the sobs and wails of parents whose children were forcibly taken to residential schools.

Terrible stories from the Carlisle Indian School in Pennsylvania found their way to Pine Ridge. They had given him nightmares as a child. Sometimes they still did. Even now, the children at the Pine Ridge boarding school could be punished for disobedience by losing the right to see their parents. He rubbed his arms to ward off the sudden chills coursing through him.

From an early age, he'd learned that conforming to white ways was the only way to survive and escape the terrors of being taken from his home and family—lessons he hoped he'd never forget.

He also credited his mother's prayers to *Wakan Tanka*, the Great Spirit, for keeping his family intact. His mother's faith had never wavered.

Rose cleared her throat and sat up straight. "I need to go. It's getting late. Judging from the letters Peter sent me at the university, admonishing me to be careful around men, I suspect he would be upset if he found me alone in the barn with you. Besides, I need to sit with Joshua tomorrow while Dr. Eastman and Miss Goodale go on a picnic."

Nathaniel had long suspected that romance was blooming between the doctor and the pretty school superintendent. What had him most concerned was his friend Peter. How would he respond if he knew Nathaniel was spending time alone with his little sister? He liked to think his friend would be fine with him reacquainting her with the language, but Peter treated his own brother badly for refusing to assimilate.

Voices and a horse's snorting echoed from outside the barn doors and crept through the thin walls. It sounded as if at least two men were intoxicated.

Rose's face blanched. "Is there another door I can leave from?"

"No, there isn't." He almost suggested she hide in the tack room but then remembered that was where his bed was. If she was caught there, it would be worse than being caught speaking their language.

He dared not breathe as he listened. After what seemed like hours, the voices faded into the night. Only then did he exhale the breath he'd been holding.

He leaped to his feet and helped Rose don her shawl. Warmth shot through him as he placed a hand at the small of her back and escorted her to the barn door. "Wait. Before you go, make sure the lights at Agent Royer's house are out."

He opened the door a crack. All the buildings along the street were dark. He guided her out into the night. The sun had long set, and darkness permeated the atmosphere. For her safety, he watched her hurry to her small home. She turned and waved before quickly stepping inside.

Nathaniel hurried to the tribal sheriff's office because he was on night duty. He thanked *Wakan Tanka* for the empty room. He prayed his thanks to the Almighty that Coyote Who Sneaks wasn't there. Nathaniel remembered the noise he'd heard outside the barn earlier, when he was with Rose. For all he knew, Coyote Who Sneaks was the one he'd heard.

He shoveled coal into the potbellied stove and dropped onto the cot provided for those on night duty at the office, hoping to quickly fall asleep.

His mind filled with thoughts of Rose and the list of duties he needed to accomplish the next day. Muck the stalls, feed the horses, and oil the tack, which reminded him of being in the barn with her.

He rolled to his side, fluffed his pillow, and inhaled a deep breath. He had to oversee the tribal members who traveled to the agency to pick up their rations. He hoped no disagreements occurred. His heart lurched every time he heard arguments between his people and agency workers, and he dreaded recording those altercations in the ledger.

Then he had to check on Sarah and see that his nephew and niece were faring well. Sarah would want a report on how well Joshua was healing, which meant he needed to stop at the clinic first. That meant he'd see Rose. Thoughts of her paraded through his consciousness like a fine-tuned marching band.

He threw off his itchy blanket. Sleep eluded him.

The office door opened and banged against the interior wall. Nathaniel's eyes popped open.

The door swung closed.

"Who is it?" Nathaniel asked.

Peter stood there, fists on his hips. "Did I see my sister leave the barn a short time ago?"

CHAPTER 6

As the sun peeked over the eastern horizon and brought light to the gray sky, Nathaniel read through the chapter of Proverbs that coincided with the day and hustled through his morning ablutions and chores.

He mucked the stalls and fed the horses. After ensuring the animals would be all right until afternoon, he stepped into the office and recorded his activities in the ledger.

He omitted any mention of his time with Rose. Her brother and the other officers wouldn't want to read about that anyway. Or would they?

A week had passed since Peter had questioned him about Rose. Nathaniel had told him that Rose had stopped by the barn to update him on Joshua's condition, which was true. He just hadn't told his friend everything, which explained why he felt so guilty.

Nathaniel shuddered. If he was honest with himself, he didn't want to be teased about his growing attraction to her. And he really didn't want to bear the brunt of Peter's likely wrath if he suspected they were courting. Which they weren't. They had met in the barn two more times to discuss the Lakota language, however.

When he finished in the office, he strode to the clinic. "Good morning, Dr. Eastman, Joshua. How is my brother-in-law today?"

"Bored and anxious to go home and be with my family." Joshua reached for a pocketknife and a chunk of wood that resembled half a carved horse.

Dr. Eastman said, "The leg is mending well, and it's only been two weeks. He's been a good patient. I hope Miss Rushing Water will be here soon. There are several children suffering from whooping cough on the edge of the reservation. I need to see them." His voice faltered. "Although I don't think there's much I can do."

"My children!" Joshua sat straight up. He dropped his carving into his lap, his eyes wide. "Will you please check on them, Nathaniel, and see they are all right?"

"Yes, I'll leave shortly." His insides twisted themselves into a knot. He'd heard how children suffered from the disease and seldom survived. He prayed his niece and nephew didn't fall prey to the terrible illness. The knot in his stomach cinched tighter.

Nathaniel cleared his throat, hoping his emotion wasn't noticeable. "Shall I fetch Miss Rushing Water for you now?"

Dr. Eastman stood and strode to the window. "There'll be no need. She and Elaine are walking this way."

Nathaniel noted the doctor's use of the school superintendent's first name. He opened the door, and the women hurried inside. He pushed against the wind to close the door. "Good morning, ladies."

Rose shucked out of her coat and hung it on a peg by the door. Miss Goodale kept her coat on and wrung her hands. "Doctor, it saddens me to say this, but two students arrived at school today and said their younger siblings are sick. I fear it's whooping cough."

The doctor blew out a sigh. "Yes, I've heard."

Miss Goodale's voice was thick with emotion. "I'd hoped we could visit them and, well, at least comfort their parents."

Nathaniel said, "Is there anything I can do? Would it be easier to treat the children if they were all here at the clinic?"

"I don't know," the doctor said. "Elaine, let's leave now." He grabbed his medical bag from the shelf and filled it with a number of bottles and envelopes of powders. "Miss Rushing Water, I don't know how long we will be gone. Will you be all right here for the day?"

"Take as much time as you need. I'll be fine. I have Joshua and Nathaniel here to keep me company." She aimed a smile his way.

"I can't stay, Rose, I'm sorry," Nathaniel said. "I only stopped long enough to check on Joshua. I'm headed to my sister's house to help her with chores, but I'll return this afternoon with a meal for the both of you." He hoped she understood.

"Thank you." Dr. Eastman offered Miss Goodale his arm. They said their goodbyes and took their leave.

Rose's head turned from Nathaniel to Joshua and back again. She stepped to the potbellied stove and fed three pieces of wood into the flames. "We must keep our patient warm. Would either of you like a cup of coffee?"

Joshua nodded and resumed his wood carving. "Breakfast would be nice too, if you wouldn't mind. There are fresh eggs and cheese in the icebox."

Rose opened the small wooden cabinet, reached around several vials of cold medicine, and pulled out a bowl containing eggs and cheese.

Nathaniel waved a hand in her direction. "I'm not hungry, Rose, but please, feed Joshua anything he'll eat. He does need his strength to heal."

"All right." Another enchanting smile lit up her face.

Nathaniel hated to leave. He'd gladly spend all day with Rose, getting to know her better, but his sister needed him. "I have to go, but I'll be back this afternoon."

Joshua locked eyes with him, pleading for assurance. "Please make sure my children are all right. If Sarah can spare the time, ask her to bring Chaske and Winuna into town. I miss them, and I like to think they miss me."

"I'll do that." Nathaniel donned his cap and reached for the doorknob. He was desperate to see his niece and nephew and hoped they hadn't fallen ill. This was as terrifying as having them taken to a residential school. What would Joshua and his sister do—what would he do—if those dear children fell sick and died?

Joshua finished his breakfast and, after taking his pain medication, drifted off to sleep. Though Rose had eaten only a piece of bread with jam before walking to the clinic that morning, she wasn't about to eat food meant for the doctor and his patient.

She kept herself busy doing the dishes, sweeping the floor, and carrying in an armload of firewood. She was tempted to use the hatchet by the stove to chop kindling, but she feared the noisy activity would wake her patient.

Hoping to help ease the hunger on the reservation, she sat at the doctor's desk and filled out an order for one dozen laying hens. She couldn't say how long it would take for them to be shipped to Pine Ridge, but she hoped they would arrive before snow fell. The odds of all twelve reaching the reservation were slim, but if only half arrived, it would make a difference and she'd count herself lucky.

With no other chores to keep her occupied, her thoughts turned into a whirlwind of activity. She fixated on the poor children suffering from an unmerciful sickness, which led her to consider praying. But she snuffed out the thought. Having been forced to pray, whether she liked it or not, didn't inspire her to do it of her own free will.

From there her thoughts spun to her sleeping patient's well-being and then whirled to Nathaniel. Her stomach growled, and she wondered how long it would be before he returned with her noon meal.

Some nurse she was. Perhaps it was boredom that fueled her anxiety. There must be something she could do besides worry. Reading was how she passed her time in Boston, but she dared not leave Joshua alone just so she could fetch a Jane Austen novel.

She straightened her skirt and strode to the doctor's bookshelf. There had to be something there for her to read. Maybe she'd find information that could help with this whooping cough epidemic. After perusing the spines, she settled on a copy of *The Year-Book of Treatment for 1890: A resource for medical and surgical practitioners*. Well, it was no *Sense and Sensibility*, but it would do.

She dropped into the rocking chair by the stove and turned to the first chapter. Though she'd finished at the top of her class in nursing school, there were plenty of words on the pages she couldn't pronounce, let alone knew the meaning of. Determined to learn more for the sake of her patients, she forged ahead. There were no gallant heroes or maidens in need of rescue, no crimes to be solved or villains to capture. Therefore, the book proved to be a very dull read.

The words in front of her seemed to blur. She rubbed her forehead and shifted into a more comfortable position. Between being up late practicing the language with Nathaniel and rising early that morning, she was more tired than she'd thought. Her eyes felt like specks of prairie dust had blown into them. She closed them, but only for a moment.

The door creaked open and shut with a bang.

The book clattered to the floor.

Joshua startled awake. "What was that?"

She stood and rushed to his bedside, offering comfort, and then turned to glare at the intruder.

Peter.

She blew out a sigh. "Did you have to make such a noisy entrance? You know this is a medical clinic. Patients here need their rest."

His face was a mask of anguish. Rose wondered what had him so distraught. A wave of compassion swam through her, and she felt sorry for her harsh words. "I'm sorry for snapping at you, Peter. What's wrong?"

His shoulders slumped. "I just came from the Ghost Dance encampment outside of town, the one by Wounded Knee Creek."

"I heard there was a large camp called the Stronghold, up near the Badlands, but I didn't know there was one much closer."

Her brother groaned. "Well, there is, and they insist on doing that dance."

Rose hadn't heard of the encampment but would ask Nathaniel about it when he returned. She glanced at the clock on the wall. It was well past noon. He should have returned by now. She didn't want to consider what might be keeping him. Sick children? Injury?

"Give me a moment, please, to tend to my patient." Rose spooned another dose of medicine into Joshua. Then she and Peter took their conversation into the kitchen.

Peter drew in a breath. "I saw Kane there."

She gritted her teeth before answering. "He prefers to be called by his full name."

"I know he does." Peter snatched his hat off and crumpled it in his hands.

"Then why don't you call him that? It's the name Papa and Mama gave him. Is it not good enough to be remembered?"

"Rose," he barked.

She stood, her hands clenched at her sides. "Have you forgotten your Lakota name?"

His chest heaved, and his mouth pressed into a fine line. "I haven't forgotten, but I understand that I need to adapt if I'm to keep my job. I've needed this job, Rose, to help keep you fed while you were at the university and Kane fed and clothed as well."

Just then, Nathaniel entered the clinic. "Sorry I'm late, Rose. Sarah fixed a nice meal for me to bring to you and Joshua. I thought we could share it and talk." He shoved the door closed, turned, and stared at Peter.

Though the two men were friends, Rose thought their expressions indicated something amiss between them.

Her stomach turned topsy-turvy, and she stared at her brother. "What's wrong, Peter? Please tell me Kaneenawup is all right."

Peter hooked his thumbs in his belt loops and turned to Rose. "*Kane* refuses to leave the camp at Wounded Knee Creek. He insists on bringing back the old ways, and there's talk of an uprising."

CHAPTER 7

Early November 1890

Rose rushed to stock medicines, laudanum, and willow bark in Dr. Eastman's bag. She stuffed boiled eggs and bread into a knapsack for his lunch. Though he'd slept only a few hours, he hurried from his quarters, snatched up his bag and the knapsack, and bolted from the clinic.

Disease had descended on the reservation like a raging tornado two weeks ago, leaving destruction in its wake.

Nathaniel had visited the clinic long enough to give her a fifteen-minute language lesson for words that pertained to sickness. *Chanhota* meant "fever," *thiyospaye* meant "throat," *t'ezi* meant "stomach." There were a few words that described "hurt," and she never remembered which one meant what. She tried to blame it on weariness, but if she was honest with herself, she'd admit that sometimes it was harder relearning the language than she had thought it would be.

She was so busy, it was a wonder she'd found time to go to Dawson's and turn in her purchase order for a dozen laying hens.

Out of necessity, Joshua had returned to his home to make room in the clinic for the influx of patients, mostly the elderly and the very young. She'd set out every extra cot she could find, and still, the sick occupied each one.

The call came at dawn, a family with an elderly relative this time, racked with either whooping cough or influenza. Rose wasn't sure which, but it made little difference to the ailing patient or their loved ones.

When she'd finished nursing school and returned to the reservation, she hadn't harbored idealistic dreams of saving everyone, but she'd hoped to at least ease the suffering of her people.

She muttered under her breath to no one in particular, "The past few weeks have been chock-full of heartache, and there's nothing I can do to alleviate it."

The supply of bottled medicines was desperately low, leaving the shelves half bare. At times she wondered if they did any good. She couldn't walk around on tenterhooks, hoping for medicine to arrive before the next emergency. Something had to be done.

She shrugged into her coat and hurried to the post office to send a letter to Bridget. As she licked the two-cent stamp and placed it on the envelope, she wondered if there would be a reply with information about Mr. Leon and if he'd faced any repercussions. That sad tragedy with the children wasn't her fault!

Shoving the troubling thoughts aside, she rushed to the administration building. Upon entering, she stormed past the complaining desk clerk and down the hall to Agent Royer's office. "Sir, I need a word with you."

The man looked up from his paperwork and aimed a disgruntled scowl at her. "What is it this time, Miss Rushing Water?"

Rose squirmed but refused to retreat. "Dr. Eastman ordered supplies, instruments, and medicine for whooping cough four weeks ago. The supplies have yet to arrive."

The agent sighed and rubbed his forehead. "I sympathize with you, Miss Rushing Water, I really do, but I can't help it if the supply wagons are slow."

Frustration burned in her middle, and without meaning to, she lashed out. "Are you sure you telegraphed Washington with the order as soon as the doctor handed you the list?"

The man's face reddened. He placed his palms on the desk, scooted back his chair, and stood to his full height. "Yes, Miss Rushing Water," he growled. "I ordered those supplies the moment the doctor gave me the list."

Rose retreated a step, regretting her words. They had angered him, understandably so, but she was exhausted and weary from watching children die. "I'm sorry, sir. I shouldn't have said that. It's just that our elders and our children are dying, and I—I feel so helpless. And I'm sure the doctor feels the same way."

Agent Royer sat and rubbed his forehead. "As do I. I hate to say it, but sometimes delivery drivers get greedy and divert supplies meant for tribes elsewhere for profit."

Taken aback, Rose sputtered before finding her words. "That's terrible." She'd suspected such things happened but didn't want to believe it. Hearing the agent voice his suspicions seemed to solidify hers. And it frustrated her.

"If it's any consolation, I'll wire the BIA and ask about the shipment. As soon as I hear something, I'll head directly to the clinic and let someone there know what they said."

"Thank you, sir. I'll tell Dr. Eastman about our conversation and to expect you—soon, I hope." This gave Rose a small measure of comfort. She said her goodbyes to the agent and the desk clerk and strode from the building.

Later that evening, a wagon lurched to a stop in front of the clinic. She yanked on her coat and bolted outside. A couple spoke frantically about their feverish child, who was lying in the rear of the wagon. Red blotches pockmarked the small boy's body.

Measles.

A disheartened sigh blew past her lips. Her people had far too many diseases to contend with. And, tragically, far too little immunity to fight them.

The boy, hardly more than a toddler, whimpered and scratched the sores. Rose wrapped him in a blanket and lifted him from the wagon.

"Sir," she said to the driver, "will you run next door and ask Deputy Gray Cloud to fetch the doctor? He's at the Running Horse residence about a half mile east of town."

There wasn't much she could do until the doctor arrived, except make the child as comfortable as possible. Though she was angry with God, desperation drove her to utter a quick prayer.

An hour later, Nathaniel entered the clinic. "Rose, I delivered the message to Dr. Eastman. He's trying to save twin girls stricken with influenza. He said he'd be here as soon as he could."

Rose thanked him and laid a cool cloth on the boy's forehead. The child's mother held his hand and prayed in their native tongue, then sang a lullaby to comfort him. Nathaniel crumpled his hat in his hands and strode from the clinic.

He hadn't said anything about the distressed woman's use of the Lakota language. This mother was desperate for her child to live and would use any means necessary to comfort him. If that meant singing a Lakota lullaby, then so be it. The woman stared into Rose's eyes, and understanding passed between them. Neither of them would mention this to anyone.

Darkness shrouded the land by the time Miss Goodale drove her wagon into town. Dr. Eastman lay sleeping in the back. Rose detested waking the weary man, but as soon as the wagon halted, she shook him from his slumber. He sat up, groaned, and then hauled himself from the conveyance and trudged into the clinic.

For the next few hours, they held vigil over the boy. His fever rose higher as the doctor administered willow bark tea. Rose wrung her hands, and his parents silently wept.

The crescent moon inched itself across the sky, and finally, the child's exhausted body could take no more. His innocent soul slipped from the earthly realm and into the arms of Jesus.

After delivering Rose's message to the doctor and returning to the clinic, Nathaniel rode to his sister's house to check on Chaske, Winuna, and Joshua.

After dinner, he and his brother-in-law played with the children while Sarah washed the dishes. At bedtime, Chaske exhibited a slight fever. Sarah was terrified that her son would get worse, so Joshua asked Nathaniel to stay in case he needed to ride for the doctor. He agreed and slept fitfully on the cold, hard floor. Thus far, thankfully, his niece had avoided sickness.

The sun peeked over the eastern horizon, casting rays of bright sunlight, a comforting warmth and hope across the reservation. Nathaniel rose and stretched his aching muscles. He stepped to where Chaske lay sleeping and placed a hand on his forehead. The child's skin was warm to the touch, not dangerously hot but warmer than it should be.

His sister bolted upright in bed. Beside her, Joshua mumbled and rose on his elbows. Sarah scrambled to her child's side, but Nathaniel wrapped an arm around her in a side hug. He assured her that the boy was alive and not worse.

His sister swiped at the tears on her cheeks. "I'll make a fresh poultice for him. That should ease the fever, right?"

"I'm sure it will. Still, I'm riding into town to see if the doctor has any medicine that might help. I'll bring lunch back for all of you. That way you can focus on your son and not have to worry about the rest of us."

She gazed at him. "Thank you, Brother."

He carried in an armload of firewood before he left. On the ride to town, he wondered how many of his people would succumb to the sicknesses plaguing the reservation. He often feared that guns and war would wipe out his entire tribe, until his people were no more, but sickness and disease swept in and seemed more likely to accomplish that morbid feat.

He adjusted in the saddle, trying to ease the ache in his neck and back, the result of sleeping on pine boards. Hunger gnawed at him. He'd have to eat breakfast after stopping at the clinic. He asked the Almighty to heal his nephew or at least provide medicine that would ease the boy's fever.

Finally, he arrived in town. Anxious to speak with the doctor, he dismounted his horse in front of the clinic. Three steps toward the door, and he heard wailing cut into the cold early-morning air. He hurried inside and saw a woman clutching the limp body of a child who couldn't have been more than three years old.

Rose stood to the side, her stricken face streaked with tears.

He pivoted on his heel and left.

Emotion, namely fear, churned in him as he strode to Dawson's store and pounded on the door, demanding they open immediately. The harried clerk yanked the door open, looking as if he'd just risen from his bed.

"What medicines do you have to bring down a child's fever?" Nathaniel cringed at the way he'd barked at the clerk, but he was desperate. For all he knew, his sister could be crying over his nephew's limp body at that very moment.

The clerk's eyes widened. "I'm sorry, sir, but I gave all the medicine I had to Dr. Eastman."

Nathaniel grunted his understanding and quickly purchased food for Sarah and her family, then strode to the deputy's office.

Peter greeted him. "Everything all right?"

"I'll be at my sister's house for a few days. If you need me, you know where to find me."

Peter waved him off, and Nathaniel stepped outside again.

He'd told Sarah he would ask for medicine, but there was none for purchase at the store. He'd have to check at the clinic, but he dreaded seeing the weeping mother and deceased child again, the sight a tragic foreshadowing of what his own family might endure if God called Chaske to heaven.

Shoving his fears aside, he tromped into the clinic. His pride wasn't the slightest bit wounded as he begged for something that would help his nephew. "Doctor, my nephew Chaske is sick. Do you have something that will bring down his fever? Please, I'll pay any amount you ask."

The doctor hung his head, and his shoulders slumped. He raised his head again, his eyes sad. "I'm sorry, but I have nothing to give you."

Rose interjected, "Try as many natural remedies as you can. Here's the last of the willow bark tea that I have. I'll ride out later this afternoon to check on him and Joshua as well."

Where was that blasted shipment of supplies?

Dismayed and frustrated, Nathaniel thanked her.

She placed her hand on his coat sleeve. Caring emanated from her eyes. "I'm here if you need me."

He thanked her again, placed his hat on his head, and left the clinic. He was almost to his sister's when she fled from her house and raced toward him.

"Brother, please help. My sweet girl has a fever."

CHAPTER 8

The reservation's meeting house was filled to capacity the second week of November. Sobs rose to an unholy crescendo and quieted a moment, as if to gain strength before rising again. Rose stood alongside one wall, trying to comprehend the enormity of the situation. Her throat and her chest tightened, hampering her ability to breathe.

Agent Royer paced the room, stopping long enough to wring his hands before stepping close to Miss Goodale and a haggard-looking Dr. Eastman. Several families clung to each other and wept bitterly. Rose was unable to hear the conversation over the din.

Four tiny coffins sat at the head of the room. Coffins so small, they were built from pieces of scrap lumber. The children who filled them hadn't been walking for more than a year before they had been carried to heaven. Their adorable tiny faces, with their pouty lips and wisps of soft dark hair, looked so incredibly serene.

The juxtaposition jarred Rose, for she knew the families of these tiny tots felt anything but serene. Each mother clutched a lock of her child's hair. Later, extended family would gather at the parents' homes. An elder would play a drum, and mournful singing would commence.

Rose made no effort to contain the tears streaming from her eyes. She pulled a handkerchief from her pocket and mopped her cheeks. This funeral was the first one she'd attended since her parents died. Her knees weakened, and she swayed.

Nathaniel wrapped an arm around her. How grateful he must be that his niece and nephew were not among the deceased. How worried he must be that they might be next. How worried every family must be, that their child, or all their children, might be next.

Nathaniel had been a source of strength the past week, visiting the clinic often to check on her. They had shared lunch together and talked of their hopes for better days ahead.

Reverend Charles Cook, a man from the Yankton Lakota, stepped to the front of the room, cleared his throat, and opened a Bible. Murmurs of discontent wafted through the crowd. Two men cursed and stomped from the building. Devastated at the loss of their children, they had grown bitter toward the government and the white man's God. She hardly blamed them.

Rose had seen the growing discord among her people and feared what might happen. Rumors of an uprising were blowing across the reservation like a mighty wind. She didn't think anyone from her tribe would commit violence, but how to convince the settlers of that?

Sobs escaped from the depths of her being. How could she not cry at the funeral of four small children? Nathaniel hugged her tighter. He smelled of horses and aftershave, and she took comfort in the warmth of his closeness.

The minister finished his speech and shut the Bible. Rose lifted her chin, determined to speak with each family to pay her respects and offer her condolences. She reached out and squeezed the hand of each parent. The haunted look in their eyes sent tremors of grief coursing through her.

"I'm so sorry," she whispered more times than she could count, but each mother there knew how much she cared. The task mercifully ended, and Nathaniel offered her his elbow and escorted her outside.

Sickness hadn't paused for the funerals. Nathaniel walked her to the clinic, where two young boys were recovering from influenza. They would live, but she feared their lungs would be weakened and scarred for the remainder of their lives.

Nathaniel said, "I'm visiting one of the families later today. Would you like me to bring dinner to you at the clinic?"

"Yes, please." She didn't know if she'd have the appetite to eat it, but she had to try. Her patients needed her, so she must keep up her strength.

When she'd left Boston, she swore she was leaving her tenuous faith behind her. With all the children who'd died since then, her slight inclination to pray had burrowed deeper into hibernation. After all, what kind of God allowed little children to suffer so?

And yet, days like this drove her to desperation. If God hadn't seen fit to heal them, she could at least ask Him why. She believed He owed these families that much, didn't He?

"Here you are," Nathaniel said when they reached the clinic.

Though there were children inside the clinic who needed care, she hesitated to pull herself from him. His strong arms wrapped protectively around her. She leaned her head against his chest and listened to his heart beating. With all the tragedy around her, it was a comfort to be in his arms.

He pulled away and cleared his throat. "I'm heading to Sarah's house when I'm done visiting. I'll have her prepare a meal for you. Is there anything in particular you'd like?"

"Just something warm." She aimed a smile at him. His eyes met hers, and her heart hammered against her rib cage. "I'll see you when you return."

"I look forward to seeing you then," he added.

She would be happy when he returned and hoped it would be sooner rather than later. Their language lessons had halted since sickness swept over the reservation. Caring for the sick had taken precedent over her relearning the Lakota language.

She entered the clinic and checked on her sleeping patients. After stoking the stove, she placed a kettle of broth on its surface. The boys would need to eat when they woke. She dropped into the rocking chair and opened her copy of *Oliver Twist*, her favorite book by Charles Dickens. At least the title character in the book had a happy reunion with his aunt in the end.

The aroma of chicken broth soon wafted through the room. Her stomach growled. She gazed at the clock and noted that only fifteen minutes had passed.

Already, she anticipated Nathaniel's return. And why was that? True, their friendship had deepened since she had arrived almost seven weeks ago and even more once they'd begun language lessons together, but if they were just friends, then why did thoughts of him continually occupy her mind?

She rose and moved the kettle of boiling soup to the back burner. She returned to her rocker, sighed, and turned to the next page in her book.

An hour later the boys woke.

"Hello there, little dears." She ladled the hot broth into a bowl and spoon-fed the boys as she regaled them with the story of *A Christmas*

Carol. This reminded her that next month, it would be Christmas. Did many members of the tribe celebrate the Christian holiday? Probably not. Nonetheless, she hoped to find presents for her brothers and Nathaniel too. She owed him something for risking the ire of Agent Royer and Peter to teach her what she'd forgotten.

There she went, thinking about him again. One of the boys squawked as she inadvertently spooned broth into his ear.

"Oh, I'm terribly sorry, Johnny." She reached for a cloth and wiped off the side of his head.

When the boys, with their bellies full, nodded back to sleep, she stoked the fire again and noted how dark it was outside. Nathaniel should have returned by now. Feeling strangely bereft without him near, she anticipated his presence more than ever.

Nathaniel spent more time than he'd planned visiting the families of the deceased children. It was nearly dark when he reached Sarah and Joshua's cabin. Exhaustion swept over him in waves as he milked the cow by lantern light. The ax seemed weightier than when he'd used it last, but he managed to chop enough wood to keep his family warm for a while.

When the chores were finally done, he bid Sarah goodbye.

"Thanks for the meal." He took the bag he planned to give to Rose and left.

He hadn't traveled more than a mile before his eyelids grew heavy. He struggled to keep them open and remain upright in the saddle. He was grateful his horse knew the way back to town, even in the dark.

Chopping firewood, milking the cow, and helping his sister care for his recovering niece and nephew and Joshua had taken far longer than he'd anticipated. He'd worked hard, splitting kindling and carting buckets of water into the house, and believed the chores would warm him.

So why was he shivering? It could be a matter of the weather turning, resulting in a mid-autumn chilly spell, but his throbbing head suggested otherwise. The cold seemed to have seeped into his bones, and in spite of the layers of clothing he wore, he couldn't get warm.

He pulled his coat tighter, wished for a knitted cap, and longed for his cot in the tack room in the barn. He was certain the heavy quilt covering his bed would warm him, but first he needed to deliver the dinner he'd promised Rose.

Sarah had filled a knapsack with fresh bread hot out of the oven, cheese, and jerky made from one of the dead mules. It was a good thing he'd placed the meal in his saddlebag, or he would have dropped it alongside the road long ago.

Why hadn't he thought to ask Sarah to fix him a meal as well?

Because he wasn't hungry.

That was odd, considering how he always developed an appetite after hard work.

He chirruped to his horse to go faster.

The sooner he delivered Rose's dinner to her, the sooner he could go to bed. It had been a long day, and exhaustion overtook him. His limbs ached, and he struggled to keep his weighty eyelids open.

Finally, he reached the clinic. He dropped from his horse with a thud and took a moment to steady himself before tying the reins to the hitching post. He staggered to the clinic and entered to find Rose asleep in her rocking chair. Propriety dictated that he place the knapsack on the counter and leave. But he was drawn to her beauty and selfishly wanted to spend time with her.

How he'd missed meeting with her for language lessons. Yet he understood that tending to patients occupied her every moment.

She stirred, and the book in her lap clunked to the floor. Her eyelids popped open, and she fixed her gaze on his. A smile that seemed to rise from her heart spread across her rosy cheeks. Lord help him, he cared for her much more than he ought.

His tongue stuck to the roof of his mouth, and his throat constricted, hindering his ability to tell her he didn't feel well.

The world around him spun and then darkened.

He hardly remembered hitting the floor.

CHAPTER 9

Nathaniel tried to speak, but his throat burned and his tongue adhered itself to the roof of his mouth. His head felt like a host of tribal singers were using it for a kettledrum. How could he be drenched in sweat and be so cold at the same time?

Chills swept through him, and he shivered violently.

Was that an angel's voice he heard?

She sounded familiar.

Rose?

The last thing he remembered was walking into the clinic to bring her the dinner he'd promised, and then hitting the floor with a painful thud. Was he still at the clinic? That would explain why he heard her voice.

"Nathaniel, open your mouth," she whispered.

He slid his eyelids open. Daylight lit up his surroundings. Pain knifed into his temples. He slammed his eyes shut, gasping until the pain subsided; then he mustered his strength and opened his eyes again, more slowly.

He lay on a cot in the clinic. A scratchy wool blanket covered him. Its weight seemed to press him deeper into the cot. How long had he been there?

Rose spoke again, appearing in his field of vision. She held a spoon to his lips. He sipped the cold water, momentarily quenching the fire in his throat. She spooned another bit into his mouth, and he swallowed painfully.

"Sarah, the children," he croaked. If this was the sickness that had taken hold of his niece and nephew, he wondered how they could still be alive.

A cool cloth was pressed to his forehead. He tried to reach for her, but his arms felt shackled with heavy irons.

"Your sister and her family are fine. Rest now, Nathaniel. I'll take care of you." Rose pulled the cloth from his forehead, and he heard splashing. He turned his head and watched as she dunked the cloth in cold water and covered his forehead again.

The tenderness in her voice lulled him, and he slipped into blessed sleep. When he woke again, darkness shrouded the clinic. How much time had passed while he lay in bed? More than twenty-four hours? Longer, perhaps? No wonder his strength was sapped.

Rose was there, spooning more water between his chapped lips. Pain still threatened to split his head in two. He continued to burn with fever and shook more violently than ever.

He locked his gaze on hers. She looked tired. Her face was paler than he'd ever seen it. Tendrils of hair had worked loose from the braid slung over her shoulder. When had she braided it? Was that fear, or worry he saw in her eyes? Or both?

He was sick. Really sick.

Again, she whispered comforting words and told him to sleep. He thought of Chaske and Winuna. They had recovered all right. Perhaps he would too. But what if he didn't? What if his spirit slipped from the earth and into the heavenly realms?

"*Wakan Tanka*," he cried again and again. He wanted to believe the Great Spirit was with him in these dark moments.

Deep, soul-wrenching groans broke loose from his middle and broke free from his parched throat. Desperate to escape the torment, he twisted, shook, and begged *Wakan Tanka* to heal him or carry him to heaven.

Death or recovery, either way, at least his suffering would end.

Rose rubbed Nathaniel's chest, hoping her words brought him comfort as he drifted to sleep. She stood and wiped the back of her hand over her sweaty brow. The water in the washbasin had grown tepid. She picked up the basin, exited the rear door of the clinic, dumped the water on the ground, then traipsed to where the well was located to retrieve more.

Fluffy snowflakes wafted to earth from the inky black sky. She paused to stare into the star-studded heavens. Even in Nathaniel's deepest agony, he continued to cling to his God. Did his God really snuggle close to those who knew Him, and offer them companionship in the midst of trouble?

What was it like to have faith like that?

The cruel nun in Boston had Rose believing that God sat on His throne, ready to fire a lightning bolt at her if she failed to meet His lofty expectations. Was He both of those entities, or neither of them? Had someone given her an incorrect description of God?

In confusion, Rose shook her head, accidentally dropping the washbasin.

"Let me get that for you."

The voice startled her. She jumped then blew out a deep breath when her brother stepped into view. She placed her hands on her hips. "You scared the wits out of me, Peter."

Gracious, how long had she been standing out there?

"Sorry." He shrugged and bent to retrieve the basin. "How's Nathaniel?"

"He's young, strong, and in good health, present illness notwithstanding." Was she saying this to give her brother hope, or convince herself that Nathaniel would recover?

Memories of him writhing in a fever-induced panic as she tried to restrain him haunted her. She didn't want to admit to Peter or to herself that Nathaniel was at the point where he would either recover or worsen and die.

Her throat constricted. She swallowed and sucked in a breath. "We should know by morning, one way or—" She swallowed again. "One way or the other."

Peter placed a small sack in the washbasin. "I brought you dinner. It's not much, just beef jerky and bread. I'll stop by in the morning to see him. If he wakes up, tell him I'm praying for him." Her brother shook his head, turned, and cleared his throat before walking into the darkness.

Rose rolled her eyes. Guilt pricked her, and she bit her lower lip. It was rude of her to dismiss another's faith, even if she had none herself.

Peter may not be outspoken about his faith, but he attended church services every Sunday when he wasn't on duty, and she'd seen a Bible on his nightstand at the deputy's office.

Christianity seemed to permeate every aspect of traditional Lakota culture. Rose wasn't sure how she felt about that. She refilled the washbasin at the well and strode back inside, determined to ask Nathaniel what he thought as soon as he was lucid enough.

She stepped into the clinic and placed her dinner on a shelf, intending to eat when she finished sponging off Nathaniel. She reached for a clean cloth and then strode to where he lay.

To her surprise, he was awake, attempting to sit up in bed. Though his eyes retained a glassy look, they seemed to focus on her. It appeared as though the fever had broken.

"Rose." His voice was steady and strong. "Will you get my Bible for me? It's on my dresser in the barn."

CHAPTER 10

Rose wiped a cold wet cloth over Nathaniel's brow for the umpteenth time that morning, even though his fever had broken and he'd drunk a bowl of broth and grumbled about missing work.

Rose had patiently tended to him while he was ill, but now she felt restless too. She needed something to do with her hands. Why was she suddenly so nervous and tongue-tied? She'd conversed with him during their language lessons just fine. Things shouldn't be different now, should they?

The feverish glint in his eyes had dissipated, and he seemed more focused when she stared at him. Heavens, she was staring at him again! Her classmates from Boston, especially Bridget, would laugh and claim she'd "dropped her parasol" for him, but that was foolishness. The few dime novels she'd read spoke of love that left heroines giddy and addle-brained. Indeed, such prose had flamed Rose's cheeks and caused her to giggle like a schoolgirl.

But Nathaniel didn't make her feel that way. Well, her cheeks did grow warm in his presence, or maybe that was because the temperature seemed uncommonly hot in the room. She'd have to be careful not to put so much wood in the stove next time it needed to be fed.

"Rose," Nathaniel said, "I don't need to be sponged off again, or my forehead will wrinkle."

"Oh, I'm sorry." When had she drawn the cloth from the washbasin again? She returned it to the basin and stood. "I'll see what I can find for our noon meal."

"I could eat another bowl of broth, if there's more, and then maybe we can have a language lesson." One side of his mouth crooked up in a half smile.

"All right." She nodded, reached for his soup bowl, and hurried to the kitchen area of the clinic. If she couldn't keep herself from woolgathering, *he'd* think she'd dropped her parasol for him. She returned and watched him until he finished eating.

He handed her the empty bowl and said, "You should know what different parts of the body are called. If someone says their arm hurts, they'll use the word *isto*. If their leg hurts, they'll say *hu*."

She set the empty bowl aside and repeated the words until her pronunciation was correct. "What are the words for head and heart? Those are very important words I should know."

"*Nata* means head," he said.

"Nata," she repeated. "Head wounds can be serious, so I'm glad to learn the word for it." She ran her fingers through his hair.

"And *chante* means 'heart.'" He reached for her hand and placed it on his chest.

His heart thrummed beneath her fingers. She locked eyes with him, wishing she could keep her hand there forever. Her breath hitched in her throat, and an unladylike bead of sweat formed at her temple.

Where was Peter? When she saw her brother at the well last night, he said he'd stop by today. His presence would provide a welcome distraction.

As if on cue, the bell over the front door jangled. She hurried up front to greet the visitor.

"Oh, hello, Dr. Eastman," Rose said with a smile. "I didn't expect to see you until much later this afternoon. How are your patients from the Oglala community faring?"

"Recovering well enough." He set his bag on a nearby counter. "Morning, Nathaniel. I see you're recovering well enough too, like I thought you would."

"Yes," Rose chirped. "I'm happy that he appears to be over the worst of it, thankfully."

She wanted to hide under her bed at the embarrassing lilt in her voice. Her cheeks burned, and heavens, why did Nathaniel affect her so? She didn't even own a parasol!

"Are you hungry, Dr. Eastman? There's hot soup on the stove. I'd be happy to bring you a bowl."

"No, but thank you. I'm changing, and then I'm off to the school to see Miss Goodale. I met with several families who have been told to send their children to the school here." Hints of pink colored his dark cheeks as he hurried to his quarters.

Rose turned to Nathaniel. He had nodded off to sleep, and try as she might, she couldn't pull her gaze from him. His long raven-colored hair framed his face, his high cheekbones prominent even as he recovered from sickness. Well over six feet and muscled, he was the epitome of the heroes in those dime romances.

She whipped her gaze to the rocking chair in the corner and fanned her cheeks, hoping to dispel the heat gathering there.

Dr. Eastman swept into the room, said goodbye, and hustled out the front door. Rose clasped her hands behind her back and meandered to the window to watch people bustling along the busy street. What could be keeping Peter from dropping in to see his friend? Although now wouldn't be a good time, considering Nathaniel was dozing. She hoped her brother wasn't preoccupied with quelling any minor conflicts.

Rose pulled herself away from the window and dropped into the rocker in the corner. She picked up her book and sighed. Another Jane Austen romance. Next time she'd remember to grab her copy of *Uncle Tom's Cabin* instead.

Nathaniel jerked awake at the jangling bell over the clinic's door. Across the room, Rose emitted an adorable squeak. Her book dropped to the floor with a clunk.

Peter entered. "Good afternoon, my friend. I meant to see you earlier today." He pressed his eyebrows together. "But Agent Royer and I had to ride out and visit a family of white settlers at the edge of the reservation. Their name is Gardner, and they're nice people."

Peter didn't have to explain the reason for the visit. Nathaniel understood why it was necessary. He glanced at Rose. She was scowling at her brother. Did she suspect the reason for the visit? The settlers' fears of an uprising?

Hoping to mollify any unease between them, he said, "Rose, will you please bring your brother a bowl of that delicious soup you made?"

"Of course." She turned and strode from the room.

Peter pulled a chair close to the bed and sat. Nathaniel pushed himself to a sitting position. The room swayed for a few brief seconds before righting itself again. He wasn't fully recovered yet, but men didn't mention such things to each other, so he held his tongue.

"I spoke to Kane. He's agreed to stop ghost dancing, at least for a while." Peter rested his elbows on his knees and leaned closer. "I hope I can talk you, my sister, and the doctor into venturing out to the camps. I'd like you to speak to the people who live there and quell any restlessness, at least for now, just until the settlers calm down."

Nathaniel didn't know if that would be a workable solution to the problem. "Maybe we can talk to more settlers, assure them that it's just a dance. We're not preparing for war."

Peter scoffed. "That's not what the newspapers are saying."

A groan crept up Nathaniel's still-scratchy throat. Those unscrupulous reporters irked him. They would print anything to sell newspapers and gave little regard to the harm their so-called news did to innocent souls. "I doubt Rose will ask our people to stop dancing. If anything, she'll advocate for them to continue."

Peter leaned back in his chair and crossed his arms over his chest. He aimed a scrutinizing stare at him.

Nathaniel squirmed. Did her brother suspect something between the two of them?

"Why would you say that?" Peter asked. "When she first arrived from Boston, she was a bit ignorant of the ways here, but since then she's been the perfect example of assimilation. I believe she'll be fine with talking to our people and showing them that assimilation is the only way to ensure our survival."

Unable to form a sentence, Nathaniel merely gulped.

Peter opened his mouth as if to speak, and then Rose strode into the room.

Nathaniel shushed his friend and wondered how much, if any, of the conversation she had overheard.

Without a word, Rose shoved the bowl into her brother's hands. The steaming broth sloshed over the side and onto Peter's fingers. He yelped, dropped the bowl, and reached for the cloth in the washbasin.

"Say now, Rose, what's this about?" Peter growled. He frowned at his sister.

By the glint in her eyes, Nathaniel guessed she'd overheard plenty.

He hoped she wouldn't unleash any additional ire until he could at least placate her brother. The last thing he wanted was a skirmish between Rose and his best friend right here in the clinic.

Rose squared her shoulders, stormed across the room, and picked her book up off the floor. "If you two don't mind, I'm heading home. I need to eat and change into fresh clothes. Once my brother has left, perhaps I'll return."

She spun on her heel and stormed from the clinic. The bell jangled obnoxiously as the door slammed shut.

CHAPTER 11

Rose scrubbed her dinner dishes with a vengeance. How dare her brother call her a perfect example of assimilation? It wasn't her fault the Bureau of Indian Affairs had shipped her to Boston. She hadn't asked the Friends of the Indian to fill her head with notions that her people were uncivilized savages who needed to be tamed. Didn't Peter understand how much it hurt to have one's culture ripped away from them?

She paused. Hadn't Peter done just that to himself? Thrown his heritage to the wind like yesterday's dishwater? He had seemingly embraced the white culture with open arms. If this bothered him, she sure couldn't tell.

A stab of betrayal pierced her. The Lakota culture had been torn from her, and those in authority hadn't given her a choice. Peter had had the option to retain his culture, like their younger brother had, but he had willingly chosen the white man's ways. If the Lakota people weren't careful, many of their traditions, oral histories, and stories would be lost forever.

And her brother didn't seem to care.

But why?

Rose dropped her hands and hung her head. She wasn't being fair. Peter was right about one thing: If her people were to survive, they needed to learn to adapt. She hoped they wouldn't have to adapt so much that their history, heritage, and customs became things of the past. There had to be middle ground somewhere, a place where the conflicts between the whites and the Oglala Lakota would be settled.

A memory wafted to the forefront of her mind.

Halfway through nursing school, one of the nuns offered Rose and her classmates tickets to a circus in the Fenway neighborhood. She'd been enthralled with the animals from all over the world, especially Jumbo the Elephant, as well as the amazing feats of strength and daring. But one act reminded her of the impossible predicament her people were in.

High off the ground, a rope stretched tight between two small, round platforms. A man holding a long bar walked on the rope from one platform to the other. If he had fallen, it would have meant his certain death.

Her people walked a narrow, precarious path between the white world and that of the Lakota Indian. Though the tightrope walker had made the endeavor seem easy, she believed he must have struggled through years of practice, suffered untold injuries, and overcome a mountain of fear before mastering the feat.

Shudders swept through her. If she wanted to walk in both worlds, she must conquer her fear and risk being hurt. It wouldn't be easy, but great accomplishments rarely were. Nathaniel seemed to understand this, and she hoped Peter and Kaneenawup would as well.

She finished rinsing her dishes, quickly dried them and put them away, and then wandered into her sitting room. With a sigh, she dropped into her rocker and picked up her copy of *Oliver Twist*. The worn pages were creased and ready to fall out with no encouragement. Though it was a sad tale of an orphan boy, she, being an orphan herself, related to the character.

The last time she'd worked at the clinic, her Jane Austen romances had left her feeling besotted. Was it any wonder? Since that awkward moment she'd had with Nathaniel, any novel containing even a hint of romance had been promptly shelved.

Still, in spite of her best intentions, her thoughts turned to him.

How was he faring at the clinic by himself? Had Dr. Eastman arrived from his visit with Miss Goodale? The man should have returned long ago. If he hadn't and Nathaniel needed something or took a turn for the worse, who would be there to help him?

Rose slapped the book shut then stood and peeked outside. The lamp burned in the clinic's front window. Nathaniel likely lit it to help guide Dr. Eastman home. Which meant Nathaniel was there alone.

A disgruntled huff blew past her lips. Being a skilled nurse meant putting aside personal feelings and tending to patients. She donned her coat and hat, retrieved *Oliver Twist* from her rocking chair, and stepped out into the cold. If Nathaniel was sleeping, she could at least read until the doctor returned. And if he wasn't sleeping?

She scurried across the hard-packed dirt street and convinced herself that another language lesson would be a fine way to spend an evening with Nathaniel.

But what if Peter found out about the language lessons? She feared her brother would be angry, and he could make their lives difficult. The near miss in the barn that night a few weeks ago still sent rivulets of fear coursing through her.

She blew out a sigh. Wisps of vapor danced in the chilly night air. She must stop being a ninny. Nathaniel wouldn't have confessed their meetings to anyone, especially Peter. If he had, her brother would have threatened him and then arrived at her doorstep with harsh words, demanding she stop.

Though Nathaniel could take care of himself, she worried what would happen to the friendship between the two if Peter found out about the language lessons. She didn't want to be the cause of either of them being hurt.

Minutes later, the wind blew her into the clinic. Nathaniel called from the kitchen, though she couldn't decipher exactly what he'd said. She strode that direction and was soon to regret her hastiness.

He stood at the cookstove with his back to her, feasting on the remnants of soup, straight from the kettle, in his long underwear.

An unladylike gasp flew from her.

Nathaniel spun toward her, dropping the kettle in the process.

Mercy, the top half of his long johns was unbuttoned to the waist!

He scrambled to button his clothing. "Rose! What are you doing here? I thought you were Dr. Eastman."

She turned away and stammered for words, but found none. Her cheeks flamed as if they had actually caught fire. Thinking the night air would cool the heat burning through her, she hurried to the door.

"Wait!" Nathaniel called.

She hoped he had the good sense to wrap himself in a blanket!

"Give me a minute, Rose, please. I need to speak with you."

"I'll be just outside. Let me know when you're, um, ready for me to come in." The bell jangled as she flung the door open and stepped into the cold. Why hadn't she announced her arrival when she entered the clinic?

Over her years of administering aid, she'd witnessed a number of patients in a state of undress and it had never been a problem. Granted, most of her patients were women, but a few had been men, and it hadn't bothered her one whit to see them in their drawers. But that didn't mean she hadn't been respectful of their privacy.

What was so different about this time?

The clinic had become like a second home to her, and she apparently had been so comfortable in her place and overcome with her desire to speak with Nathaniel that she hadn't thought things through.

Where was Dr. Eastman anyway? The man really shouldn't be out this late with Miss Goodale, or he'd damage the woman's reputation.

Thankfully, Peter wasn't anywhere to be seen, and he likely wouldn't, because he was visiting settlers.

She sat on an empty medicine crate beside the door, not caring that her skirts were hitched up and her ankles and feet stuck out in front of her.

Nathaniel hastily finished buttoning his long underwear. He shoved his legs into his trousers and nearly fell over in the process. He dropped onto the cot to keep from tumbling to the ground, grumbling over his weakness. Inhaling a deep breath, he slowly stood, placing a hand against the wall to help him remain steady. He tried to convince himself that sickness had made him dizzy, but truth be told, he was embarrassed that Rose had seen him in such a state of undress.

What was she thinking, waltzing into the clinic like she lived there? Shouldn't she have knocked before entering and announced her presence?

His face heated at the memory of her standing at the kitchen door, her mouth open like a freshly caught fish gasping for air.

How to rectify the situation?

Best deal with Rose now rather than later.

Once he regained his bearings, he lumbered to the front door and opened it.

She was sitting on a wooden crate and quickly stood. Her lips curved into a delightful smile, and her cheeks were a deep shade of pink. From cold or embarrassment, he couldn't tell.

"I'm sorry," she said. "I've grown so accustomed to being at the clinic that I just burst in without considering your privacy."

Nathaniel shifted his weight from one foot to the other. That was true enough, but he was just as much to blame for the fiasco. Several people had run of the clinic, and anyone could have waltzed right in. He would have been a sight more embarrassed if Miss Goodale had barged in, or a mother with a sick child in search of Dr. Eastman. He decided to be more mindful and not go traipsing around in his underclothes.

"I'm sorry, Rose. Can we forget this happened, please?" His face heated again, so he ducked his head to conceal any telltale blush.

Her hand rested on his arm. "Not to worry. I won't mention it if you don't."

He nodded and thanked *Wakan Tanka* for Rose's grace with the situation.

She continued. "I want to apologize for my behavior and my unkind words from earlier today. I was rude, and I'm sorry." Her booted foot traced a small rock on the pathway.

He retreated two steps and invited her in. She entered and sat in the rocking chair in the corner. He strode into the kitchen to mop his now-cold dinner from the floor. In the darkness, he inadvertently stepped on a cooked potato and stifled a groan as it squished between his toes. He fumbled along the counter until he located a towel and wiped the mess from his foot.

When he returned to the front of the clinic, he discovered that Rose had rocked herself to sleep. Her hair framed her face, and her lips were pulled into an adorable pout. He could have stared at her all night long were it not for propriety. Though she made an enchanting picture, it was scandalous for her to be here, alone with him, this late at night. He needed to rouse her and ask her leave.

Voices that didn't belong to Dr. Eastman reverberated from across the street. It wouldn't bode well for either of them if they were caught like this—her sleeping in the rocker, him traipsing about in his long johns with nothing but his trousers to cover him.

Nathaniel crossed the room to extinguish the lantern when a shadow darkened the doorway outside. Perhaps this was the doctor after all. Nathaniel yanked the door open.

Peter poked his head in through the door.

Rose murmured drowsily from her place in the rocker.

Peter's head turned in her direction.

Nathaniel muttered under his breath. Even to him, this looked bad.

His friend's face filled with fury.

Rose's eyes popped open, and she stretched.

Peter stomped to where Rose sat, took his protesting sister by the hand, and pulled her from the clinic, slamming the door behind him.

CHAPTER 12

Though the sun had reached its zenith, the barn's interior hadn't warmed enough to melt the water in the horse's trough. Nathaniel and Peter hadn't left the structure since dawn. First they had broken the ice in the trough and filled it with lukewarm water. Next they mucked the stalls and filled them with fresh slough hay. By this time, Nathaniel was winded and needed to sit. It bothered him that he needed rest after only a half day's work. He hoped he regained his strength soon, because a plethora of chores needed to be done.

Peter repaired a broken bridle while Nathaniel oiled the leather saddles.

The wagon owned by the tribal police needed to be repaired, and it was a job for two, but he hadn't heard one word from Peter. He didn't want to push his friend into a conversation he didn't want to have, but stewing over unresolved issues wouldn't solve problems.

Nathaniel sensed trouble between him and Peter, but every effort to draw his friend into conversation had been met with a grunt or a shrug. He was almost glad Peter hadn't peppered him with questions about Rose, but an awkward silence stretched taut between them, and that didn't bode well for their friendship. It would have been easier if Peter had yelled at him for being alone with his sister late last night and in his long underwear. He would almost prefer that compared to the frosty tension thickening the air.

Peter dropped the pitchfork, muttered under his breath, and picked up a stray horse brush from the floor. They were the first words Nathaniel had heard from his friend all day.

Encouraged by the hope of conversation, Nathaniel said, "Didn't catch that, Peter. Mind repeating it?"

"Just found something that needs to be put away." Peter turned, tripped over the pitchfork, and thudded to the ground.

Nathaniel rushed to his friend's side, intending to help him up. "Are you hurt? Should I fetch the doctor or your sister?"

Peter was on his feet in an instant, his eyes emanating fire, and his mouth formed a thin line. With each deep breath, his chest rose and fell.

Chills that didn't have anything to do with the freezing temperatures in the barn swept through Nathaniel. He held his hands up in a gesture of surrender. "Look, I'm sorry if I offended you."

That much was true.

Peter thumped his index finger against Nathaniel's chest. Reflexively, Nathaniel stepped back, but that didn't assuage his friend's wrath.

"Then why was she at the clinic last night while you were in nothing but trousers and long johns?"

"I know it looked bad, but it wasn't what it appeared to be. There's nothing untoward going on." Nathaniel's heart jerked a beat. Just what did Peter think was going on between him and Rose? Dare he ask?

Peter clenched his fists. He paced the empty stall like a corralled, unbroken mustang. "I'm not stupid."

Nathaniel shrugged. "I didn't say you were."

"I see the way you two look at each other. Half the town does too. We've been friends for a long time." Peter's shoulders sagged. His eyes and voice softened. "Please, don't hurt my sister. Don't engage her in anything that will harm her."

How to answer a request like *that*? To whitewash the truth would be a lie. But if he answered truthfully, Peter would reach for the pitchfork and put it to good use!

The barn door creaked open, and Rose entered. "I fixed beef stew and added potatoes that Miss Goodale gave me. I thought after working in the cold all morning, you two could use a break and eat a warm meal."

Her head swiveled from her brother to Nathaniel and back again. Her eyebrows rose, and she lifted her chin. "What's going on here?"

"Nothing." Peter leaned the pitchfork against the stall, pushed past Nathaniel, and muttered, "We'll discuss this later."

"Okay." Nathaniel followed, wondering if Rose would receive the same icy treatment, or worse, an interrogation. He hadn't meant to put her in a position of being interrogated by her own brother.

Frustration swirled in his middle. The more the government pushed for the eradication of all native culture, the more determined the native people became. Several families he knew were secretly keeping the Lakota traditions alive, believing that once tensions dissipated, the regulations would be loosened.

Others had fully assimilated out of fear of repercussions, such as loss of rations, removal of their children, or being arrested. Bile collected in his stomach, making him wonder if the stew would unsettle him further.

Nathaniel slowly paced the length of the street, giving Peter time to speak with his sister in private. His thoughts drifted back to earlier that morning, when he and Peter were working in the barn and Dr. Eastman had returned.

The doctor had handed his horse's reins to Nathaniel. "I'm headed to the clinic to sleep. Will you take care of my horse for me, please?"

"Sure. I'll pray you have a relaxing nap." He didn't believe that Peter would question his sister at the clinic while the doctor was trying to sleep. With the people he was caring for at all hours of the day and night, the man needed his rest.

A noise startled Nathaniel, and he turned.

Rose strode toward him. "We need to talk. I don't know how much Peter knows, but I know my brother. I'm sure he suspects something is going on between us." She glanced across the street and peered around him, then clutched his coat sleeve. "I'm not sure what to tell him regarding our language lessons. I need to be able to communicate with our people."

"Maybe we can halt the lessons, at least for the time being."

Her shoulders sagged, and the light diminished from her eyes. "If you think that's best, but we can still see each other, right?"

Nathaniel gazed past her to ensure Peter wasn't close by. Then he wrapped an arm around her. "Yes, we can. I don't know what excuse we'll give your brother, but we'll think of something."

Rose washed the dishes that evening, much more relaxed and at peace than the night before. She hummed a popular Irish folk song, "Molly Malone," that Bridget had taught her in Boston.

Much as she liked Nathaniel, she couldn't allow herself to grow sweet on him. Nursing was too important to her, had cost her so much, and she didn't want to give it up if she married, like most women in Boston were forced to do. Bridget had married her beau two days after graduation. Her husband ordered her to stay home and clean their grand house, and she never spent one day practicing her skills.

What if she married and her new husband ordered her to stay home as well? She couldn't allow a man to rob her people of the health services they desperately needed. Members of the Lakota tribe deserved good medical care as much as anyone else.

Rose finished the dishes and strode to her sitting room. Her shipment of chickens had arrived at Dawson's General Store, but there were only eight of them. Whether the other four had died, were stolen, or were eaten was hard to say, but she'd begin work on a chicken coop as soon as possible.

She'd also received *Little Men* and *Jo's Boys*, the second and third books in the series about the March family. Delighted to finally have the entire series by Louisa May Alcott, she placed them on her shelf and admired how they looked.

Next, she reached for her letter and a new medical book. She set the book for Dr. Eastman aside and ran her fingers along the envelope containing news from Bridget. What if her friend had written distressing news? There was only one way to find out. She tore open the envelope and unfolded the stationery.

> *Dear Rose,*
>
> *I have news. I hope this doesn't distress you, but another student has come forward with allegations against Mr. Leon. While it's disturbing that the man would do such things, it lends credibility to your accusation that the man is a skunk. Though it won't undo the terrible wrong those children suffered, every female student is praying that he's held accountable for his actions.*

Vindication threaded through Rose, but it didn't undo the damage. She read further and was pleased the missive ended on a brighter note. She learned that her friend would become a new mother in a few months. Though Rose was excited for her friend, she also felt a twinge of sadness.

Now it was even less likely that Bridget would ever practice nursing.

Rose set the letter aside with the intent to pen a reply later. She reached for the medical book and flipped through the pages. Though she loved reading, this one looked like it would induce drowsiness.

After adding more wood to the stove, she dropped into her rocking chair and opened the book once again.

Rose startled awake, and the book dropped to the floor with a loud thud. She glanced at the clock and realized an hour had passed. The book had indeed put her to sleep.

Someone had knocked on her front door. That someone might need medical assistance. She jumped from her seat and hurried to answer it.

Peter stood there, his hat in his hands, in spite of the cold.

"Rose, I want to apologize for my behavior earlier. And I need to talk to you about Kane."

Her stomach dipped. "What is it with Kaneenawup this time?"

Peter huffed, scowled, and appeared very unamused.

Her hand flew to her chest. "What's wrong? Is he all right?" If anything had happened to her baby brother, after she'd been away for so long and only now had the opportunity to know him better, it would devastate her.

"He's fine. We've managed to keep our uneasy truce. He's going to refrain from dancing, at least for a little while longer."

"What! Why? Peter, why are you making him do this?" Rose dropped her hands to her sides. Her fingers curled into fists.

Her brother's eyebrows knit together in a fierce expression. She wondered if he would ever master the ability to rein in his anger.

"Because I want to keep you both alive!" he stormed. "I've had enough of this. Trying to placate the settlers while rogue Indians do everything they can to stoke their fears."

"We're not trying to rile up anyone! We're trying to hang on to our way of life!" Rose practically wailed with frustration. "Why can't these settlers understand that?"

"I'd like you to go with me tomorrow to speak with a worried white family so you can see why they're afraid," Peter said. "Maybe then you'll understand why we need to be careful when we practice our customs. If the settlers are happy, we should be all right practicing a few customs, as long as we're responsible about it."

Rose was stunned to hear her brother talk like this. Was he saying that if they could persuade the settlers not to be afraid of the dancing and singing, he wouldn't mind keeping their traditions alive? Perhaps she would go along with him. Maybe she could help them understand.

"All right, Peter. I'll go with you."

He placed his hat on his head. "Good. I'll pick you up after breakfast tomorrow. We have a long drive ahead of us."

Though Rose relished the thought of spending time with her older brother and becoming better acquainted with him, she also wondered how this would affect her language lessons.

Would her brother use this time alone to question her about Nathaniel?

CHAPTER 13

Rose clutched the wagon seat as her brother drove to what had once been part of the reservation before the government opened up the land for settlers. Ahead, maybe a half mile or so, she spotted a cabin. Smoke curled from the chimney.

Minutes later, Peter tugged on the reins, and the horses stopped in front of the small structure.

A tall white man exited and quickly pulled the door shut behind him. He cocked his rifle, aimed it at the sky, and placed the barrel against his shoulder. His lips pressed together, and a frown marred his pale features.

The fine hair on Rose's neck prickled. She squirmed at his scrutinizing stare. This man appeared distrustful and didn't seem happy to see them.

She whipped her focus to Peter, hoping he would say something to calm the troubled settler. Uneasiness skittered over her, but Peter didn't look the least bit troubled.

He wrapped the reins around the wagon's brake handle and held up his hands, his palms facing the settler. "Hey, Matthew, this is my sister Rose. We've come to pay you a visit. See how you and the missus are doing."

The settler lowered his weapon. Rose exhaled with relief, but an odd feeling quivered in her middle. Her brother's words and tone sounded cultured and refined, and he hadn't even been sent East! A discomforting thought slammed into her. Both Peter and Nathaniel said that the Indians' survival depended on them abandoning their traditional way of life and fully adapting to the white culture. Considering how true that could be sent tremors through her.

Anger bubbled until the man fixed his gaze on her. His eyes were haunted, as if something awful troubled him and he didn't trust them. As a child she'd seen Indians who didn't trust the whites, and many times in Boston she'd seen white people display distrust toward her. The animosity between the races bothered her greatly, but ideas for how to bridge the gap escaped her.

Peter continued. "Rose, this is Matthew Gardner. He and his wife, Ellie, live here."

She swallowed hard and forced a smile to her trembling lips. "Hello, Mr. Gardner. I'm pleased to meet you."

Peter jumped from the wagon. "What's got you so afflicted?"

Mr. Gardner swiped a hand through his hair. "Me and Ellie been hearing them Indians hollering and beating their drums again. It's scaring my wife, and with her in the family way, I'm worried sick for her and the baby."

Any distrust Rose had toward the man quickly evaporated. She hitched up her skirts and jumped from the wagon seat. "Sir, I'm a nurse, trained at a fine Boston university. I'm happy to see to your wife and do what I can to allay her fears."

She drew her medical bag from the rear of the wagon. Mr. Gardner's expression faltered, and she imagined how his feelings must be warring within him.

Finally, he grumbled, "C'mon inside. We don't got a fancy place compared to Boston, but it's our home."

He opened the door and ushered them inside. Rose squinted in the dim light and saw a pale woman sitting in a rocker near the cookstove. The woman looked up from her knitting, and alarm registered on her face. Worry jabbed at Rose. She wanted this woman to trust her, for the sake of the child, if nothing else.

Mr. Gardner made the introductions. "Ellie, you remember Peter Rushing Water. This is his sister, Rose. She's a nurse, trained in Boston."

The woman had the same hard glint in her eyes as her husband. She looked ready to deliver at any time. Setting her knitting aside, she moved to stand. "You want coffee?"

Rose noticed a cold edge in the woman's tone. Hoping to ease any fears, she stepped forward. "Please don't get up on our account. You need your rest. My brother and I are fine without coffee, but thank you for your kind offer."

Mrs. Gardner dropped back into her chair. Her gaze traveled from Rose's moccasin-covered feet to the crown of her braided hair. "You say you're a nurse? Trained in Boston?"

"Yes." Rose shifted under the scrutiny but lifted her medical bag and smiled. As wary as this family seemed, she didn't want them to fear her. The unborn baby was just as important a patient as the expectant mother.

"I'm Ellie. Do you got young'uns of your own?" The woman rocked and rubbed a thin hand over her rounded abdomen.

Peter cleared his throat and said, "Matthew, why don't you show me the hole in the roof of your barn? I'd be glad to help fix it."

Mr. Gardner hesitated a moment, clearly worried for his wife and child. Then he said, "Ain't that big of a hole, but it lets the cold in, and that ain't good for my stock." He shoved a hat onto his blond head, and he and Peter left.

Rose sat beside Ellie. "Have you seen a doctor? Do you know when your child is expected?" She pulled a Pinard horn from her bag, hoping to place it on the woman's abdomen to hear the child's heartbeat. This late in the pregnancy, she should be able to hear it and assuage any fears Ellie might have about her baby.

"Spoke to my granny before moving here, when my monthlies were three months gone, but that was in May. This is the middle of November. Wasn't much Granny could do then, anyway. I sure do wish she was here now."

Rose spoke as gently as she could. "Perhaps we could send for her when your time comes."

The woman shook her head. Tears wet her cheeks. "Got a letter from Pa the other day. She passed on in August."

Compassion moved through Rose. "I'm so sorry."

The woman looked up. Her lower lip protruded in a frown. "My aunt and cousin were killed by a band of Indians. It's been ten years, and I still miss my cousin. We were playmates and best friends."

Rose didn't want to frighten the poor woman. She wanted to earn her trust, to help her feel at ease. "Again, Ellie, I am so sorry. I lost both my parents when I was just twelve years old. Losing a loved one does leave a huge hole in one's heart."

A slight smile lifted the corners of the woman's lips, as if to say she understood.

"What are you knitting? Judging from the pale yellow yarn, I'd say you're making something for your baby?"

Her smile grew. "I am. I picked this color because it reminds me of daffodils in the springtime."

"Oh, I love daffodils." Rose put a little sway in her stance, remembering the rows and rows of bright yellow blooms springing up from the cold Boston earth, a hint that warmer weather and planting season were on their way.

Ellie's smile drooped, and her eyes darkened. "I'm only making one thing, though, on account of I lost—"

Rose was by her side in an instant and knelt beside her. "Ellie, I'm here to help in any way I can. You're safe with me. If you'll allow me, I'd like to examine you?"

"Sure." Ellie stuffed her knitting into a satchel by the rocker and motioned for Rose to draw closer.

An hour later, Rose had completed her examination and placed a thin coverlet over Ellie so she could stay warm while she rested. Rose then busied herself by peeling potatoes and preparing a stew. The men would like a hot meal when they finished repairing the barn's roof. She placed a pot of water on the stove to heat and fished a bit of tea from her medical bag.

When the sun crept closer to the western horizon, her brother and Mr. Gardner entered the house. They stomped their feet on the rag rug in front of the door, cupped their hands, and blew on them.

"Whew," Peter said. "It's cold out there."

"Yeah. Thanks for your help." Mr. Gardner nodded. "I can't afford for my only milk cow to get sick and die, not with the baby coming."

"Matthew," Ellie said, "Miss Rushing Water listened to the baby's heartbeat. She said he or she sounds just fine. She even made a stew for us."

"Thank you kindly." Mr. Gardner nodded in Rose's direction.

Peter rubbed his hands over his arms. "Rose, you ready to go? I'm sure the Gardners want to eat in peace."

"Yes, I'm ready." To Mr. Gardner she said, "Your child moved about the womb and kicked strongly. He or she appears to be fine, and I don't foresee any complications with the delivery."

Peter grimaced, likely from her delicate comments to the father-to-be, but it couldn't be helped. Her brother muttered a goodbye, reached for her arm, and guided her out of the house and to the wagon. He helped her climb onto the conveyance. Soon they were headed across the wind-whipped prairie.

"You're quite the handyman," Rose said. "Will you help me build a chicken coop? I have eight laying hens, and they can't stay in those crates forever."

"Okay, but on one condition." He leaned closer to her. "Share a few eggs with me."

She gave his arm a playful swat. "Deal."

With the prospect of her chickens being cared for, Rose thought about what Ellie had told her about her family.

Did the Indians have just cause to attack her aunt and cousin? Had they been riled up by white people nearby? Or had they been a band of bitter, cruel men bent on destruction? It was something Rose would probably never know.

And yet, thinking like this bothered her.

Both brown and white people had done terrible things to each other. She hoped that one day they could live peacefully with one another.

Nathaniel held the board as Peter hammered the nail into place. Still weak from his recent illness, he leaned against the coop's frame, winded again after only a half-day's work. He lacked the strength for manual labor at that moment, but he could pray for Rose's chickens to do well.

"Why don't you sit and rest a spell." Peter finished sawing the last board that would complete the structure's frame. From there, they'd nail wider boards in place to complete the coop.

"Good idea, especially since I'm headed to Sarah's house to help with their chores."

Peter grimaced. "Just don't overexert yourself. We don't need to be down another deputy. Did I tell you Coyote Who Sneaks hasn't been seen in a while?"

Nathaniel shrugged. "I didn't notice, but I've been sick and busy trying to catch up on chores. So I haven't been to the office in a few days."

"Either way, we're short on deputies, so don't you go dying on me." Peter kicked a pile of sawdust his way.

Nathaniel stood and helped him hold the next board against the frame as Peter pounded in the nails.

Later, at Sarah and Joshua's cabin, he dropped the ax to his side then leaned against the handle for support. During the time he was laid up, too many chores had gone undone. Joshua was able to walk now, albeit with a limp, but still used his crutches for support. They needed to clean the barn, and there hadn't been a stick of kindling or a piece of chopped firewood when he'd arrived at his sister's house that morning. In spite of the numerous tasks, he was careful to take Peter's advice and not overexert himself. He didn't want to get sick again.

With a groan, he hefted the ax and swung at the wood on the chopping block. The metal zinged as it split the wood into chunks.

He thought of Rose and how she'd tended to him while he was ill. It had been a long time since they'd practiced any language lessons, and he missed their time together.

He worried that she'd inadvertently spill the proverbial beans to one, or both, of her brothers. Kane wouldn't care. He'd likely cheer them on and then ask to join the party.

But Peter? He already suspected something between him and Rose. Nathaniel chortled. However, he feared igniting his friend's wrath and the threat it posed to his job as a tribal deputy. He reached for the badge pinned to his coat and stroked the gold-colored metal.

Rose and Peter were spending the day together, visiting the Gardner family. Ellie was in the family way, and both he and Peter hoped Rose could assist the woman and ease any fears she had about the ghost dancers.

Nathaniel mopped his sweaty brow with his shirtsleeve. *Please, God, help Rose see things from the settlers' point of view. They're not bad people. They just don't understand our ways. Despite how angry she is at You, she has a good heart.*

Joshua grabbed the chopped wood on the ground. When he stood, he locked eyes with Nathaniel. "You seem to have a mind full of important things. Would one of those things be your friend's sister?"

Nathaniel squirmed. "You're very intuitive." If Sarah or Joshua found out about the language lessons, they wouldn't report him. They would keep his and Rose's secret. Though it would lift a weight from his shoulders, he wasn't selfish enough to burden them with the issue.

"I'm not the intuitive one. That's your sister." Joshua stacked an armload of chopped wood next to the house.

Nathaniel swung the ax, and another chunk of wood split into pieces. His shoulders and forearms ached. "I need a rest. I'm going inside to see Sarah and play with the children."

Joshua reached for the ax, a grin spreading across his face.

Nathaniel entered the front door and shut it behind him. "What are my favorite nephew and niece up to? Being under your mother's feet, I suppose."

Chaske and Winuna rushed to greet him. They squealed as they crashed into his legs, nearly upending him. He emitted a playful growl and then tumbled to the floor, tickling one child and then the other.

"Let me fix you a meal. It's the least I can do." Sarah sliced bread and spooned steaming broth into a bowl.

Minutes later, with his energy spent, he dropped into a chair, gasped for breath, and rubbed his aching head. He was overtaxing himself. Sarah set the meal before him. He whispered a quick prayer of thanks and reached for the spoon.

"Thank you," he muttered. She didn't reply but merely harrumphed and moved to tend to her children. Chaske and Winuna took turns stacking the blocks Joshua had recently carved for them.

Nathaniel continued to shovel food into his mouth to keep from encouraging a conversation with his sister. The broth and bread were quickly devoured. He gulped the last bite, leaned back in his chair, sighed, and patted his stomach.

Sarah's skirt swished as she tromped over to him, hands on her hips. "I know what's troubling you, Brother. I know you have a secret, so there's no use trying to hide it."

His heart transformed into a heavy stone and sank into the depths of his torso. He stared at his sister, his hands sweaty and his mind whirling. How had she found out about his time with Rose? Or had Sarah discovered something else about them? Or something about Rose that not even he knew?

Unable to meet his sister's gaze, he reached for his cup and gulped down some water. When he was finally able to look her in the eyes, she stood there with a knowing smirk, her arms folded over her chest. "I know you're in love with Rose Rushing Water," she said.

He blew out a long breath and scrubbed his hand over his face. That much might very well be true, but that was a whole other knot to untangle. He couldn't exactly deny it, not when she occupied his thoughts from dawn until long after the sun had set.

But was it love? He scoffed.

Sarah's grin remained as she continued. "I'd like to invite you, Rose, Peter, and even Kaneenawup here for dinner next Sunday after church. I've already spoken to Joshua about it, and he would like it also."

Nathaniel shot to his feet. "Now see here, Sarah—"

So intent on denying any love for Rose, he almost reconsidered his earlier decision to keep the truth from his sister and brother-in-law. No. Though he could trust them, he couldn't risk them slipping and inadvertently informing any government or military officials who visited the reservation.

Strong gusts of wind blew into the house when Joshua entered. He leaned his crutches against the wall. "Whew, it's cold out. The stock is fed. Here's tonight's bucket of milk." He set the pail on the floor. "I'm in for the day."

Sarah faced her husband. In a teasing tone, she said, "Nathaniel doesn't think he's in love with Rose Rushing Water."

"But we heard you and Miss Rushing Water whispering and giggling in the barn one night on our way home from the clinic," Joshua said. "You two sounded pretty cozy, and we didn't hear any other voices. If you're not secretly meeting for, uh, company, why were you together?" Joshua's eyes narrowed as he furrowed his brows.

Under their watchful expressions, Nathaniel squirmed and dropped onto his chair. Sarah raised her eyebrows and lifted one corner of her mouth in a sly grin. The secret pressed on him like pent-up steam in a teakettle, demanding release. Though his stomach churned, he could stand it no more.

Nathaniel jumped to his feet again and squared his shoulders. "I've been meeting with Rose in secret, giving her lessons, reacquainting her with our language and customs. And I'm not sorry for it either."

Chaske and Winuna suddenly halted their play and looked up at him. Sarah gasped. Her eyes grew wide, and she dropped her hands to her sides. Joshua leaned against the wall, his lips pressed into a thin line.

At least neither of them appeared angry, though the cabin was as silent as a recent snowfall.

"Does Peter know?" Joshua asked.

"Of course not." Nathaniel hung his head, dejected. "It pains me to ask this, but please, don't tell Peter, or we'll all be in big trouble."

CHAPTER 14

Mid-November 1890

Rather than have a meal at Sarah and Joshua's house, everyone decided to meet at Rose's. That would spare Sarah having to prepare a meal, and Rose's house was conveniently located in town.

While the settlers celebrated Thanksgiving, she, her brothers, and Nathaniel's family decided to honor the season of harvest. Nathaniel had shot a wild prairie chicken near White Clay Creek and brought it to her. The roasted bird sat in a pan on the counter, cooling off and waiting to be carved.

Rose wiped sweat from her forehead as she hustled around the warm kitchen; then she stirred the gravy, trying to remember what else needed to be prepared.

Peter, Nathaniel, and Joshua carried on a lively conversation in the sitting room about horses. Kaneenawup had been disgruntled at her invitation, claiming Peter wouldn't welcome having a meal with him. She prayed he'd reconsider. How thankful she would be to have both of her brothers under her roof enjoying a hot meal together.

If only she'd known how much work it took to prepare an elaborate meal for so many people. The cafeteria workers at the university made cooking for a crowd look so easy. Her friends in Boston, mainly Bridget, with whom she'd shared a Thanksgiving dinner one time, seemed to prepare the feast with ease.

"Is there anything I can do to help?"

Rose glanced up and saw Sarah standing in the doorway.

"Yes, please." Relief flooded through Rose. She pointed to a kettle of boiled potatoes on a nearby table. "Will you mash those, please?"

Sarah stepped forward and leaned over the pot. She lifted the masher from the table and turned it this way and that. Then she gazed at Rose, confusion written in her expression.

"What does it mean, to mash potatoes?" she asked.

Rose bit her lower lip. Potato mashers were a relatively new thing in Boston, so how could she expect Sarah to know about them? A memory from her university days sprang to mind. She had volunteered to help the head cook in the kitchen in exchange for extra portions at mealtimes. After several mishaps, the woman had ordered her from the kitchen with instructions to never return.

When a new head cook replaced the old one, Rose did return, and under the woman's patient tutelage, she'd become a decent cook. All she'd needed was time and patience.

Rose breathed in and slowly exhaled. Carefully moderating her tone, she said, "Add a few splashes of milk to the pot and a spoonful of butter, then take that utensil and use it to mash the potatoes until they're creamy. I'll be over in a moment to help you."

She turned back to the stove and continued stirring the gravy.

Sarah retrieved butter and milk from the icebox. Then she sidled over to Rose and whispered, "Nathaniel told Joshua and me that he's given you a few lessons on our language and customs."

Rose sucked in a breath, and her heart thudded in her chest. She dropped the spoon into the pot of bubbling gravy and stared into Sarah's eyes. The consequences she and Nathaniel could face whirled in her mind like autumn leaves in a tornado.

"Ouch!" Rose pulled her hand away from the hot pan and reached for a wet cloth.

Sarah wrapped an arm around her. "Don't worry, my friend, your secret is safe with Joshua and me. After everything you and my brother have done for us and our children, we'd never do anything that would put either of you in danger."

Rose blew out a deep sigh and reached for Sarah's hand. "Thank you."

An understanding seemed to knit Rose to this strong woman, and their friendship deepened. She used a fork to fish the spoon from the gravy. After rinsing the spoon, she resumed stirring.

Finally, the meal was ready. The aromas permeated the house as Rose placed the last dish on the table and everyone gathered around and seated themselves. There wasn't enough room at the table for Chaske and Winuna, so they sat next to an overturned crate, waiting for their plates. Nathaniel said the blessing, and then the food was passed to her guests.

Peter said, "Wow, Sis, I didn't know you were such a good cook." He cleared his throat. "I, uh, spoke with Kane the other day. He said you invited him. If he shows up, I hope he behaves himself and isn't dressed like a Sioux warrior."

Rose's fork fell from her grasp and clattered to the plate. She glared at her brother. "You mean you hope our brother Kaneenawup dresses accordingly, forgets the old ways of life, and every word of the Lakota language! One more thing. We're not snakes in the grass, as the French would say. We are *Lakota*."

Where had that outburst come from? Rose bit her lower lip and turned to Nathaniel. Their gazes locked, his eyes as round as her pie pans. She glanced back at Peter, who chewed his food very slowly and swallowed.

"Don't be so dramatic, Rose." Peter set his fork aside. "Another newspaper wrote an article about the Ghost Dance, and a few settlers are riled up again. Matthew came to town and spoke with me about Ellie. It's nearly her time, and he's worried."

Rose hadn't thought of that. She needed to visit the woman and assure her that no war parties were afoot. She risked another exchange of looks with Nathaniel.

Peter glared at Nathaniel and reclined in his chair. Nathaniel shifted in his seat. Peter turned his head to face Rose and then again locked eyes with Nathaniel.

Sweat beaded at her temples. She glanced at Nathaniel and fanned her face with her napkin. Heaven help her, Peter suspected something. She tried to think of a lie, but none came to mind, nor did the courage to tell one, even if it had presented itself.

"What are you hiding from me? There's something going on between you two, isn't there?" Peter glowered at Nathaniel.

Joshua and Sarah leaned over their plates and gobbled their food so fast, Rose feared they'd choke.

She reached for her cup of coffee, sucked in a gulp, then aimed her sweetest smile at her brother. "Peter, it's not what you think. Nathaniel and I are spending a lot of time together, but we're just friends."

Nathaniel choked, cleared his throat, and stared at her. She knew what he was thinking. It was one thing for Joshua and Sarah to know about the language lessons, but Peter? He'd go straight to Agent Royer with any misgivings he might have and talk the agent into ordering them to stop.

She couldn't let that happen. "Peter, calm down. There's nothing to be upset about. I'm a grown woman, and I'll see whom I please, for whatever purposes I please."

He stared at her, his mouth hanging open. Then he shrugged. "You are an adult, Rose. I guess you can do what you want, as long as you don't break the law, if you get my meaning. I know Indians who have been arrested for refusing to assimilate."

Rose stood to her full height and placed her hands on her hips. "You're right. I am an adult, and my choices are my own, and if I choose to make inappropriate ones, I'm fully aware of the consequences. Now, if you'll excuse me, I need to check on the pie in the oven."

She strode into the kitchen and held a wet cloth to her face, taking pleasure in the coolness on her heated cheeks. She and Nathaniel would have to be more careful. She'd never forgive herself if she got him in trouble.

He stepped into the kitchen and stopped directly behind her.

"I have an idea," he whispered. "Why don't we let your brother think we're seeing each other romantically? That should throw off his suspicions, right?"

She turned and stared into his dark eyes, noting the emotion smoldering there. To convince her brother of something that wasn't true would be akin to lying to him with her lips. She refused to partake in such dishonesty. If Peter wasn't being such a traitor to their people, it wouldn't be an issue. For several long moments, anger at her brother boiled in her middle.

Someone banged on the front door. Reluctantly, Rose pulled herself from Nathaniel's gaze and stumbled to the front door. She smoothed her hair before pulling the door open and losing her breath.

"K–kaneenawup," she stammered.

Nathaniel stealthily eyed Rose's younger brother. Not surprisingly, he wore buckskin trousers, but at least he wasn't wearing his ghost dancing shirt, and he didn't appear to carry any weapons. Though it was cold outside, Kane lacked a coat, scarf, and gloves. Nathaniel hoped it prodded Peter to pity his youngest sibling and kindled a desire to make peace with him.

Kane stepped forward and embraced Rose, then shook hands with Peter.

Kane handed her a package wrapped in brown paper. "Here is some meat for you, Sister."

"Thank you." She hugged him again, then hurried into the kitchen. Moments later, she reappeared at the dining table, her cheeks flushed pink with what had to be happiness.

Nathaniel's teeth clanked onto his fork with more force than intended. He steered his thoughts toward ways to keep Peter from discovering his language lessons with Rose. If Kane decided to come into their lives on a regular basis, that would be two people to keep the secret from. Nathaniel didn't think Kane would be upset with them, but it would put another person in an awkward position.

What if Rose confided in Kane and not Peter, and Peter later discovered their secret? Wouldn't that drive a deeper wedge between the siblings? That was the last thing Nathaniel wanted, considering the tension was thick enough between the two brothers.

He glanced up and noticed his sister and Joshua staring at him. He hung his head, ashamed of the predicament he'd put them in.

Still, he believed the best course of action would be to tell everyone that he and Rose were romantically involved. Most people thought they were sweet on each other anyway.

Nathaniel kept his thoughts to himself as Peter and Kane droned on about horses and hunting. Kane even mentioned the Stronghold near the Badlands, and thankfully the conversation didn't result in them shouting at each other. They had Rose, the sensible peacemaker, to thank for that.

Peter stretched. "I'm stuffed. Can't eat another bite."

"Rose," Sarah said, "I'll help with the dishes."

The two of them moved to clear the table while Nathaniel, Peter, and Kane meandered into the sitting room. There weren't enough chairs to go around, so Kane sat on an old buffalo skin on the floor. Chaske and Winuna sat next to him, and he regaled them with stories of the buffalo hunts of yesteryear.

Peter said, "Chaske seems particularly taken with my younger brother."

Nathaniel logged a mental note to keep an eye on his nephew, to see that he didn't venture too far into traditional Lakota culture.

Much as he liked Kane, he didn't want Chaske or Winuna to acquire any habits or ideas that would displease any schoolteachers or government officials. His entire body tensed. It bothered him that his innocent nephew had to be instructed on such matters, and he swallowed the lump in his throat, attempting to listen to the discussion.

Later, the two women entered the room. Rose looked radiant. Her cheeks and eyes glowed, and her lips turned up in a grin. Nathaniel's attention was so fixed on her that everything else in the room faded.

Fearing that his growing feelings for Rose would be evident, Nathaniel stood. "I'm going outside to the woodpile for an armload. I'll return in a minute."

"Thank you." Rose's eyes shone as she spoke.

He smiled at her and then noted Peter giving him a look that said *we'll talk later*. He turned away and strode out the back door. After taking a few minutes to allow the frosty air to bring him to his senses, he filled his arms with firewood. Once inside, he added a chunk to the potbellied stove.

As dusk approached, Joshua shook hands with Peter and Kane and reached for his coat and those of Sarah and his children. "We must go now. The children have been sick, and I want them home before the ride gets too cold."

Sarah agreed and helped Joshua bundle them up.

Rose called over her shoulder as she hurried to the kitchen, "Let me prepare a basket of food for you folks."

Nathaniel would have to remember to thank her the next time he saw her. He hoped that would be tomorrow.

"Joshua," he said, "I'll follow you home."

"Thank you." Joshua buttoned his overcoat.

"Yes, thank you, Brother." Sarah pushed a lock of hair from her face and tugged mittens onto her daughter's small hands.

Soon the children were in the wagon, nestled under two wool blankets. He hoped they would fall asleep on the ride. There were things he wanted to discuss with his sister and brother-in-law. Should he tell them that he and Rose would try to convince Peter they were, what. . .*courting*, as the white people called it?

He shook his head and reconsidered. The less Joshua and Sarah knew about him and Rose, the better.

Nathaniel was so lost in his thoughts, they arrived at Joshua and Sarah's homestead before he could formulate any answers to the questions that tumbled through his mind. He carried his niece and nephew into the house and tucked them into their bed.

"Goodbye," he said to Sarah and Joshua. "I'll return tomorrow to help with chores."

He donned his hat and rode into town. After leading his horse into the barn, he combed the beast and then led it into a stall. He grabbed a change of clothes and trudged to the deputy's office. There, he dropped onto a cot. Exhaustion overwhelmed him, and he told himself that he was taking too many night shifts.

He tried to sleep, but thoughts agitated in his mind like churning river waters. Images of Rose filled his thoughts.

Her long dark hair shone like a curtain of black silk. Her eyes were as dark as the night sky and sparkled like the brightest stars in the heavens. When flustered, her cheeks turned an enchanting shade of pink, creating in him a desire to pull her into his arms and chase away whatever flustered her. When she pulled her lips into a pretty rosy pout, it was as if they begged to be kissed. When he imagined kissing those lips, his heart thrummed in his chest.

His wool blanket suddenly became too warm, and he threw it off, wiping the sweat beading on his brow. It wouldn't be so bad if he and Rose became romantically involved. And convincing her wasn't what troubled him.

He reclined on his cot and, without the aid of his blanket, tried to sleep.

By the time the rooster crowed, he'd slept little. He climbed from his bed, splashed his face with cold water from the washbasin, and ran a comb through his hair. He quickly dressed, though *not* in his Sunday best like the heroes of those romance novels Rose read.

The sun had crested over the horizon by the time he strode to Rose's house with confidence in his step, hoping she was up. Had it been spring, he would have robbed a flower bed of its blooms and offered them to her. With an uncomfortable shift in his footing, he feared he was more like those romance heroes than he cared to admit.

Smoke wafting from the chimney and a lit lantern in her kitchen window told him she was awake. He knocked, and when she pulled the door open, he said, "Rose, we need to talk."

CHAPTER 15

Rose stood in the doorway in her nightdress and robe, the cold wind blowing in. Her pulse ratcheted up a notch. In the early morning quiet, she heard someone whistling as they approached on horseback.

"Wait outside for a minute while I change."

She quickly shut the door, hoping Nathaniel had the sense to duck around the corner of her house, where the shadows and semidarkness would help hide him. She quickly donned her day clothes and then peeked out a window to ensure the rider passed. She then raced to the front door and opened it.

"Good morning," she said, ushering him inside. She could imagine what he wanted and licked her lips as if that helped her muster courage.

"Nathaniel, why are you here so early in the morning? It couldn't be a medical emergency, or I'd be speaking with Dr. Eastman instead of you."

His expression spoke of befuddlement. "I enjoy our time together, and I care for you, Rose, very much, and I like to think that you care for me too. If we give it a chance, I think our feelings for one another can grow. Considering how we feel about each other"—he waved a hand in the air—"being romantically involved wouldn't be far from the truth."

Indecision nibbled at her. He was right. Her feelings for him deepened every day, but where would it lead? Where *could* it lead? Marriage, and thus, the end of everything she'd worked so hard for, sacrificed so much for.

No, not yet, anyway. She needed time to make a difference in the lives of her people before calling an end to her occupation. She wrung her hands. More than once she'd envied Dr. Eastman. If he and Miss Goodale married, he'd be free to continue practicing medicine. Women weren't afforded the same luxury. At least that was what she'd been told in Boston.

She squared her shoulders and lifted her chin. "Nathaniel, I care for you, and yes, I'd enjoy getting to know you better, but I worry about where it will take us."

He frowned. "What do you mean?"

"Two days after we graduated from the university, my friend Bridget was married. Then, her husband asked her to stay home and take care of the house. I couldn't believe it when she agreed to it. After all the hard work of earning a nursing certificate, it's now going to waste."

He tilted his head to the side. "Rose, you don't know that."

"Well, now she's expecting a baby, and I'm happy for her, but I really don't see her working in a hospital while her husband stays home to care for the child." She cringed at the sarcasm in her tone. She hadn't meant to be rude. "I'm sorry, Nathaniel. Would you like some coffee? We can sit and talk for a while."

"Yes, please." He sat in a ladder-back chair and placed a foot on his opposite knee.

Rose strode into the kitchen and filled the pot and then quickly returned to the sitting room and placed it on the stove.

Nathaniel said, "I usually read the Bible in the morning. I'd like to read it with you, if you have one."

"I don't, but I have a lot of other books to choose from. We could turn this into a language lesson." She strode to her new bookcase and perused her volumes. Several medical books sat at one end of the shelf. If she considered them dull, Nathaniel likely would too.

A Christmas Carol. That would be perfect. She pulled it from the shelf and handed it to Nathaniel. "Would you mind reading this one? It's fairly short. It has a good moral message, and it's perfect for this time of year."

He opened it. "You want me to read it out loud, right now?"

"No better time to start, and please, replace as many English words as you can with Lakota ones." Rose sat in her rocker, eager to learn as much as she could.

For a quarter of an hour, Nathaniel read. When the coffee in the pot finished percolating, Rose reached for a tea towel and pulled it off the stove. She filled two cups with the brew and they continued.

By the time they heard the clanging of hammer on metal from the smithy's, Nathaniel had nearly finished the book. A wagon rattled and creaked as it passed her house. She rose and glanced out the window to see that it had stopped at the blacksmith shop.

Nathaniel gasped, quickly slamming the book closed as he sprang from his chair. "I need to go before I'm late for work."

Rose hated to see him leave, but she also had work that day. The shipment of medical supplies Dr. Eastman ordered had arrived, and she'd volunteered to help sort through them and take inventory. Perhaps she'd find something that would help ease Ellie Gardner's labor pains. She needed to make another trip out to see the woman soon.

"Nathaniel, I've brought you lunch at the agency a few times, but I can't today. I'm busy at the clinic."

"Don't worry. I'll make myself a sandwich." He shoved his hat on his head.

Rose peeked out the window and let him know when no one was looking. He hurried out the door.

Keenly feeling his absence, Rose closed the door and leaned against it. Her clock chimed, and she noted the time. She hurried into her bed chamber, ran a brush through her hair, and quickly plaited it. She shrugged into her coat and reached for the pot of still-warm coffee, intending to share it with Dr. Eastman.

Moments later, she breezed into the clinic and set the coffee on the stove. The doctor was already sorting through the crates of goods. Three Lakota men, wrapped in tattered blankets, stood at the window, waiting for cod liver oil—their "brown bottle" medicine.

The doctor used a crowbar to wrest the lid from the crate containing the cod liver oil. The dejected expression on his face and in his eyes spoke of how much it bothered him to give the men this medicine.

Perplexed, Rose leaned close and whispered, "Why does it make you sad to give cod liver oil to those men?"

Under his breath, he explained, "It saddens me that the men drink it for the meager amount of spirits the medicine contains. How hopeless and desperate they must feel."

Sighing deeply, he pulled three bottles from the crate and handed them through the window to the men waiting outside. Rose blinked back her tears and kept working.

Hours later, Miss Goodale entered the clinic with a warm meal for the doctor. He smiled and thanked her. Seeing the way they gazed longingly at each other, the way their hands touched when Miss Goodale handed the doctor his plate, Rose had no trouble surmising there was romance between these two. She'd even heard patients discussing the matter.

Not wishing to dwell on the business of others, she pushed the thoughts aside and focused on her job.

When the supplies were cataloged in the ledger, she placed them on the shelves and put the temperature-sensitive ones in the icebox. Her mind wandered to her time with Nathaniel that morning. Perhaps it wouldn't be so bad if there was a real romance between them. Maybe he wouldn't ask her to quit her nursing duties, at least for a while.

But what if they had children? Would Nathaniel trust her with them if he knew what had happened in Boston? Her breath hitched when she recalled those frightening days, the sick children, the lack of medicine, and those who blamed her for the shortage of it.

Dr. Eastman entered the room, and her thoughts lurched to a stop.

"I'm heading out to visit Chief Red Cloud," he said. "To see how his eyesight is doing. I shouldn't be too long."

"Give him my regards. If I need anything, I'll send for you."

He left, and she finished putting away the medicines and then seated herself in the rocker. She closed her eyes, hoping for a few minutes of sleep.

She startled when Peter stormed into the clinic and slammed the door. "What was Nathaniel doing at your house this morning *at dawn*?"

Rose stammered, panic sweeping over her. What exactly had her brother seen?

Peter's face turned red, and his eyes blazed with fire. "Don't deny it, Sister. I saw him leaving your house at sunup!"

Nathaniel had rushed through feeding and watering the horses and mucking the stalls. He'd stepped into the deputy's office, and to his relief, Coyote Who Sneaks wasn't there. The man was hardly ever there but still managed to collect his government paycheck.

Peter hadn't arrived for work yet either. That was odd, considering he was always at work before the sun peeked over the eastern horizon and stayed until long after it sank in the west.

Nathaniel tamped down his anxiety and started a pot of coffee. While waiting for the brew to heat, he lowered himself into a chair and read through yesterday's ledger.

The door swung open, and Peter entered, his face a mask of storm clouds.

Nathaniel reclined in his chair, the front legs lifting from the floor.

Sensing his friend's anger and hoping to alleviate it, he lifted a hand. "Hey, Peter."

His friend stomped toward him, placed his booted foot on the chair, and gave it a shove.

Nathaniel flailed his arms and fell over backward, his head bouncing on the hard wood floor with a painful thud.

"Ow!" He sat up and rubbed the back of his head, already feeling a goose egg forming. "What was that for, *friend*?"

Peter threw his arms open. "What do you think it was for? I saw you at my sister's house *early* this morning when I rode by. What were you doing there?"

Nathaniel noted his head was bleeding, so he yanked a bandanna from his pocket and held it to his throbbing head. "We were just reading a book together."

"That doesn't change the fact that you were in her house unchaperoned while it was still dark!" Peter leaned over him, his hands clenched into fists. "I'm telling you now, I won't have my sister's reputation sullied, particularly by someone I consider my best friend. The reservations are brimming with white men who dishonor our women. I won't have that happen to my sister, even by one of her own people."

Nathaniel held his hands up, palms facing his friend. "I wouldn't think of harming Rose." He cared deeply for her but wasn't about to admit *that*. Not now, anyway. But Peter was right. "I'm sorry. I'll be more mindful of when I'm meeting with her."

"My sister is the one you should be apologizing to." Peter retreated two steps, then spun on his heel and stormed from the office. He slammed the door so hard the glass rattled.

Nathaniel stood and righted the chair. Blood wet the nape of his neck, so he lumbered from the building to the clinic to have it checked.

The bell over the door jangled, and Rose glanced up from her work. Her eyes were wide, as if she guessed what had transpired between him and Peter.

"Rose," he began, "I'm sorry I arrived at your house so early this morning. I should have been more mindful of your reputation. From now on, I will be."

"That's all right. I'm as much to blame as you." She smirked. "I take it Peter has been to see you."

"Yeah." He steered the conversation to a more pressing topic. "I hit my head, and it's bleeding. It hurts, and I think it needs medical attention. Is the doctor here?"

"He's paying Chief Red Cloud a visit. Let me look at it." She stepped closer, tilted his head, and examined the wound. "It's not bad enough to need stitches, but it does need to be cleaned and bandaged."

He winced and stifled a cry as she dabbed his wound with a solution he thought for sure must be turpentine. With the job complete, they sat at a small table and ate lunch—watery bean soup, since the rations were late again.

When they finished, his belly was only somewhat full. He set the empty bowl on the table and stretched out his legs. His thoughts drifted to his predawn visit with Rose. Contentment overwhelmed him, though he would have to be more mindful of her reputation when they were together.

Sleepiness washed over him in visions.

Her pretty face ebbed into his dreams.

"Nathaniel!"

"What, what?" He sat up straight and then stared at the person who'd called his name.

Peter pulled on his hat and shoved his hands into his gloves. "I'm headed to see the Gardner family. Rose is going with me to check on Matthew's wife. We'll return before dark."

"All right," Nathaniel said.

Peter's mouth flattened into a hard line. The fire in his eyes could have melted a snowbank. "Agent Royer wants to meet with us tomorrow to discuss a serious matter. He wouldn't tell me what it was."

"Okay." He couldn't help but wonder what the man wanted.

"Since you're so keen on being up and visiting people before dawn, I figured you'd be all right with us meeting Royer first thing in the morning. I'm going to hitch up the wagon. See you in the morning." Peter stormed out the door.

Nathaniel jumped to his feet. "Rose!" he called out.

Her footsteps resounded from the kitchen before she entered the clinic's front room. She held a basket with what he presumed to be food. Her lips parted as her jaw slackened. "What's wrong?"

"You're going with your brother to the Gardners'."

She nodded.

"When you return, after Peter goes to sleep at the deputy's office, I need you to meet me in the barn."

"For a language lesson?" She looked and sounded befuddled.

"No. Peter and I are meeting with Agent Royer in the morning. I don't know what it's about, but it doesn't sound good. We can't lie, but we want to make sure we have our story straight."

"Good idea. I'll be watching and will sneak into the barn when the coast is clear."

Peter's voice boomed from outside, and then the bell above the front door jangled as she left.

CHAPTER 16

Darkness permeated Rose's house as she watched from behind a heavy curtain for Peter to leave town. Though it'd been his turn to stay at the deputy's office, Agent Royer had asked him to patrol a worried settler's homestead west of Pine Ridge, where several Indians had been hunting for game. Or so her brother had claimed.

She watched him exit the barn, mount his horse, and ride off into the night. The jingling of the bridle echoed in the cold darkness and then faded as Peter rode away. The deputy's office remained dark as well. Either the building was empty or another tribal deputy had volunteered for the night shift.

If someone currently occupied the office, what if they woke and discovered her and Nathaniel in the barn? She already harbored a number of secrets from her time in Boston. Innocent children suffered irreversible harm, all because she made the mistake of trusting Mr. Leon. Scandal was the last thing she needed.

Hence the reason they *must* remain quiet, to keep any hint of scandal from happening again.

Rose donned her coat, slowly pulled her front door open, and peered outside. Ears perked, she listened and heard nothing. Then she lifted the hem of her skirt and sprinted into the night. Reaching the barn, she opened the door and flinched when it creaked loud enough to be heard in Boston.

"Rose."

The scratchy whisper caused her to jump, and she let out a croaky gasp. Placing a hand over her chest to still her racing heart, she rasped, "Nathaniel? Is that you?"

He was at her side in an instant.

Her breath caught in her throat.

"Shh." He stepped away and lit a lantern.

In spite of her warm winter coat and gloves, it was cold in the barn. She shivered and rubbed at the goose bumps forming on her arms, though they were from fear as much as the brisk temperature. What if Agent Royer discovered her language lessons with Nathaniel? Would the man blame her and not one of his trusted tribal police officers? She'd asked herself that question a thousand times. And now, that possibility had become a reality. Fear wrapped icy tentacles around her, and the air seemed to freeze in her lungs.

Nathaniel said, "I'll carefully consider my words to try to leave you out of the conversation with Peter and Agent Royer tomorrow morning. I won't lie, but I'll do everything I can to keep from mentioning the reason we've been meeting. I think if Agent Royer wanted Peter to know, he would have already told him."

"I appreciate that, but we're going to have to tell Peter the truth soon. I don't like keeping secrets from what little family I have left, and I can't risk losing his trust." Her voice cracked. Tears pooled in her eyes. In spite of her best efforts, a sob escaped her lips, and she swiped at the tear that slid down her cheek.

Nathaniel stepped forward and pulled her into his arms. "It's all right, Rose. God will watch over us and take care of us."

She scoffed at the notion but placed her head on his chest anyway. The sound of his heartbeat met her ears. She took comfort in it. An old Lakota lullaby from childhood, one her mother had sung to Kaneenawup, floated into her mind. She sang the lyrics, and Nathaniel joined her.

"*Chante waste hoksila. . .la khe istinma. . .*"

When the song ended, he whispered, "'Kindhearted young boy, fall asleep.' My mother sang that to me when I was a boy."

He took her hands in his, squeezed them, and then led her to a chair near the stove. She sat and peered up at him. He squatted beside her and tucked a loose tendril of her hair behind her ear.

A coyote howled in the distance, and others replied with a series of yips. Walking home with the creatures afoot didn't stir reassurance within her, and she flinched.

He strode to the barn door and opened it, and a cold gust of air sailed inside. He peered out into the darkness and drew his revolver from its holster. Mercy, were the coyotes that close?

In spite of sitting near the stove, she shivered.

He closed the barn door, laid his revolver on the table, and returned to where she sat. "I didn't see anything out there. Let's practice a few names, shall we? Those ought to be safe enough, in case we're overheard by someone."

She nodded. "Good idea."

"How do you say Dr. Eastman's Lakota name?"

Rose closed her eyes to focus. "*Ohiyesa*. It means 'the Winner.'"

"That's right," Nathaniel said. "How about Sitting Bull?"

"The Lakota translation for Sitting Bull is *Tatanka Iotake*, meaning 'Buffalo Who Sits Down.'" She opened her eyes.

"Very good." The dim light in the barn reflected in his eyes, causing them to shine. He grinned and placed a hand on her shoulder. "Would you like to learn the Lakota translation of your name?"

She hadn't heard it since childhood, right before her parents died. Did she want to draw those memories to the surface? Well, she couldn't go her whole life avoiding them. Rose sat straighter and squared her shoulders. Though her Indian name had never escaped her, she longed to hear him say it. "Yes."

"*Wa-ka-cha-sha Minnihaha.*" The words were a gentle whisper from his lips. He took her hand and squeezed it gently.

Her heart fluttered. "Red Rose Falling Water." The breathy words escaped her lips. The barn's interior must have warmed considerably, because her cheeks heated so much she longed for a breeze to cool them. They continued, listing the Lakota names of their friends and family and the English translations. From there, they spoke of places they'd seen and hoped to visit someday. According to a windup clock on the table, they'd practiced Lakota words for nearly thirty minutes and should be ending the lesson soon.

Rose yawned, then stood and stretched. "I need to go. Will I see you tomorrow?"

Growling echoed through a crack in the structure's wall. In a flash, Nathaniel dashed to the table, grabbed his revolver, and returned to her side.

The barn door flew open.

He pressed her close to him, his strong arms comforting her. Fearing it might be the pack of hungry coyotes, Rose clutched handfuls of his shirt in her fists and pressed her body to his, seeking the protection of his embrace.

He swiftly pulled back the hammer and took aim at the barn's entrance.

Peter entered and held a lit lantern high. "First I catch you leaving my sister's house at dawn, and now I find you snuggled up to each other this late at night, and all alone."

Nathaniel's mouth went drier than a pile of sun-bleached bones. His throat constricted. He would have preferred facing the coyotes to Rose's furious brother. He swallowed, hoping a logical explanation would pop into his mind.

None did.

Light illuminated the barn's interior. The lantern swung slightly, casting eerie shadows against the hay bales and stalls.

Rose sputtered, "Peter, what are you doing here?"

"I could ask you the same thing," her brother growled. "I don't see any books in either of your hands, so don't tell me you're reading to each other again. The barn is no place for such a thing anyway, don't you agree?"

Peter placed the lantern on a nearby table next to the clock, then crossed his arms. Nathaniel feared a fight brewing between him and the man he called his best friend. If fists flew, Rose could be caught in the middle and injured. Worse yet, if the horses were spooked, they could trample her. The thought of that scared him more than his friend's wrath.

"Peter," Nathaniel said, "don't take your anger out on your sister. She's innocent. If you want to be mad at somebody, here I am."

Peter guided his sister toward the door with a gentleness that belied the fury on his face.

"Go home, Rose," he said.

She yanked her arm free, straightened her spine, and stood to her full height. "I'll do no such thing. I'm an adult, capable of making my own decisions, and that includes meeting with Nathaniel anyplace or anytime I please."

"Rose!" Nathaniel's stomach flipped and flopped so hard he thought he'd be sick. He was afraid Peter would tell Agent Royer. The man had the power to put both of them in jail until the federal authorities could transfer them to prison. Would he do that?

Peter's voice rose. "This isn't Boston, little sister, where your chaperones would simply admonish you for speaking your native language. Out here, Indian agents will arrest you for doing that. And don't try to tell me that wasn't what you were doing. I heard you."

Distressed to see his friend turning on his own sister, Nathaniel said, "What are you doing here, anyway? You said you were going to patrol around some scared settler's house. I saw you leave."

Peter raked his fingers through his hair. "I sent another deputy to take care of that, because I sensed something going on between you two. So I told you and Rose I was leaving. About a half mile out of town, I picketed my horse and ran back here."

"So you tricked us." Rose's eyebrows lifted, and a second later they angled into a frown. "You lied to us."

Peter glared at her, clenched his fists, and paced the length of the structure. "Now I know it's something more than just romance. I heard both of you speaking the Lakota language. What if Agent Royer had been the one to walk in here? Do you have any idea the trouble the both of you would be in?"

"It's not as bad as you think." Nathaniel gulped. But it was what Peter suspected. The emotions within him seesawed up and down. He refused to lie to his best friend. His faith and his respect for the man wouldn't allow it. He and Rose were speaking Lakota and growing closer with each lesson, and now they would suffer the consequences. What could he say that would dispel his friend's anger?

Peter faced him. His eyes blazed. "My sister has just been returned to me. I don't want to lose her again!"

She threw her hands in the air. "I'm tired of keeping this from you, Peter. Nathaniel and I have been conducting more than language lessons. He's been teaching me some of the customs I'd forgotten."

Terror crawled up Nathaniel's spine, rendering him mute.

"First thing tomorrow, me and the both of you"—she wagged her finger between him and Peter—"are going to meet with Agent Royer.

He'll find out that Peter knows about the lessons, and we'll let the chips fall where they may."

Nathaniel stood stunned, at a lack for words, though he admired her spunk.

Rose spun on her heel and stormed from the barn. The door slammed shut with a loud bang. He immediately thought of the coyotes in the area and voiced a prayer for her safety.

Nathaniel turned to his friend, hoping to calm the tension pulsing through the air.

A fist shot out of nowhere and smacked him square in the jaw.

CHAPTER 17

The next morning, Nathaniel stood in Agent Royer's office with Peter and Rose. He rubbed his aching jaw. Though his friend's fist had left a good-sized bruise and it had swollen enough to hurt when he ate his breakfast, he couldn't blame Peter. If Joshua had behaved that way with Sarah before they were courting, he'd be angry too. At least none of his teeth had been knocked loose. That was a mercy.

Rose had discussed everything with the agent while his clerk took notes. "So you see, Mr. Royer, I was correct when I said there is a benefit to the language lessons. I've been doing a better job of assessing what's wrong with those patients who don't speak English very well."

Nathaniel admired her bravery but still worried about the consequences.

Agent Royer scowled and thumped his fist on his desk. "I could hold you responsible for not heeding my warnings to keep this quiet, but I'm not angry enough to have you two arrested. This town needs medical professionals and deputies. We need the both of you."

Nathaniel moved his gaze to the rough-hewn pine floorboards. He twisted his hat in his hands and shifted his weight from one foot to the other.

The clerk was a different story. He had faced each person as they spoke and seemed to study them with interest throughout the whole conversation. It was a change in his demeanor, because he usually disregarded anything the Indians had to say.

"May we be excused now, please, Agent Royer?" Rose asked. She tilted her head and leveled a smile at him. "Nathaniel and I promise to be careful about where and when we speak our language. I will only use it with patients who don't speak English."

"Please see that you do, Miss Rushing Water. Remember, I could still have you arrested at any time for this infraction. Now, if you'll excuse me, I need to speak to Mr. Gray Cloud and your brother about an important matter."

Rose strode from the room, closing the door behind her.

Agent Royer drummed his fingers on his desk. He faced Nathaniel and then turned to Peter. "Agent McLaughlin is planning to arrest Sitting Bull for allowing ghost dancers on his farm. If there is any way you can convince your people to stop this nonsense and act civilized to avoid the risk of violence, I would rest a lot easier."

Peter muttered something under his breath.

Nathaniel cut in. "We'll see what we can do, sir. May we go now?"

"Yes, go." He waved them from the room.

Peter pushed away from the wall and sidled over to Nathaniel. "You two are getting off easy, and you better be careful."

He stormed from the room, nearly bumping into his sister, who stood just outside the door. Peter's footsteps resounded from the hallway. The front door opened and slammed shut, rattling the glass pane. Nathaniel loathed seeing his friend so angry but was at a loss for how to fix the animosity brewing between them.

To the agent, he said, "Thank you, sir." He stepped into the hallway and offered Rose his arm. She placed her hand in the crook of his elbow. The pained look in her eyes didn't escape his notice. He ached for her, but the agency wasn't a place to discuss delicate matters.

They left the man to his business and strolled outside into the chilly air.

Peter waited on the boardwalk. "I hope Kane doesn't find out about Agent McLaughlin's plans for Sitting Bull."

Rose dropped her hands to her side. "What plans? And what do they have to do with our brother?"

Peter relayed the agent's words. "I think it'll push Kane over the edge."

"Yes, I think it will too," Rose said. "But will you please call him by his *real* name? It's Kaneenawup, and he's only recently, grudgingly, agreed to halt his dancing for the time being. If he's told to stop forever, it'll only encourage him and the rest of our tribe to dance all the more."

Nathaniel's middle swirled with a mixture of emotions he struggled to separate. Thankful for the agent's mercy, he agonized about the growing tensions between his people, the government, and the frightened settlers. To lose his language and be forbidden to practice his Lakota traditions left a painful gaping hole in his heart. The thought of being jailed or killed for refusing to abandon his heritage haunted his sleep at night.

Years ago, while he and Peter had been out hunting, two separate wolf packs had surrounded them. One group paced to the left of them, the other to the right. Both packs growled and bared their teeth. Each pack wanted to make them their next meal.

He and Peter had drawn their pistols. Peter fired to one side and he had fired to the other. Two wolves dropped, and the rest scattered.

Nathaniel sensed that he and his people were in the same situation. Trapped between two determined forces, only this time, he and Peter couldn't aim a gun at the parties threatening them.

Peter blew out a defeated-sounding sigh and leaned close to his sister. "The last thing we need is for *Kaneenawup* to make a run for the Standing Rock Reservation and join Sitting Bull."

She lifted her chin and stuck her hands on her hips. "You don't need to use such a nasty tone when saying his name, Brother. Maybe we can halfway assimilate until things blow over, just enough to calm the settlers and the agent."

Peter shuddered and shook his head. "I've got a bad feeling about this."

"I do too." Fear shone in Rose's eyes. "I'm afraid for my people," she wailed. "I'm afraid of losing what little family I have left."

The sound tore at Nathaniel's heart. He wrapped an arm around her, hoping the gesture brought her a measure of comfort. He silently thanked God that Joshua and Sarah had adapted to white culture without too much difficulty. If his sister had been as resistant to assimilation as Kane, his heart would have shattered into pieces. But premonitions of impending doom seemed to hover over the reservation like dark storm clouds. No matter how much he prayed, the feelings didn't dissipate.

Peter donned his hat. "I'm off to find Kaneenawup and invite him to stay with us at the deputy's office where we can keep an eye on him. You don't have any objections to this, Nathaniel?"

"Fine by me." He pulled the collar of his coat tighter around his neck. Mercy, it was cold out. "I'd like to have someone in the barn helping me care for the horses."

Rose's face brightened. "That's a wonderful idea. I think he'd love that. Thank you both, Peter and Nathaniel." She reached for Nathaniel's arm and gazed at him with eyes that shone. Her cheeks were the color of prairie roses in full bloom.

Peter mumbled something under his breath that Nathaniel wouldn't repeat.

He cleared his throat and turned to Rose. "Would you like to go for a ride and a picnic? I have the day off, and I know a nice wooded area a short ride from here."

She squeezed his arm tighter. "Yes, that would be lovely."

Peter reached for his horse's reins and climbed into the saddle. "While you two are being amorous with each other, I'm off to the nearest dance camp to find my brother."

Rose said, "Check the one east of Pine Ridge, near Wounded Knee Creek."

Peter rolled his eyes, shoved his hat on his head, and rode off.

Nathaniel prayed his friend would dispel any notions of an uprising. Hoping to calm Rose's fears, he walked with her along the street. "Do you have food to pack a picnic lunch? I have a few things I can add."

"I'll run home and fix something. I have boiled eggs and some cheese and bread, but I'm afraid there isn't much more."

"That'll do. Don't forget to dress warmly and pack a blanket or two. It's quite cold out, and I think this will be an all-day excursion."

"I'll do that and return shortly." She buttoned her coat around her middle and jogged across the street.

He watched her duck into her house and then turned toward the barn. Inside, he blew on his hands to warm them so he could more easily hitch the mounts and hook them to the wagon owned by the tribal police department. Other officers had borrowed it, and he didn't think anyone would mind if he took it.

The horses seemed to sense his uneasiness. No matter how many soothing words he spoke, no matter how many times he gently rubbed their sleek warm necks, they whinnied, snorted, and stomped on the ground as he put the bridles on them and adjusted the reins.

Rose had returned by the time he'd finished. "I'm ready."

"So am I. Will you open the barn doors, please?"

She did, and then strode to his side with a bounce in her step. He assisted her into the wagon and climbed onto the seat next to her. After chirruping to the skittish horses and steering them from the barn, he jumped from his perch and closed the barn doors. When he returned to his seat, he snuggled as close to Rose as propriety allowed.

They were nearly a mile out of town when she asked, "Are you all right? You seem unusually quiet. Is something bothering you?"

He shrugged. "I have a sense of foreboding at the pit of my stomach that I haven't been able to settle, and I can't guess why." Was God trying to warn him of impending danger?

"Oh." She folded her hands in her lap and stared straight ahead.

Nathaniel wondered if she too wrestled with anxiety. She had to be worried about her brothers.

They rode another few miles over the rolling prairie in comfortable silence, and then he spotted a stand of trees alongside White Clay Creek. It was a private place he liked to go when he wanted to be with God, a place where he felt free to pour his heart out to his Savior.

Rose's voice was almost a whisper. "It's beautiful out here, Nathaniel. So peaceful and serene."

"Yes, it is."

"Kaneenawup used to play here as a child. It's where I found him when our parents died. I remember that tree—it's shaped kind of like a cross."

He placed his hand over hers for a moment and then guided the horses along a faint path that led to the bank of the small creek. After helping Rose down, he tied the horses to a nearby tree branch. The skittish beasts tugged at the lines until he petted their necks and spoke softly to them.

He strode to where Rose had laid a blanket on the ground and placed their lunch atop it. He sat, prayed over the meal, and helped himself to the bread and cheese she handed him.

Rose said, "When you finish your sandwich, I have a surprise for you."

Minutes later, he'd eaten his meal and brushed his hands on a cloth napkin. "So," he said, "what's the surprise?"

She reached into her basket and pulled out a small cake. "I bought this at the mercantile to celebrate our ability to practice our language without fear of being arrested."

His heart softened like butter on a hot summer day. "That's nice."

She sliced a piece and offered it to him.

The horses whinnied.

He jumped to his feet and glanced over the embankment. In the distance, he spotted a company of soldiers. Two of them had their weapons drawn.

Rose shifted from foot to foot and chewed her fingernail as she watched Nathaniel jog toward the soldiers, his arms up in a gesture of surrender. Did these men in army blue suspect she and Nathaniel were up to something nefarious? Obviously, or they wouldn't be aiming their weapons at them! Her stomach convulsed, knowing these men had the power to give them trouble. Her experience with Mr. Leon had proved that much. How would she explain that to Peter?

Did Nathaniel know either of these soldiers? Did he have any clout with them, being a tribal deputy? She hoped so. She released a deep breath when the belligerent-looking soldiers holstered their weapons. Nathaniel waved at them and jogged back to the creek bank.

"They're just a small company out on patrol. Nothing to worry about."

Rose released another breath and sat down on the blanket. Her stomach was full of savory cheese, bread, and cake, and sitting beside Nathaniel, she should be content. So why did feelings of anxiety remain? Could it be lingering distrust of the soldiers?

She should be relieved that their secret was out in the open. But however grateful she was that the truth had been revealed, the situation was still fraught with danger—like the threat of being arrested at the slightest misstep!

What if Agent Royer had a change of heart and ordered them to face the consequences of their actions? Who would help Dr. Eastman care for her people if she was in jail, or worse, sent to prison? The repercussions of her choices weighed on her.

She smoothed the wrinkles from her dress, at a loss for words.

Nathaniel stood and strolled to the nearest tree. Two branches grew from the trunk, one on each side, about three-fourths of the way up. Stripped of leaves, the bare tree did indeed resemble a cross.

He ran his fingers over the bark and then tilted his head to the heavens, as if expecting the angel Gabriel to appear. Why was he so silent?

Rose longed to tell him all her hopes and fears, even if the two of them were never more than friends. Did he not trust her with his feelings? The thought drove a spike through her soul. If she had done something to lose his trust, it would crush her, and of course she'd want to make amends for it.

Rather than cajole him to confide in her, she let him be.

He turned and stared at her, his eyes shining with an emotion she couldn't label. "I was just thinking of my relationship with God."

She hopped to her feet. Considering her feelings about God, it was no wonder he didn't want to talk to her about what beleaguered him.

He grinned and once again turned his face to the sky. "You don't think much of God, do you, Rose?"

"Well. . ." She swallowed hard. "It's not that I don't believe in Him. It's just that—" Shivers that had nothing to do with the cold wind swept over her, and she huffed. "If God is so loving and merciful, then why are some Christians so cruel to us?"

He lowered his head and leveled his gaze at her. "Because God gives man free will."

She blew out a hard sigh. "So, he *allows* people to hurt us. And you want me to trust Him?" She stifled a scoff but couldn't resist folding her arms over her chest and rolling her eyes.

He continued. "In the Garden of Eden, God gave Adam and Eve the choice whether or not to obey Him. In the New Testament, Jesus says He stands at the door and knocks. He doesn't kick the door open and barge inside. He gives people the free will to decide for themselves if they want to answer the door. Too many Christians forget that and try to shove Jesus through the door, regardless of what the inhabitants of the house feel." He lowered his head and sighed.

"There are people who want to see us exterminated." She practically spat the words.

"Yes. And I believe God is angry with how cruel some people are to us, but He gives us free will too, Rose."

"I don't understand. If He commands people to love one another, why do they disobey Him and inflict cruelty of unimaginable proportions on blameless victims? Why would I want to love and serve a God who allows His so-called followers to harm people? You think I haven't heard of the Sand Creek Massacre?"

Nathaniel backed up a few steps. His eyes held the same haunted expression, but now he looked as though she'd slapped him. She'd hurt him. Guilt seeped into her.

"Nathaniel, I'm sorry." Ashamed of her harsh words, she stepped toward him, hoping to make amends. She reached for his shirtsleeve, and to her surprise and relief, he didn't pull away.

He took her hand and led her to another tree. It had many more branches, though they were bare and blew in the gusts of wind. He motioned at the copse around them. "Do you see all these trees?"

Unable to grasp his meaning, she tapped her foot on the cold, hard ground. "What are you talking about, Nathaniel? Of course I see them. What do they have to do with our conversation?"

A bright smile lit up his face. "Aren't they beautiful?" Excitement infused his tone.

She craned her neck for a better view of the branches overhead. "Yes, even though they are bare, I must admit, they do possess a haunting beauty."

Nathaniel pointed upward. "And they have a purpose. Wood from these trees is used for more than just firewood to heat our homes. It's used to build our homes and barns to keep us and our animals safe and warm. It's used to build furniture, like the beds we sleep in, and your rocking chair. It's also used to produce paper for the letters you write to your friend in Boston, and for the books you so love to read."

Rose tapped her foot, feeling her patience slipping away. "I know that, but what's that got to do with your faith?"

The sparkle in his eyes dimmed. "Wood has also been used for horrible things, like the paddles white teachers used to beat us with when we spoke our language. Wood has been used to perpetuate evil, like burning people at the stake and as whipping posts for slaves." The words tumbled from his mouth.

After a pause, he continued. "Are we to stop using wood to build homes, barns, and furniture because evil people use wood for things the Good Lord never meant His creation to be used for? Are you going to stop using paper to write to your friend and quit reading the books you love so much because greedy, selfish, arrogant people misused it and built slave ships?"

She shook her head.

"Rose, *Wakan Tanka* made these trees for us to enjoy, to glean fruit and nuts from them. He meant them for good, like many things in life, and much like Christianity. But people often misuse these things, wood and religion, for evil that does great harm."

The puzzle pieces of his explanation fit together in her mind. Warmth kindled in her middle and radiated outward as she began to understand. She couldn't move into a cave rather than live in a house built with boards, or refrain from using firewood because evil men used wood to commit horrid atrocities.

It made no sense to do something like that.

Should she reject Christianity because evil people used it as a weapon to hurt and control others? Is that what she had been doing? It hurt to think that maybe she had.

Finally, she found her voice, though it was just a whisper. "We don't blame the creator of the wood that's used for evil. We blame the person using the wood for evil purposes."

Nathaniel continued in soft, almost hoarse utterances. "In a time when the world seems to be going crazy and there's so much fighting between people, we can't allow the evil actions of a few to keep us from enjoying the good things God has to offer us. That's something I try to not lose sight of."

CHAPTER 18

December 15, 1890

For the past few weeks, Nathaniel had regularly driven Rose to White Clay Creek for a picnic. They spent their time talking about the goings-on in town, books, and his favorite, their childhoods. His heart had nearly wrenched in two when she told him about when her parents died. And she had laughed when he told her that he and Sarah had fashioned bows and arrows out of twigs so they could go hunt buffalo.

The memories of their time together warmed his heart, especially since they had spent time discussing his faith again.

Cold wind blew across the prairie, drawing him back to their present time together. Usually, focusing his attention on his Lord and Savior brought warmth to his heart, but now icy gusts that chilled him to his core whirled around him and Rose. Or did he shiver because that odd sense of foreboding had returned to haunt him?

He glanced at Rose, intending to tell her it was time to go. Judging from the way she tilted her head to the side and tapped her chin with her forefinger, she appeared to be mulling over their conversation about his faith, and he didn't want to interrupt her. That she'd actually listened ignited hope that someday she'd invite Jesus into her life.

It seemed heartless to disturb her, so he busied himself by buttoning up his coat and donning a pair of gloves. A companionable silence stretched between them. He would have enjoyed discussing his faith with her further, but he felt God prompting him to return to town. The feeling weighed heavily on him.

The wind increased, demanding his attention. He gazed upward. Strong gales roared and whipped through the trees, causing even the larger branches to sway and creak. Alarm needled him.

"Rose, we need to go." He slapped his hat on his head and tightened the string under his chin to help keep it in place. Rose looked in his direction and then pivoted in a circle. She hastened to pack the remains of their lunch, then ran to the wagon, where he helped her step up onto the seat. He quickly undid the horse's reins and leaped onto the seat beside her.

Fearing a tornado, he flicked the reins and hollered at the animals.

His people were ill-equipped to survive a tornado. He had helped Joshua dig a small root cellar when they built his cabin. It wouldn't do the man much good if he was working far from the house. At least Sarah and the children could find refuge there, providing they were in close proximity and able to reach it before calamity struck.

"Ha! Ha!" he called to the already-galloping horses. Guilt welled in him for pushing them so hard, but he sensed something was terribly wrong.

"Nathaniel, please slow down!" Rose cried. She bounced on the wagon seat and clung to it as if it were a lifeline. Her long braid bounced against her back as she ducked her head.

Reluctantly, he eased up on the reins. His hat was lifted by a sudden gust and threatened to take flight. He emitted a sigh and retightened it with one hand while holding the reins with his other. Reducing their speed didn't ease his mounting trepidation.

The town finally appeared on the horizon, bringing a small feeling of relief.

Was that a horse he saw galloping toward them? He squinted into the darkening atmosphere, attempting to decipher what he saw. Rose voiced her own confusion.

A minute later, he recognized Peter approaching. Rose gasped. Had something happened to her younger brother, or was Peter seeking them for a completely different reason?

Nathaniel sat straighter. He hoped he hadn't done anything to warrant another argument with his friend.

He pulled on the reins, halting the horses as Peter drew closer and tugged on his own horse's reins. The horse neighed and reared up on its haunches. A second later, its front paws hit the ground with a thud. "I've been looking for you two. Nathaniel, you're needed at the agency."

"What's wrong?" Rose asked. "Is Kaneenawup all right?"

Peter glowered at her. "Our brother is distraught and angry, but as safe as he can be, considering the circumstances."

"What circumstances?" Nathaniel's curiosity rose, but he dreaded the answer.

"Agent Royer received a wire from Agent McLaughlin. It's Sitting Bull." Peter yanked his hat off and slapped it against his thigh.

Scenes collided in Nathaniel's mind. Ghost dancers, frightened settlers, conflict that resulted in skirmishes, the potential for lives lost. The contents of his picnic lunch threatened to come up. In spite of the icy gales, sweat beaded on his forehead.

Rose leaned forward on the seat, her tone panic-stricken. "Tell us what happened to Sitting Bull!"

Peter released a loud, agony-filled groan and pointed his face at the charcoal-colored sky.

"He's been shot dead. Murdered by his own people, the tribal police."

Rose clutched the wagon seat to keep from falling to the ground. Sitting Bull, the Lakota people's great leader? The wise and kindhearted man she'd met and tended to in Boston? The one she'd wanted to meet again and have a chance to listen to his stories?

Dead?

No, she couldn't believe it. Oh, why had she delayed in writing to him? She should have traveled to the Standing Rock Reservation to visit him.

She didn't want to believe the news, but at the same time, she knew it had to be true. Her heart volleyed between thudding wildly in her chest and periodically lurching before resuming its jerky cadence.

Nathaniel steered the conveyance into town, through the muddy street, and into the barn. They lowered themselves from the wagon seat and onto the barn floor. A slew of emotions muddled within Rose.

Disbelief. The Great Chief couldn't be dead.

Anger. All the man wanted was peace. Why would someone shoot him?

Sadness. What were her people going to do without their respected leader?

Nathaniel proceeded to unhitch the horses and remove the bridles.

Rose bolted from the barn and toward the agency's administration building. Her boots slapped against the wet ground as she ran, and she didn't care if she was muddying the hem of her skirt.

Behind her, Nathaniel called, "Rose, wait!"

But she couldn't. This had to be a mistake, and she had to know for sure. The administration building was just ahead. She burst through the door. Nathaniel bumped in behind her. He reached to steady her and mumbled an apology.

Agent Royer stood in the front lobby, beside the clerk, dictating a message for the telegraph.

"Is it true?" Nathaniel gasped. "Has Sitting Bull been killed?"

The man stared at them and nodded. "Yes, he has, and furthermore, his camp has been disbanded. Now we can put this ghost dancing craze behind us and get on with our lives."

"B–but, sir—" Rose stammered.

"Considering these circumstances, I think it's best if you stop language lessons and any discussions of native customs, at least for a while." The man shuffled a handful of papers and strode to his office. The desk clerk looked as bereft as she felt.

Eerie silence filled the room.

Rose wanted to argue but thought better of it and placed a hand over her mouth. She darted from the building and sprinted across the street toward her house.

Nathaniel called her name again, his footsteps echoing behind her. The last thing she wanted to hear was his declarations of faith. If God cared about her people, He would show some mercy and understanding for their grief.

Rose burst through her front door without bothering to close it behind her and for a few seconds tried to distract herself with the knowledge that she could escape into a book. She imagined reading all night, but dawn would break and the sun would rise, and with it, the painful reminder. Another person symbolizing her heritage had been taken before she had the chance to fully know him. Another piece of her heritage, the Ghost Dance, had been stripped from her before she had the chance to participate in it.

"Rose." Nathaniel stood in the doorway and locked eyes with her. "I won't ask if you're all right, because I know you're not. But I will say that

I'm sorry this happened."

She began sobbing, and he pulled her into his arms. She placed her head on his chest and wept, crying for the loss of their leader, for his family, for each piece of her heritage that was being stripped away bit by bit.

He ran his fingers through her tangled hair. "I'm sorry, Rose. Sitting Bull was a proud and wise man. His death is a great loss to all of us."

Rose didn't know how long she stood with her head against Nathaniel's chest, listening to his heartbeat. Her throat ached and her lungs burned with the knowledge that things would never be the same.

News of Sitting Bull's death must have reached other members of the tribe, because drumbeats and songs of mourning echoed from outside and floated into the interior of her home.

Rose snapped to the present. "Where are my brothers?"

"Guarding each other, I hope. Peter is probably comforting Kane, likely begging him to refrain from seeking vengeance."

"You're right." She stepped out of his arms. "I better put on some coffee. I have a feeling it's going to be a long night."

While she scooped the last remnants of grounds into the coffeepot, someone knocked on her door. She hurried into the sitting room in time to see Nathaniel usher Peter inside.

"Did you bring Kaneenawup with you?" she asked. "I'd like to see him. I'm sure he's crazy with grief. I'd like to console him, if he'll let me."

Peter raked his fingers through his short hair and paced the floor. "I don't know where he is. I told him to stay in the deputy's barn while I looked for you, but when I returned, he was gone."

"We have to find him," she wailed. "There's no telling what he'll do."

"I'll help you search for him," Nathaniel said. "But first, we need to talk about where he would go, and then we need to split up to cover more ground. Rose, finish making that coffee, please."

She rushed to do as he asked. Peter answered a second knock at her door. From her kitchen she heard Agent Royer speaking to the other two men.

"I'm sorry about Sitting Bull," she heard him say, "and I sympathize with you Indians, but I didn't want any bloodshed."

"None of us did," Peter retorted.

Nathaniel concurred.

Peter added, "We'll do what we can to keep more blood from being spilled."

The conversation ended, and the agent left.

Rose pulled two empty coffee ration bags from her kitchen drawer. She tucked slices of bread and cheese into each one so Peter and Nathaniel could eat while they hunted for Kaneenawup.

They stepped outside a short time later. The wind blew fiercely, as if the air itself twisted and writhed with grief at the aching loss of Sitting Bull.

"You stay here in case Kane comes back," Peter said to her. "If he does, don't let him leave." He shoved his hat on his head, buttoned his coat, then hugged her and strode toward the barn.

Nathaniel held her close for a long moment and then followed her brother.

Darkness encroached, spurring her desire to find Kaneenawup quickly.

She watched Peter as he rode west and thought of the place where her young brother had run to when their parents died. She prayed Peter would find him there. Minutes later, she waved at Nathaniel as he headed east.

Easing into her rocking chair, she tried to read. She attempted three different Jane Austen romances but lost her focus with each one after a mere two paragraphs. Sighing, she set her books aside and stood. Three times she circled her sitting room, pausing at each rotation to look out her window, searching the horizon for Nathaniel and her brothers.

She kicked off her shoes and padded to the kitchen, then washed dishes and wiped the counters. Seeing no other housekeeping chores that needed attention, she stuffed the stove full of wood and dropped back into her rocker.

Hours later, Peter returned. She opened the door, and he breezed inside.

The first thing she noticed was his attire. "Why are you dressed in civilian clothes and not in your deputy uniform?"

"Because it was tribal police who shot Sitting Bull while trying to arrest him," he huffed. "A lot of people don't trust tribal police right now, so I changed before going to look for our brother."

"That's understandable," she muttered.

Peter blurted, "I found Kane at the camp at Wounded Knee Creek. He's asking for you."

She exhaled with deep relief and rushed to don her socks and shoes. She grabbed a blanket and yanked her coat off the hook before following her brother outside.

In the barn, Peter said, "I'm leaving a note for Nathaniel, informing him of the situation and where to find me in case I'm needed. I'm also telling him to keep the stove in your house filled. Do you have any objections to that?"

"None at all. When we bring Kaneenawup home, I want the house good and warm for him." Rose helped quickly hitch the tribal deputy's wagon, and then Peter assisted her onto the seat. She hung on as they rode into the night.

When the moon was high overhead, they reached the camp.

After questioning someone about her brother, she finally located him, huddled in one of the tepees, with a bedraggled group of people who were sobbing and wailing songs of mourning. Rose held Kaneenawup close and whispered what she hoped were words of comfort. And still, he wept just as he had when their parents died.

CHAPTER 19

The sun eased itself over the eastern horizon and slowly climbed higher into the magenta-colored sky. The air was so cold it sank deep into Rose's core whenever she ventured more than a few feet from a fire.

She shivered even though she'd bundled herself tightly with every piece of winter clothing she owned. She longed for her warm house and hoped Nathaniel had found Peter's note and stoked her stove. Her chest ached as she helped Kaneenawup pack his meager belongings. A tattered buffalo skin, a leather pouch filled with trinkets, and an old beans ration bag he clung to, containing a threadbare shirt and a pair of dingy white socks with holes at the toes and heels.

"The minute we get home, I'm fixing you a nice hot meal and darning your socks." Rose tried to sound cheerful, hoping it would ease her brother's despondency.

Kaneenawup muttered a monotone reply. "I'm not hungry. I don't care where we go, as long as it's warm and I can lie down and sleep."

Her eyelids fluttered as she folded his ghost dancing shirt, unable to meet his gaze as she tucked it into the bag with his socks.

She understood that he grieved, but something had been snuffed out of her younger brother too. It seemed he'd lost his will to cling to the Lakota traditions. He sounded defeated and without hope. That not only worried but frightened her.

Fearing that a sudden snowstorm could hinder their journey to town, she wanted to leave posthaste. She went looking for Peter and found him speaking with a gray-haired elder.

"Can you help our brother into the back of the wagon, please? I'll carry his things."

"Sure." Peter followed her to the tepee, looped his arms under

Kaneenawup's, and hefted him upright. They traipsed to where the wagon sat. To her consternation, her younger brother hadn't protested or so much as uttered a word. He just crawled into the rear of the wagon.

Rose covered her brother with his buffalo skin, and her heart wrung itself tight when he curled into a ball and pulled the skin over his head. She patted his back and set his belongings beside him.

She tried to tell herself that all he needed was time to work through his grief, a hot meal, and a good night's sleep. Or a day's sleep, in this case, but that hope didn't burn very bright.

"Come, Rose. We need to go." Peter took her hand and helped her climb onto the wagon seat. As he settled beside her, a woman raced toward them and grabbed the wagon wheel.

Tears streamed down the stricken woman's cheeks. "Are you the medicine woman who works with Dr. Eastman? My child is sick. Will you help us, please?"

Never before had Rose felt so torn. Much as she wanted to take her brother home, a sick child needed her. Kaneenawup, she believed, would understand and be content to wait.

She reached for her bag and then laid a hand on Peter's shoulder. "I'll be just a few minutes. Will you wait?"

He shrugged. "All right, but try not to be too long."

She dropped to the ground and followed the woman into a small tepee. A little boy with a sweaty face looked up at her with glassy eyes. He couldn't have been more than four years old. She ran her fingers through his hair and whispered the words of the Lakota lullaby she'd recently relearned.

Her quick examination of the child revealed no cough or congestion in the lungs. No soreness in the throat or rashes anywhere on his body. His slight fever should be easy enough to remedy.

She fished a white pill from her bag and handed it to the woman. "This is a new medication that helps with fevers. Give him one quarter of the pill now, and another quarter before bedtime, and he should be right as rain by tomorrow morning."

The woman grasped her hands and beamed. "Thank you." She whispered her thanks to *Wakan Tanka*. "What of the other half?"

"Save it, in case his fever returns," Rose said.

The woman thanked her again and offered a small palmful of no more than eight or nine dried beans. Tears brimmed in Rose's eyes. She had to swallow twice before the lump in her throat dissipated. She'd gladly starve before exacting those beans from this mother as payment for helping her child.

She folded the woman's hand closed and pointed to the child. "Feed them to your boy, so he can grow into a big strong warrior."

The woman hugged her, and Rose reciprocated the embrace, feeling warmth course the length of her body.

She gathered her things and shoved them into her bag, then exited the tepee and hurried to the wagon where Peter and Kaneenawup waited. As soon as she was seated, Peter flicked the horses' reins and drove the team away from the camp.

Later, when the town came into view, she tried to rouse her brother. He grunted a reply but remained buried under his buffalo skin. Rose squeezed his shoulder. She no longer worried about her brothers arguing over Lakota traditions, but she feared what Peter might say to their emotionally fragile young brother.

As soon as he steered the horses onto Main Street, Rose breathed a sigh of relief. Nathaniel stood outside her home, holding a pot that she hoped contained a warm meal. Smoke puffed from the stovepipe. Nathaniel must have done what Peter asked and stoked her woodstove.

Considering Kaneenawup's state of mind and how he needed warmth, she was grateful for Nathaniel's actions. Any other time she would have scolded him for invading her space.

"Whoa, whoa, boys." The horses stopped, and Peter set the brake and jumped down. He pulled Nathaniel to the side and spoke something to him. Rose was busy descending from the wagon and didn't pay attention to the specifics of what they said.

It didn't seem to matter.

Nathaniel handed her the pot of food. "Peter left ingredients for this in the barn and asked me to make it for you and Kane, so you should thank him."

Nathaniel stepped to the rear of the wagon and helped Kaneenawup to the ground.

She entered her warm, cozy house and placed the heavy pot atop the cookstove in the kitchen. Lifting the lid, she was pleasantly surprised to see bits of meat swimming in thick broth with a few carrots and potatoes.

All from Peter. How could she have thought her older brother didn't care about their young sibling?

She reached for a spoon to stir the contents but was overcome with emotion. Peter had wanted their brother to stop behaving like a traditional Indian, and now he'd gotten his wish. She couldn't help but feel that Sitting Bull's death wasn't the only tragedy that had occurred. Anger and pity warred for control of her heart.

Moments later, Nathaniel entered. "Peter is caring for your brother. Mostly, he's worried about Kane, but he's genuinely heartbroken about Sitting Bull's death too."

Rose choked back tears. "I hope we can all heal now."

But she wasn't entirely convinced they could.

The next morning dawned with a chilly bite in the air. Nathaniel worked in the barn. It wasn't very cold in there, since he kept the stove fed. He covered the horses with blankets to help keep them warm. Next, he poured water into the troughs. With those chores complete, he proceeded to muck the stalls and fill them and the mangers with fresh hay.

How could he not think of his Savior while working around the mangers, especially at this time of year? He whistled one of his favorite Christmas hymns as he wielded the pitchfork.

When he finished, he contemplated whether or not to speak with Agent Royer to see if he'd heard any rumors of an uprising. A few Indians might seek retribution, especially against tribal police. Most Indians were saddened with the tragic news, but it was hard to say how grieving people would react.

He held the lantern high as he exited the barn and swung the large door closed. There were no lights on at the agency, so he tabled his plan to speak with the agent. That suited him fine. He needed to check on Rose and her brother anyway.

A light shone in her front window. That likely meant they were already up and awake. Perhaps going there wasn't a good idea. He didn't wish to intrude on their private time, but he cared about Kane and wanted to see to his well-being.

Nathaniel shoved his hands into his pockets to shield them from the wind and charged across the street. His foot slipped on a frozen puddle, but he righted himself. This was one of those times when he wished the agency would invest in streetlights. Pine Ridge wasn't exactly Boston, but people needed to see where they were going, especially in the dark.

He knocked on Rose's door, wishing he'd thought to bring gifts, mainly for the saddened Kaneenawup. To his surprise, Peter answered.

"Morning, friend." Peter stood in his long underwear but had draped a blanket over his shoulders and was rubbing sleep from his eyes.

Nathaniel thought of the day Rose had barged into the clinic and seen him in the same state of undress. His cheeks heated at the thought, even now. "I came to check on Rose and Kane. How are they doing?"

"All right, I guess. Can you run to Dawson's for me and pick up some salt pork and flour so Rose can bake bread for breakfast, please?" Peter reached for his trousers and fished a few coins out of his pocket.

Nathaniel held up his hands. "You don't need to pay me. I'll be back with them soon."

Thankfully, the mercantile owner kept early hours. Lanterns shone in every window, illuminating the interior. Nathaniel strode into the building and inhaled the aromas of spices and the wild sage that many Indians used sometimes when the tobacco supply ran short.

He quickly gathered the items Peter had asked for and a handful of potatoes, then carried them to the counter. He nodded to the clerk standing there. "Did you hear that Sitting Bull has been killed by his own people?"

The man drew a pencil from behind his ear and tallied up his purchases. "I did. Sorry to hear it. I hope no Indians seek revenge."

"I hope that too. You'll let me know if you hear anything of the sort?"

"Sure." The man scribbled the total in his ledger.

After paying him, Nathaniel walked outside and paused in front of the store for a moment, noticing the quiet blanketing the town. No children scurried to the schoolhouse. No wagons rumbled through the streets. No clanging of metal on metal resounded from the smithies. Lights were extinguished in practically every other building. He guessed most people weren't up this early.

It seemed as though time itself had frozen in this place, the residents too saddened to move forward without their respected and beloved leader.

Nathaniel's deep sigh left puffs in the icy air. His friends needed breakfast, so he hurried on his way. By the time he reached Rose's house, the three siblings were up and dressed. Kane sat near the stove, holding his hands to the blaze. Peter brought in an armload of firewood, and Rose prepared a pot of coffee in the kitchen.

Nathaniel said, "Hello, Kane. I'm sorry about Sitting Bull, but I'm happy to see you're here and safe."

"Thanks," the young man mumbled.

To Nathaniel, he seemed to stare at the wall without really seeing anything. Nathaniel shot Peter a look. His friend shrugged and tossed wood into the stove. Nathaniel turned and headed into the kitchen. He handed Rose the sack of breakfast items.

A short time later, after the stove emitted enough heat for them to sit around the table, Peter said the blessing. Nathaniel dug into his helping of potatoes and eggs. He assumed Rose was saving the salt pork for the noon meal, which was fine.

"Rose," he said, "you're sure a wonder in the kitchen."

Her lips curved into a smile. "Thank you. Having a few laying hens does help keep us fed. I'm not getting many eggs now, but I hope that changes when spring arrives."

"I hope so too," Peter added.

"I'm not sure what kind of Christmas this will be," Rose stated. "With everyone so distraught about Sitting Bull, I don't know if much of a celebration will be planned."

Nathaniel swallowed his weak coffee. "I want to purchase gifts for Sarah and her family, especially the children."

Peter set down his fork. "When I was at the agency yesterday, I heard rumors that someone is in charge of buying presents for the children at the boarding school. If that's true, I'd like to contribute."

"So would I, and I'm sure Dr. Eastman and Miss Goodale would as well. She's probably the one to speak to." Rose rolled her eyes. "I'm not sure about Agent Royer though."

Throughout the meal, Kane never uttered a word. He slowly ate everything on his plate and then ambled to the sitting room and crawled under his buffalo hide.

Nathaniel glanced from Rose to Peter. Concern emanated from their eyes, and the sight broke his heart.

He scooted his chair back. "I need to go. Peter, are any other deputies on duty today?"

"Nah," his friend replied. "There's a young kid named Ezra that Agent Royer is looking to hire. We could sure use the extra help."

Rose stood. "I need to tell Dr. Eastman about the woman I saw at the camp yesterday, the one with the sick child. And, I'd like to ask him about. . ." She turned her head to the sitting room, where Kane rested, and then stood. "If you'll excuse me, Brother, Nathaniel."

"Let me help you before I go." Nathaniel reached for the dishes and followed her into the kitchen. When he was sure they were out of earshot of Peter and Kane, he said, "When I see the agent today, I'll ask him what's to become of the people at the camp at Wounded Knee Creek. Perhaps we can bring them here for medical assistance and supplies."

"That would be lovely, Nathaniel. They could live in their tepees outside of town, or by the boarding school or the Episcopal church. Several families already live in tepees near the school so they can be close to their children."

She was right.

But what about food? He didn't know what supplies were at the rations office, but there had to be something. He couldn't let the people at the camp starve or suffer any more than necessary. Would the agents in charge share their goods?

Though he made a good wage being a deputy and he didn't mind helping support his family and friends, he couldn't financially support the entire Oglala tribe. If only the whites hadn't killed off all the buffalo. His people could feast every night rather than starve.

To his way of thinking, the government handouts were poetic justice. The buffalo were intentionally eradicated to force the Indians onto reservations and facilitate their dependency on the government. If only the politicians and buffalo hunters could have foreseen what a can of worms they opened up.

Well, the Indians were now completely dependent on the government, and look where it had gotten those politicians. They forked over tens of thousands of dollars every month to feed and clothe his people. Not to mention the shipping costs and wages for the agency staff.

Poetic justice indeed.

CHAPTER 20

Rose sat beside Nathaniel on the return ride to the camp at Wounded Knee Creek, where they'd found Kaneenawup the previous day. The tribal police wagon held as many medicines as the clinic could spare, which weren't many, but Rose hoped to learn about natural remedies from the elders in the camp. She was weary of seeing her people sick and dying and didn't care if the government approved of her actions or not.

The short wild grasses were coated with frost, and the air held a hint of snow. Having white Christmases in Boston had always been welcome, but here, an onslaught of snow would only create obstacles for her people's survival. Sickness and hunger were made worse by freezing temperatures.

She and Nathaniel hoped to bring as many people back to Pine Ridge as possible but believed many would not want to come because of the noise and lack of privacy that resulted from living in town. Others wanted to distance themselves from government officials so they could be free to behave how they pleased.

Rose was anxious to see the people, especially the sick little boy and his mother. She also wanted to return to Pine Ridge as soon as possible to tend to her younger brother.

Several Confederate soldiers, she remembered, had come to the Boston University Hospital in a catatonic state of mind. Their families were desperate for a cure, but none was to be had. Rose shivered and couldn't make herself believe that Kaneenawup would suffer the same fate. Surely all he needed was time.

The camp came into view. When they reached the perimeter, Nathaniel tugged the reins and hopped down.

He offered his hand and said, "Let me help you. The ground and wagon wheels are slick. I don't want you to fall."

Rose placed her foot on the wheel, and the cold penetrated the sole of her boot, chilling her instep and toes. She immediately thought of her warm stove at home and then wondered how the people here survived such temperatures. She reached into the rear of the wagon for her medical bag, and the woman with the sick boy emerged from her tepee and looked overjoyed to see them. She hastened to Rose's side and tugged her toward the dwelling.

Rose carefully tramped behind the woman, worried that she might slip and fall on the slick ground. "I'm sorry, ma'am, but I didn't catch your name yesterday when I was tending to your son."

The woman paused at the tepee's entrance. "I am *Wetu Zeent Kala*, or what whites say is 'Spring Bird.' My son is *Cikala Chatan*, which means 'Little Hawk.'"

"Pleased to see you. Again, I'm Rose Rushing Water, Kaneenawup's older sister." She ducked into the tepee and saw the boy sitting on a tattered blanket and playing with a carved wooden bird. He seemed better. Rose checked his temperature and noted that the fever was gone.

She stood and addressed the mother. "I've brought some food and a little medicine for your son. I'll be right back with them."

Spring Bird thanked her and said, "My husband and my brother are out searching for game so we'll have something to eat tonight. He is a proud man, but we'll take any food you give us. We lost our two other sons when they were babies." Tears shimmered in her eyes. "It would break my heart to lose Little Hawk too. We'll do anything to keep him strong."

Rose trudged to the wagon and returned with an armload of supplies. Spring Bird commenced to prepare fry bread.

Rose left the dwelling and breathed in the cold air; then she spotted a Catholic church on a hill above the gathering of tepees. Children ran in circles and laughed, likely overjoyed at the prospect of a meal. The priest walked the length of the church and seemed to smile at the sight of the children playing. She thought of Nathaniel. Playing with Chaske and Winuna had brought him such joy.

She turned away from the happy scene, and a pang sliced through her at the thought of not having children of her own. Peter and Kaneenawup would make fantastic uncles to any children she had. Was it fair to rob them of that joy?

Rose shook her head. She had nursing skills that would help the Lakota people survive. Her occupation helped keep her family fed, and that was nothing to feel guilty about.

By this time, the sun was high overhead. Spring Bird's husband had returned to camp singing a happy tune. He and his comrades had shot a small antelope. He beamed at his wife. Little Hawk raced to his father, who ruffled his son's hair.

Rose couldn't help but think her people and the whites weren't so different. They all laughed and cried. They worked hard to care for their loved ones.

Nathaniel announced it was time to go. "If anyone wants a ride into Pine Ridge, we will fit as many as we can into the back of the wagon."

Three couples with small children stepped forward. They quickly packed their meager belongings and thanked Nathaniel for the ride to town.

"No need to thank me. Rose and I are headed there anyway."

One of the mothers was expecting a baby soon. The other two had young girls with coughs that seemed to rattle their small chests. Rose chewed her lower lip with worry. These children weren't more than two or three years old. She would make sure they were seen by Dr. Eastman as soon as possible.

Spring Bird stepped forward. "My husband says our family has food, and Little Hawk is all better now. So we will stay behind, but I will visit you next time we travel to town for our rations." The woman grasped her husband's hand and pulled her child close.

The wagon was packed so full, Rose wondered if the horses would be able to haul the load all the way to town without being overexerted. She glanced at Nathaniel, who seemed concerned as well.

After some debate, Rose said, "The men can walk, and I'll drive the wagon. The women and children will ride with me."

Nathaniel added, "The men have bows and arrows and can use the opportunity to shoot additional game. I'll walk with the men. Rose, are you sure you can handle driving the wagon?"

"Yes, I can manage. Will you be all right?" What good would the amenities of town be if the women lost their men? If she lost Nathaniel? A pang shot through her heart.

He waved his hand. "We'll be fine."

His lopsided grin sent a wiggly feeling along her spine. She swallowed hard, tugged at her collar, and looked away.

He added, "We can walk fast enough to make it to town before it's too dark."

"All right. We'll see you there. Be safe."

Their hands touched when he handed her the reins, and a jolt shot from her fingertips to her heart. She shook the reins, and the horses pulled ahead, but she dared not glance back at Nathaniel lest he see the longing for him in her eyes.

Nathaniel had helped the men load as many supplies as they could into the rear of the wagon. They'd need their hands free to shoot any game they encountered. If they walked briskly, they would arrive in Pine Ridge in a few hours. Wolves were scarcer in recent years, due in part to the lack of buffalo as prey. Nonetheless, he asked Wakan Tanka that none attack them during their long trek. Why hadn't he thought to bring his gun?

Though the men had bows, they had only so many arrows. Not wanting to borrow trouble, he relegated the unsettling thoughts to the recesses of his mind and increased his pace to keep up with the men.

"Hey, wait for me." Nathaniel breathed in the cold air and prayed that his illness wouldn't revisit him.

The men chuckled.

The tallest one said, "We don't ride around the reservation on horseback. We travel long distances on foot in search of game. We're used to walking."

Nathaniel gulped. The only hard work he did was caring for the deputy's horses and helping Joshua and Sarah with their homestead. Now that Joshua had fully recovered from his injuries, Nathaniel wasn't doing those chores anymore. Determined not to be called a sluggard, he walked faster.

As he remembered that Rose would be there waiting at the clinic for them, likely with a hot meal, his steps became much lighter. He dreamed of filling his belly and falling into his bed in the tack room.

The sun sank over the western horizon, and the last dregs of sunlight illuminated the atmosphere just enough to see Pine Ridge ahead.

The men began to run, and Nathaniel tried to keep up. In minutes their long journey ended when the men reached the town and hollered for their wives.

Children emerged from the clinic and excitedly sprinted to their fathers. The men embraced their wives, and for a moment, Nathaniel's heart tugged. He didn't often dream of marrying and starting a family, but something about the scene before him caused him to consider it for a moment. Having a wife and children would be nice if he could guarantee they wouldn't be taken away and sent to a boarding school far from him.

Like Dr. Eastman had.

Like Rose had.

Rose. With her eastern education, any children she had likely wouldn't be removed. Or would they? If they were, she could probably go with them, since she was familiar with the eastern culture. But would the government allow it?

Why was he thinking of children with Rose? He wasn't even married to her. But he sure did think of her a lot.

By this time, he'd reached the street in front of the clinic. Nathaniel bent at the waist and sucked in breaths. He'd need to chop wood and muck stalls more often! Rose's sweet voice drew him to the moment.

"There's warm beef stew, but not a lot of it, so come in and eat what you can." She stepped aside, allowing him to enter the crowded clinic, then handed him a bowl half full of broth with a few vegetables. He downed the meal, vowing to purchase goods from the mercantile and give them to Rose to help feed these families. Maybe he'd bring Sarah and her children into town. Sarah could shop, and his niece and nephew could play with the little ones running around the clinic.

The men carried their supplies behind the clinic and set up tepees while the mothers sang songs to the children, preparing them for bed.

By now the last dregs of sunlight had faded into darkness and the stars appeared in the inky black sky. Nathaniel walked Rose to her home. He shouldn't have been surprised to see Peter there, caring for Kaneenawup. He was happy to see Kane in the sitting room, on the floor, eating bread and a piece of beef.

"Vegetables are in short supply," Rose said. "Nathaniel, would you help my brothers and me start a garden in the spring?"

"I think that would be a good idea." He looked at Peter. "What do you think?"

"Sounds good to me. Most people on the reservation don't have a lot of luck with crops, and neither do the white settlers, but maybe a raised garden bed will be different."

Nathaniel clapped his friend on the back. "We'll have to pray God blesses it, won't we? I need to leave. It's my turn to care for the horses and do chores in the barn."

The Rushing Water family said goodbye, and he stepped out into the night.

When he entered the barn, he was happy to see that it had been well kept during the day, so there weren't many chores to do. He gave the structure a good once-over. From there, he strode into the deputy's office and recorded the day's events into the ledger and wondered what tomorrow would bring.

CHAPTER 21

The day before Christmas dawned clear with an azure-blue sky and nary a cloud to be seen. Though the day was beautiful, there was an icy bite in the air. Cold seemed to seep in through the cracks of every structure in town. No amount of firewood could warm the interior of the clinic that morning or Rose's house that afternoon.

She set the coffeepot on the stove, rubbed her arms, and stamped her feet. She left the stove door open, hoping it would help heat the room at least a little bit. The thought of going outside to retrieve more firewood didn't appeal to her at all.

Kaneenawup sat on the floor near the stove, staring at the dancing flames. At least he was eating and sleeping now, but he continued to cling to his buffalo hide. Was it his way of hanging on to the old way of life? Not that she blamed him. Many of her people were in anguish that their lifestyle was being torn from them, like an old bandage ripped from a deep wound.

"I'll see what I can put together for our noon meal." She moved to the kitchen, wondering what she would find. She thought wryly that those in Boston were purchasing gifts and feasting on meals fit for royalty, while here on the reservation, her people would be lucky to have any food at all in their bellies on Christmas Day.

Her stomach growled, and a question rumbled in her soul. If the Savior of the world cared so much for people, why was He not providing food to keep them from starving?

Fearing that her recently arrived chickens would die in the freezing temperatures, she checked them several times a day. Though the creatures survived, they hadn't laid many eggs. The thought of going outside still didn't appeal to her, but she was hungry and hoped to find a bounty in the hen's nests.

Bundled in her wraps, she stepped outside and gasped from the cold. The icy air penetrated deep into her lungs and stole her next breath. She sensed a hint of snow in the atmosphere. Shivering and stamping her feet, she quickly tossed several pieces of firewood into the house and then bolted to the chicken coop.

Mindful of her steps so as not to slip on the frost-covered ground, she hurried to the coop that Nathaniel and Peter had skillfully constructed. There, to her delight, she discovered three eggs beneath the clucking hens and quickly wrapped them in her apron. Careful not to drop or crush them, she ran to the house as fast as she'd left it.

Perhaps Nathaniel's God had heard her prayers after all. After removing her coat, scarf, and gloves, she stood in her kitchen and took stock of the ingredients available.

There was no sugar to be had in town, but she'd spied a bottle of molasses at Dawson's and snatched it up. Though there were enough eggs for breakfast, she hoped that tomorrow there would be enough for breakfast *and* enough to make cookies.

If she scrambled the eggs, that would make one and a half each, for her and Kaneenawup.

A Christmas hymn was on her lips as she cooked the eggs and placed the heel, the last of her bread, in the skillet to toast. Three eggs and one slice of bread crust to split between two people. This meager meal wouldn't fill their bellies, but it was more than what most families on the reservation would eat that morning.

Thoughts of the Christmas Eve service popped into her mind. Of all the church services she'd been required to attend in Boston, the ones she'd actually enjoyed had been the ones on Christmas Eve.

This would be her first Christmas since returning to the reservation. She was sure there would be services here, and decided to ask Nathaniel or Peter about it, depending on who she saw first. If Kaneenawup agreed to go, she hoped it would draw him from his doldrums.

She wanted very much to attend, and not just to be with Nathaniel. Questions about his God swirled in her mind since their conversation at the cross-shaped tree, and she wanted to know more about Him. Perhaps the reverend would have a few answers for her.

If only she hadn't left her Bible back East. She mentally kicked herself for doing so and contemplated ordering one. She had ordered several books and had them shipped to the reservation. Why not a Bible?

From the kitchen, she heard the potbellied stove door creak open, followed by the noise of Kaneenawup tossing in a few pieces of wood and closing the door again. She drew herself from her musings, scooped the bread and eggs onto plates, and carried them into the sitting room.

Silence surrounded them as they ate. He still said very little. It saddened her to see her once-energetic brother so withdrawn. She hoped, prayed, that something, anything, would draw him from his melancholy. She debated whether or not to ask him to attend church with her that night. Would he be angry that she asked, or acquiesce? She didn't want him to go just to please her.

Rapping on the door startled her. She jumped from her seat, nearly knocking her plate to the floor, then hastened to the door and tugged it open.

Peter stood on the porch, a grin on his face and a burlap bag in his hands. "I brought presents for you and Kane."

Rose didn't correct his nickname for their baby brother. She didn't want the Christmas mood ruined, so she tamped down her annoyance. It was enough that he'd thought of them and responded with kindness.

He stepped inside and withdrew two paper-wrapped gifts from the bag. "I saw a Christmas tree at church last year. Would you like to have one? If so, I can locate one for you."

"I don't have one, but I remember the university had them all over the place. I thought they were pretty, so yes, having one of my own would be nice."

"Okay. By the way, here's Christmas dinner." He handed her the burlap bag.

She hadn't anticipated how weighty it was and nearly dropped it. "Oh, Peter, this is heavy!"

He puffed out his chest. "I ordered it long before Thanksgiving to make sure it arrived on time. I couldn't have my little siblings going hungry on Christmas."

"And you must have spent an entire paycheck on it." Her heart softened. "Thank you."

"You're welcome. It's the least I could do."

Peering into the bag, she drew out a small canned ham. Three pounds would be enough to feed them, with leftovers for ham and bean soup. There were three sweet potatoes and a miniature can of cranberry sauce. Warmth swept through her. They would feast like kings tomorrow.

She was about to hug her older brother, but instead she watched him stride into the sitting room and sit next to Kaneenawup. Peter even wrapped his arm around their troubled brother. Kaneenawup laid his head on Peter's shoulder. Tears filled her eyes.

Nathaniel escorted Rose to the Holy Cross Episcopal Church. Peter and Kane followed close behind. Hearing rumors of candy and gifts, Joshua agreed to bring Sarah and the children. Still raw from the death of Sitting Bull, Nathaniel hoped his people would find solace here with God.

Candles inside the building illuminated the windows and cast light into the darkness. The sky above held a million stars that lit up the night like diamond dust flung across the inky canvas.

Music reverberated from the open doors. A dilapidated piano and handbells created a delightful melody that resounded through the air.

"This is beautiful." Somberness infused Rose's tone.

"It is," Peter agreed.

Embers of hope filled Nathaniel that Rose would choose to surrender her life to God that night. It pleased him that she and her younger brother had decided to join them that evening, but he worried because Kane still said few words.

They reached the church and climbed the steps.

Reverend Cook greeted them. "Welcome to Christmas Eve service."

Nathaniel nodded. "Merry Christmas. I'd like to introduce my friends, Rose Rushing Water and her younger brother, Kane."

"Pleased to meet you." The reverend gave a slight bow.

Rose offered a polite curtsy.

"Good to see you back, Peter. It's been a while." Reverend Cook shook hands with the men, and then the group strolled inside and found an empty pew. Surprisingly, many people filled the building for this white man's holiday. Nathaniel hoped they were there because they actually wanted to be and not because they feared repercussions if they didn't participate.

The interior had been decorated for the holidays. A star fashioned from tinfoil hung above the pulpit. A Christmas tree that couldn't have been more than three feet tall sat in one corner. Green garlands were strung throughout the interior and above the windows. Wreaths graced the walls. Their piney fragrance filled the air and tickled his nose.

Nathaniel waved to Dr. Eastman and Miss Goodale, who were stringing paper chains around the tree.

Joshua and Sarah arrived with the children. Chaske and Winuna ran to Nathaniel and wrapped their arms around his legs. He had to grip a nearby pew to keep from toppling over. He laughed and gathered them into his arms, then stood. Laughter bubbled from them, and he lowered them gently to the floor so they could join the doctor and Miss Goodale in decorating the tree.

He turned to his sister. "I'm glad you and Joshua could make it."

Sarah beamed. "We're happy to be here," she said.

Reverend Cook stepped to the pulpit and announced that it was time for the service to begin.

Nathaniel and his family took their seats next to Rose and her brothers.

The reverend said, "Please stand with me as I thank our Lord and Savior, Christ Jesus, for coming to earth as a baby and making a way for us to be saved."

Beside him, Rose bristled but stood, as did Peter and Kane.

Once the prayer concluded, they sang his favorite Christmas hymn, "O Holy Night." He had never heard Rose sing before but delighted in the sound. She sang beautifully, and he hoped the reverend could talk her into singing in church more often.

When the music ended, they sat, and the service continued. Nathaniel loved hearing the Word of God being preached, especially at Christmas. The story of Jesus' birth in the book of Luke always spoke something new to him. All too soon, the service was over.

Miss Goodale rose and began distributing small paper bags to the children. His nephew and niece were each handed one. They pulled pieces of candy from their sacks and squealed. Each family was also given a small can of meat and a one-pound bag of beans.

Peter declined to take the food. "My family and I aren't starving," he said. "Please give this to someone who needs it more."

The air in the church grew stuffy with so many people milling about. Nathaniel longed for the cool, fresh air outside and excused himself.

Minutes later, Reverend Cook joined him. Nathaniel asked, "Sir, will you please pray for Peter's brother, Kane? He hasn't been the same since Sitting Bull was killed."

The reverend laid a hand on Nathaniel's shoulder. "Many people are struggling. Of course I'll pray for him."

Joshua, with Sarah and the children in tow, exited the church soon after.

To Rose, Nathaniel said, "I'm having Christmas dinner with Joshua, Sarah, and the children tomorrow. I'd love to stop by afterward, if I wouldn't be imposing."

"That would be fine. It'll be just the three of us, me, Peter, and Kaneenawup, but I have presents for everyone, so feel free to stop by after your visit with Sarah's family, if you want."

She smiled up at him, her eyes shining. Her cheeks were pink, which sent his pulse racing like a runaway mustang. Peter nudged him with an elbow and aimed a lopsided grin at him. Was that Peter's way of saying he approved of a courtship?

"Rose," Nathaniel said, "I'd be happy to. Thank you for the invitation." He started whistling one of the Christmas hymns they'd sung in church. His people had endured bad times, but he prayed those were behind them and that God would bring good things to the reservation in 1891. Perhaps there would even be peace between Indians and whites.

Peter, Kane, Rose, and Nathaniel stayed behind to help the minister straighten up the church and lock the doors. Nathaniel offered Rose his elbow, and they descended the church steps then meandered toward her house.

"Merry Christmas," Dr. Eastman called to them.

Rose replied, "And you as well, Doctor." She leaned closer to Nathaniel. "I saw Miss Goodale holding Dr. Eastman's arm in church, and they had their heads together. Perhaps both snow *and* romance are in the air."

He cleared his throat and walked a smidgen faster. Snow didn't bother him, not much anyway. Romance tended to be more complicated.

By the time they reached Rose's house, he wanted to kiss her but hesitated, not wanting to be too forward. Should he ask her brothers for their blessing? He didn't want to create any more tension in the family.

She tilted her head up and met his gaze. "Thank you for taking me to church tonight. I have much to think about where faith is concerned."

"If you have any questions or thoughts, I'm happy to listen and give you answers, if I have them." In spite of the cold, his middle warmed considerably. She wanted to talk about faith. Praise God, this was what he'd been praying for.

Playful shouting echoed in the night. Peter and Kane barreled down the street, right toward him and Rose. It pleased him to see the brothers enjoying each other's company, but that didn't mean he wasn't perturbed. Their antics had interrupted his tender moment with Rose.

Before Nathaniel could give any more thought to a good-night kiss, Peter dragged Rose inside. Nathaniel chose not to protest. He would see her tomorrow.

They said their goodbyes, and Peter closed the door.

Nathaniel tugged his cap on more snugly and hustled to the deputy's office. Mercy, it was almost as cold in there as it was outside. He stomped his feet and slapped his hands to his chest to help warm himself. Once the fire in the potbellied stove emitted heat, he wrapped the presents for his nephew and niece. For Chaske, he'd purchased a set of toy animals and could almost hear the boy making sounds like lions. Winuna would be pleased with the small cradle and blanket for her doll.

He climbed into bed that night with a full heart.

The next morning, when he woke, it was Christmas. He took a half hour to thank Christ Jesus for coming to earth to live, die, and thereby save all of mankind, then read through the book of Luke as he always did on Christmas morning.

Next, he spent another half hour praying for his people, especially Kane. But no matter how hard he prayed, no matter how much he poured his feelings out to the Creator, that same strange sense of foreboding he'd felt earlier enveloped him like dark clouds hovering over Pine Ridge.

He had a busy day ahead, so he closed his Bible and did his best to shake off the feelings of despondency.

Then he dressed, mounted his horse, and headed to his sister's house. When he stepped inside their cabin, he was greeted by Chaske and Winuna.

"What did you bring us, Uncle Nathaniel?" they chimed in unison.

He ruffled their hair. "You'll have to wait until after dinner to see."

Joshua had shot a small wild turkey, which Sarah had roasting over the fire. To this, Nathaniel added yams and jam for fresh bread. The aromas wafting through the cabin made his mouth water.

He placed the children's presents under a tree that couldn't have been more than two feet high, its branches bare twigs. A lump formed in his throat when he noted a gift with his name on it. He hoped Sarah had fashioned a homemade gift and not spent precious cash on something for him. They still hadn't financially recovered from the loss of produce and the dead mules. At least he'd been able to help Joshua repair the damaged wagon.

When the turkey finished roasting, they sat down at the table. Joshua said the blessing and prayed for their people. During the prayer, the sense of disquietude Nathaniel had felt that morning returned and swept over him like a prairie wind. He didn't know what the feeling meant, but he didn't like it one bit.

Was God trying to tell him something? Prepare him for something?

"Amen," Joshua said. "Let's eat."

Sarah passed around the bowls of food, and they ate as the children chatted with excitement and anticipation to open their gifts.

After dinner Joshua helped Sarah wash the dishes while Nathaniel entertained his niece and nephew. Then they opened their presents.

Nathaniel was delighted with his knitted scarf and socks. "Sarah, you made these? When did you learn to knit?"

"I visited Ellie Gardner and helped her deliver her baby. In exchange, she taught me to knit. It's really not that hard, and she was pleased that I caught on so fast. I hope to teach Winuna the skill soon."

Nathaniel thanked God that there seemed to be a peace growing between the settler family and at least a few Indians.

The sun had passed its zenith and was well on its way to the western horizon. "I must be going now. I'd like to stop at Rose's house and wish them all a Merry Christmas."

Sarah gave him a knowing smile. So did Joshua as Nathaniel wrapped his new scarf around his neck and left.

CHAPTER 22

Christmas night, Rose stared at the batch of sugar cookies she'd baked, intending to give a dozen or so to Nathaniel when he arrived. That was, if her brothers didn't devour them all first.

She had almost given up on seeing him, but finally, there was a knock on the door. She pulled it open, and he rushed inside, bringing with him a dusting of snowflakes.

He shook the snow from his coat. "Merry Christmas, Rose."

"Merry Christmas to you too." As she shoved the door closed, she noticed him unwinding what looked like a new scarf from his neck. She couldn't help but admire the handiwork.

"That's pretty, Nathaniel," she said.

"Thank you. Sarah made it and gave it to me for Christmas. Ellie Gardner taught her how to knit. I'm sure she'd teach you too, if you'd like to learn."

"I think that would be delightful."

He turned and greeted her brothers. "Hello Peter, Kane."

Rose wished everyone would call her youngest brother by his given name but let it slide this time. "Have a seat with the others, and I'll make a fresh pot of coffee."

She didn't want to tell Nathaniel this would be the fourth time the grounds were being used. He would find out soon enough when he sipped the weak and bitter brew. When she'd asked Agent Royer about the last shipment of medical supplies, he'd said that wagons had a harder time traversing across the prairie in the winter. That was understandable.

When the coffee finished brewing, she filled three cups, placed them on a tray, and padded into the sitting room.

"Thank you," Nathaniel said. The twinkle in his eyes shone almost as bright as the stars.

Her brothers thanked her as she sat down in her rocker. Forgoing a book, she chose instead to listen to the men's conversation. They bantered together much like the men did in Boston.

Peter asked, "How are Sarah and her family doing? Did you all have a nice Christmas?"

"They are well. We had a nice Christmas," Nathaniel said. "Have our horses been fed and watered?"

Peter nodded and sipped his drink. "They have."

Kaneenawup seemed interested in the conversation, though he didn't engage in it. Though he'd rallied from his despondency last night, he seemed to have somewhat slipped back into it again. Rose guessed these things took time and hoped this meant he was healing from grief.

She smiled as she rocked, hoping, praying, that 1891 would be better for her people.

All seemed well in her world. Peter and Nathaniel conversed in the kitchen about how much wood to chop and stack in the lean-to. Kaneenawup slept in a corner, seemingly at peace, under his tattered buffalo hide. He clutched the hunting knife that Peter had given him for Christmas. The fishing pole Nathaniel gave him leaned against the wall.

Her eyelids grew heavy, and she closed them, daring to dream of spring.

Her rooster crowed, rousing her from slumber. The house contained a chill, and she shivered, though someone had placed a blanket over her while she slept. Probably Peter. She scanned the room and didn't see him. He must have returned to the deputy's office or to the barn to sleep near the horses.

Rose stood, and the blanket slipped to the floor. Cold surged through her feet and up to her middle. She shivered again and stamped her feet to get her blood pumping, then rushed to stoke the fire in the stove and add wood.

Next, Rose donned her coat, hood, and gloves and stepped outside to check the chickens. Delighted, she counted five eggs, which meant, thankfully, she and her brother would eat that morning. With rations cut nearly in half, she'd learned to be grateful for every morsel of food she could procure for herself and her family.

How thankful she was for the leftovers from Christmas dinner. Her family would have something to eat that night as well.

Rose stepped inside and decided against preparing a pot of coffee. After several rounds through the percolator, the brew wouldn't be much more than hot water, and bitter-tasting stuff at that. She'd have to remember to check at Dawson's and see if they had any. If not, she'd invest in tea. At least that would help keep her family and her patients warm. With a sigh, she wondered why she hadn't thought of that earlier.

Last night she'd placed a cup of dry beans in a kettle of water to soak overnight. That wouldn't make much of a lunch for her and Kaneenawup, but it would have to do.

Without draining the beans, so as not to lose any of their nutritional value, she set the kettle on the stove and fed the fire underneath. She cracked the eggs into the cast-iron skillet heating on the small stove and stirred. Beans and eggs didn't normally go together for meals, but it was that or go hungry.

Her teeth clenched as she thought bitterly of the Indian children who were literally going hungry that morning. How many of her people had nothing to eat on Christmas Day? How many of them would have nothing to eat for the next few days?

The acrid smell of something burning wafted to her nose. "Oh," she exclaimed, and yanked the pan off the burner, then stirred the eggs with fervor. They weren't black, but they'd be a bit crunchy. Kaneenawup wouldn't mind. He, like so many other Indians, was grateful for anything to eat.

Her brother ambled into the kitchen. "No coffee?"

"No, sorry. I'll stop by the store today and see if they have any. If not, I'll buy some tea. I like it just as well."

He laughed. "Tea. Now I know Boston refined you."

Kaneenawup wandered into the dining area and sat at the table. She scraped half the eggs onto a plate, added a spoonful of beans, and carried the meal into him. He reached for his breakfast.

Without really thinking, she whispered a prayer of thanks for the meal. She eyed her brother, not knowing what to expect. The prayer surprised her, but since the Christmas Eve service, she had pondered her ideas about God. Nathaniel and Peter would be pleased, though she wouldn't say anything just yet.

Kaneenawup's eyes shot daggers at her, and then he shifted in his seat and shoveled the eggs and beans into his mouth. It took him less than a minute to finish eating. He scooted his chair back, stood, and stomped away from the table. She watched, dumbfounded, as he gathered his things and headed to the door.

He called over his shoulder, "I'll be at the Wounded Knee camp for a few days. You're welcome to come see me if you want." The door closed behind him with a heartbreaking thud.

Tears pooled in Rose's eyes. She already missed him and longed for his return. He'd gone to the Christmas Eve service, so she hadn't thought a prayer would be an issue. At least she hadn't asked him to join her in it.

Perhaps she should take his example and visit the camp again. Little Hawk and his family or someone else there might need medical care. Maybe she could entice Dr. Eastman to go with her.

With a sigh, she finished her meal and washed the breakfast dishes. She was needed at the clinic that day.

An hour later, she assisted Dr. Eastman in boiling his instruments. The doctor turned away those who asked for brown bottle medicine, because there wasn't any. Rose folded clean sheets and placed them on a bare shelf next to where the medicines were usually stored.

Dr. Eastman said, "I'm going to speak with Agent Royer to see when the shipment might arrive."

"All right. I'll be close by." While he was away, she cared for the expectant mother, White Flower, who'd come into town with her and Peter the day they'd picked up Kaneenawup. She put her Pinard horn to good use and predicted a healthy baby. Next, she used a stethoscope to check the children's lungs. By God's grace, their breathing sounded clear.

When things quieted at the clinic, she scribbled a note for the doctor and left for her house. The small amount of leftover breakfast beans would have to serve as her noon meal.

Several children played in the street. All four had bare feet, and not one of them had a coat! An exasperated groan flew from her lips. The government couldn't see fit to send food, so why would she think they'd send adequate footwear and coats for children? Though they were healthy enough to play right now, she thought, was it any wonder these poor dears succumbed to sickness and disease?

She admonished the children. "You shouldn't stay outside for very long. Finish your game and then go inside where it's warm so you won't get sick."

The children's stricken faces sent a wave of guilt through her. She hadn't meant to frighten them. They nodded and ran toward the clinic. They would be hungry soon, if they weren't already. It seemed that Indian children were always hungry.

Reminded of her task, she hurried to her house and into the kitchen. She searched her cupboards and found enough flour and lard to make two, maybe three pieces of fry bread, and small pieces at that. There was nothing else to feed those who were staying at the clinic.

She saved the remnants of Christmas dinner to feed herself and her brothers, though she berated herself for being selfish.

After counting every coin she had, she discovered she had enough to feed herself and Kaneenawup until the next month's rations arrived, but nowhere near enough to feed three hungry families at the clinic. Perhaps her brothers could shoot wild game.

Frustration and despair fought for control of her heart. She jumped to her feet. First chance she had, she'd order vegetable seeds to plant that spring. She likely couldn't grow enough to feed the whole Oglala tribe, but it would make a difference to at least her and her family and maybe the patients who came to the clinic for medical care.

With renewed hope, she finished mixing the bread dough and set it aside to rise, then strode back to the clinic. The children were inside listening to an elderly woman tell stories of when the buffalo covered the plains and the brave warriors hunted them.

Rose noticed how the woman neglected to tell the children that after a buffalo hunt everyone ate like kings and went to bed at night with full bellies. Whether or not the omission was intentional or forgotten, Rose couldn't say. Whatever the reason, it was a mercy. Hungry children shouldn't be reminded that Lakota stomachs weren't always empty.

"Rose."

"Yes, Doctor?" She'd been gathering wool, again.

He raised his eyebrows. "I'm taking these children and their mothers—except White Flower, of course—to meet Miss Goodale. We hope to enroll them in school. I'll return later this evening."

"Yes, sir. If anyone stops by, I can see to their needs. If it's anything serious, I'll know where to fetch you."

The doctor blushed and hurried out the door. The women and children followed him outside. Rose busied herself straightening the clinic.

When she finished, she browsed through the doctor's medical books to see if any new ones had arrived. None had. No matter, she'd simply reread one she'd perused earlier.

She lifted the volume from the shelf and settled into the rocking chair in the corner. Not more than five minutes elapsed before the words blurred on the page. She rubbed her eyes as her thoughts meandered to Spring Bird and her family. Though she was grateful the woman's husband had procured game, a small antelope could feed only so many.

Would Kaneenawup have anything to eat that night, or was he going hungry? Knowing her brother's pride, she thought he'd rather starve than eat food that could feed the children. Why hadn't she thought to give him something before he left the house?

When would Kaneenawup return? And where was Peter? She hadn't seen him all day. He and Nathaniel were likely riding from settlement to settlement across the reservation, doing their best to keep the peace. Tensions were running high because the ghost dancing had increased. According to Peter, Agent Royer had received a telegram from Agent McLaughlin. Chief Spotted Elk had fled Sitting Bull's camp and was running from the army to avoid arrest. The chief was heading south some three hundred miles to Pine Ridge. Agent Royer had been instructed to alert the army if Spotted Elk arrived there.

Peter added that Agent Royer had requested military assistance. If Kaneenawup encountered soldiers, she hoped they would convince him to return home.

She must have dozed off, because something startled her awake. When she sat up in the rocking chair, she noticed twilight had fallen. Shouts echoed in the night air.

Nathaniel was startled to hear shouting from the street. Fearing trouble, he dropped the brush he'd been using to comb a horse. The beast snorted and shook its head, but with gentle soothing words, he calmed the animal, then hurried outside. There were men milling in the street, and Peter was dismounting his horse in front of the agency. His face was a mask of worry as he entered the building.

Sensing the need to investigate, Nathaniel rushed inside, past the wide-eyed desk clerk, and entered the agent's office.

Peter said, "I don't know all the details, sir, but there's been a skirmish, just north of the Wounded Knee camp."

Agent Royer groaned and dropped into his chair. "Any casualties?"

Peter shook his head. "None dead, just a few with minor wounds."

Nathaniel stepped forward. "Thank God. Do you need help calming settlers or bringing the wounded into town? Rose and the doctor are close by."

"It wouldn't hurt to have the wounded looked at, but I don't want my sister in the middle of all that." Peter rubbed his hands together and held them over the potbellied stove in the agent's office.

"I don't blame you." But however much Nathaniel agreed with his friend, Rose would find out about this somehow.

Agent Royer said, "I'm sending a wire to Fort Robinson right away, letting them know what happened."

He leaped from his chair and hollered for his clerk, leaving Peter shaking his head and Nathaniel wondering what would happen next.

Peter twisted his hat in his hands. "I knew we should have stopped the ghost dancing. I need to get to the camp right away and bring Kane back, even if I have to drag him."

Rose bolted into the room, her medical bag in hand. "A man came into the clinic and told me there are wounded men who need medical attention. Where are they? Is Kaneenawup one of them?"

Nathaniel looked at Peter. "That didn't take long."

Peter placed his hands on his sister's shoulders. "Kane is fine. Nobody needs medical attention. The military doctor is with the wounded soldiers, and they have already been cared for. Nathaniel and I are riding to the camp as soon as we can."

Rose exhaled. "When will that be?"

Peter shrugged. "I promised the Gardners that I'd visit them tomorrow with updates on the military's arrival in the area, so it'll have to be the day after tomorrow, and I'll bring Kane back."

She harrumphed, and her cheeks reddened. "What if *Kaneenawup* doesn't want to come with you? You can't drag us kicking and screaming where we don't want to go."

Peter growled and slapped his hat against his thigh. "Rose, the reason soldiers are roaming the prairies is to suppress the dancing. I've even heard rumors that they plan to disarm the Indians, and I know that won't bode well. I told you the government would do this if we insisted on clinging to our traditional ways of life. And now"—he spread his arms wide—"here we are."

Rose gasped. Maybe she'd never seen her brother like this before, and even Nathaniel had to admit, he rarely saw his friend this angry. Hoping to quell Peter's obvious frustration rather than escalate it, he aimed a look at Rose, silently imploring her not to say anything that would upset him.

She must have taken the hint, because she licked her lips and ducked her head.

Agent Royer entered. "I'm locking up the office. You folks need to turn in. We'll meet back here in the morning and see what's to be done."

They exited the building, and Nathaniel said to Peter, "You take care of the horses. I'll walk your sister home."

Rose grabbed her brother's arm. "Peter, I want to go with you to the Gardners'. I need to check on Ellie and her new baby. I'm a woman. I can answer any questions she might have."

"Good idea, Sister. I'll pick you up after my meeting with Agent Royer." He turned toward the barn.

Nathaniel placed his hand at the small of her back. "Let's go."

When they were out of earshot, Nathaniel leaned close and whispered, "I know you're worried, but I'll do everything I can to keep both of your brothers safe."

Rose looked up and met his gaze. "I have every intention of going with you to the camp, and neither you nor Peter can stop me. I'll walk the whole fifteen miles if I have to."

She opened her door, entered her house, and closed the door before he had the chance to protest. And yes, he believed that, if necessary, she would indeed walk to the camp.

CHAPTER 23

December 27, 1890

The morning sun crept over the horizon but did little to warm the frost-covered prairie. Though Rose desperately wanted to go with her brother to the Gardners', an army officer had requested her presence for a stomach ailment and she wasn't sure if she'd be finished with the patient in time.

Rose stuffed her medical bag with natural remedies that would aid digestion, since none of the treatments given by the army doctors seemed to be working. Together, she and Nathaniel strode to the white tents housing the army personnel.

To her dismay but not her surprise, a heated discussion ensued.

To the army officer, Nathaniel said, "While the military wants to arrest the dancers, I believe they should be left alone. If given enough time, they will move on to entertain another tradition."

Rose straightened her spine. "I agree, and I heard Dr. Eastman say as much also."

The officer seemed skeptical but thanked Rose for the herbal remedy. She returned to the clinic to care for the families there.

One of the teachers from the residential school stopped in during recess to have her heart checked. Rose listened to it but didn't detect anything amiss and suspected a case of nerves.

Later that afternoon Rose closed the clinic's door and hurried to her house to feed more wood into the stove. She wondered about Kaneenawup. Was he warm and safe? Did he have anything at all to eat that day?

Her chickens seemed to be affected by the cold too. There were only two eggs that morning. One for her breakfast, and the other she saved for lunch.

She thought of all those potatoes and carrots that had spilled from Joshua and Sarah's wagon wreck when she'd first arrived in town. What a blessing they would be now. Again, she longed for warmer temperatures and the chance to plant her garden.

Rose returned to the clinic and focused on caring for patients. White Flower and her children were in good health despite the lack of rations and the biting cold. It was a small mercy that the children weren't sick from playing outdoors without adequate winter clothing.

Foreboding rolled over her like dark storm clouds. Everyone seemed to feel it. Nathaniel and Peter were spending more time in prayer. They'd even stopped at the church yesterday to speak with Reverend Cook.

Dr. Eastman entered the front room. "I'm off to see Agent Royer."

"I hate to say it, but will you ask him about the supply wagons again? If they don't come soon, half the town will starve."

"I know." The doctor sighed and donned his hat. "If I have time, I'll take my rig out to meet the supply wagon and bring back what I can as fast as possible."

"Thank you." Rose watched him leave the building and disappear down the street. One of the small boys coughed, a deep hacking rattle and then a deeply inhaled gasp of breath. Shudders welled in Rose's middle and radiated outward. She scurried to the child's side, pulled the stethoscope from around her neck, and placed the end on the boy's small chest.

She tried not to count his thin ribs as she listened to his breathing.

Just as she feared.

Whooping cough.

Though this seemed like a mild case, she still spent the rest of the morning preparing a poultice and applying it to his chest. For all his small stature, he was strong, and she believed he'd pull through. Now she was even more adamant about ordering and growing healing herbs, as soon as the seeds could be shipped to the reservation. Never again would she be this unprepared for winter.

Dr. Eastman hadn't returned by the time the sun passed its zenith. Maybe he was headed to meet the supply wagon. If so, she hoped he'd return with food and other rations. Food wasn't the only scarcity in town. More blankets were needed, as well as medicine, shoes, and warm clothing.

Shouts outside reached into the clinic. White Flower, who rested on a cot nearby, rose to her elbows. The children sat up and looked to her.

In a calm voice, Rose said, "I'll go see what all the fuss is about and be right back." She donned her coat, hat, and mittens and stepped into the frigid atmosphere. The cold caused her to shiver as she hurried to a group of men gathering in the middle of the street in front of the agency.

"Nathaniel, Peter, you're back from the Gardners' already." She waved and stepped carefully toward them.

Both men spun around, their faces etched with worry. The sense of foreboding returned, settling in her middle. She reached for Peter's coat sleeve. "What's wrong?"

"We need to speak with Agent Royer and give him the report he asked for this morning. You can come." He took her arm and led her into the agency's administration building.

They filed past the clerk and entered the agent's office. The clerk strode behind them with paper, ink, and quill.

Peter said, "The whole Ninth Cavalry has made Pine Ridge their home since last month, and they continue to make their presence known around town. One of them said the Seventh Cavalry is on its way to the camp at Wounded Knee."

The agent shoved his hands into his pockets and nodded at the clerk. "No notes will be necessary. I'll continue to sleep easier knowing the troops are close by. You all can go now."

Nathaniel and Peter hustled her outside. "Why is the army so watchful over us?" she asked, alarmed.

"There are rumors that the Seventh Cavalry, led by Colonel Forsyth, has been commanded to confiscate all the weapons at the camp," Peter informed her.

Nathaniel added, "I hope they have sense enough to make this as peaceful as possible."

"Regardless, the men in the camp will not be happy about this," Peter said. "They need their rifles to hunt, especially with the supply wagons running late every month."

"What can we do?" Rose asked. A feeling of trepidation rose up in her middle. This was her worst nightmare playing out before her. There were no plans or talk of an uprising. To her way of thinking, the settlers had nothing to be afraid of.

Worry lines etched her brother's face. "I'm heading to the camp first thing in the morning. If I'm lucky, I can persuade the men that this situation is only temporary."

"Maybe we can speak with Colonel Forsyth first and make sure this *is* just a temporary thing," Nathaniel said. "And I can go with you. Two deputies are better than one."

Peter nodded. "If we leave early enough, we can reach camp and return before it gets too dark. I'm late in getting to the Gardners', but I won't stay long and will return as soon as I can." He climbed into the saddle and rode out of town.

Rose watched him disappear over the prairie, wishing she could go with him, but she was hesitant to leave the sick boy at the clinic and wanted to be nearby in case anyone else needed medical care.

Dr. Eastman approached. So he hadn't gone for supplies after all. Aggravated, she dropped her hands to her sides. That meant the supply wagons weren't close enough for him to ride out to meet them.

"Is everything all right out here?" the doctor asked.

Nathaniel explained what was happening at the Wounded Knee camp. Dr. Eastman blew out a sigh, and his shoulders slumped. He shook his head and then faced the school building. Rose imagined he was thinking of Miss Goodale.

Rose said to him, "I'm headed to the camp tomorrow morning with Nathaniel and my brother. I'm sorry, but I must see that Kaneenawup is all right and beg him to come home."

"How long will you be gone?" Worry laced the doctor's tone.

"Not more than a day, and I will return as soon as I can."

He shifted his medical bag to his other hand. "Remember, we have patients at the clinic."

She placed a hand on his shoulder. "One of the boys has a cough, but it doesn't sound serious. I've already spoken with the women there. They have experience delivering each other's babies. I've examined White Flower and don't foresee any complications."

The doctor took a deep breath. "Very well. I can manage. Have a safe trip." He tipped his hat and strode away.

Anxiety emanated from Nathaniel's eyes. "If you insist on going to Wounded Knee Creek, Peter won't like it one bit."

Her hands clenched as she squared her shoulders. "I don't care. I'll borrow a wagon from someone if I have to, but one way or another, I'm bringing my brother home where he'll be safe."

For a long time, he just stood there, gazing at her. Judging by his features, he was feeling protective of her.

Finally, he sighed. "Okay, I guess it can't be helped. Come with me."

She followed him to the barn.

Nathaniel opened the barn door and ushered Rose inside. Though the interior was warmer than the exterior, it was still much colder than inside her home.

Nathaniel blew into his hands, trying to warm them. "Your brother isn't going to like the idea of you going with us tomorrow, but I can understand why you want to go."

He held out his arms, and she stepped into his embrace. "I'm worried sick about Kaneenawup," she said, looking up at him, "but also, there might be people there who need medical attention."

He agreed. She would be a welcome sight to those who were sick. "This doesn't mean I'm not worried about you going, but at least if you accompany us, we won't have to worry about you riding across the prairie alone."

She leaned into his embrace and then stepped back. "I must go for now. I'll be at the clinic if you need me."

Nathaniel watched her go, then brushed down the horses and got everything ready for the night. When he was done, he plopped onto his bed in the tack room and pulled his Bible from the nightstand.

He startled awake with the open Bible lying on his chest when he heard someone open and close the barn door. When he came out of his room, he saw Peter and Rose standing by a horse stall.

"What's going on?" he asked them.

Peter acknowledged him with a wave. "I stopped by the clinic to tell Rose that Ellie Gardner and her baby are doing fine."

"That's wonderful." Warmth radiated from Nathaniel's middle.

"She and Matthew are sad about Sitting Bull's murder, but relieved that the army is close by and ready to protect settlers if necessary. Tensions are running high between Indians and the soldiers, but I told the Gardners they have nothing to fear."

Rose exhaled. "Of course they have nothing to fear, but I can sympathize with Ellie. She has a new baby, and mothers are supposed to protect their little ones."

Nathaniel's respect for Rose grew. He admired her empathy for the settler family. The first chance he had, he'd tell her so.

Peter nodded in her direction. "You're right." Then he turned to Nathaniel. "The reason we're here is that we need to plan our trip to the camp."

Rose sprang into action. "I can gather a bit of food to share with those at the camp, but not much. Do you think anyone was hurt badly in the skirmish and might need more serious medical attention?"

Nathaniel sighed, bent at the waist, and placed his hands on his knees. He thought of Spring Bird, her husband, and their young son, Little Hawk. Had they been caught in the middle of something?

Would these frightening skirmishes ever end? *Please, God, let it be so.* He was weary of the distrust between whites and Indians, but what else could be done, except feeding the hungry and supplying the needy with warm clothes.

He stood and stretched, then said, "I don't think we'll know the full extent of injuries until we actually arrive at the camp. I have two, maybe three, blankets I can spare. Both the agency and Dawson's are closed and won't open until daybreak, so there's nothing we can do for food until then."

Peter raked his hands through his hair. "We can't leave tonight anyway. It's fifteen miles to the camp. We'll collect a few supplies in the morning and head out at first light."

"Let's take the tribal police's wagon," Nathaniel said.

Peter turned to his sister. "Rose, can I stay with you tonight?"

"Yes, of course," she replied.

Snowflakes floated around them. Nathaniel shivered, and not just from the cold. The foreboding feeling returned and caused his middle to tighten and his heart to hammer. Dread seemed to materialize and hover behind him, intent on reaching out and placing a gnarled hand on his shoulder. He shuddered at the imaginary icy grip and tried to wrench himself free of it.

While Peter took care of his horse, Nathaniel walked Rose back to the clinic. They were both too occupied with their own thoughts to speak, but he gave her a warm hug before she entered her house.

"I'll see you in the morning." He spun and traipsed to the barn.

Peter had unhitched his horse and led it into a stall. With the horse cared for, he muttered something about checking in at the agency and left the barn.

Frigid wind whipped through the open door.

Nathaniel closed it and made sure it was secure against the wind. Minutes later, he dropped onto his bed in the tack room and instantly fell asleep.

What seemed like seconds later, he jolted awake when the barn door opened and he heard the horses whinny.

Peter was leading the team to the tribal police's wagon. "Rose is preparing eggs and bread for our breakfast, but we only get one egg each. She's going to beg Agent Royer for extra rations that we can take to the camp."

Nathaniel stood and stretched the kinks from his body. "I hope the man's feeling generous, but I'm not betting on it."

"Me either," his friend replied.

Nathaniel went to the trunk where he kept his personal supplies and pulled two blankets from inside. One had two holes in it, but if it was cut in half, it would cover two small children. He pulled his knife from its sheath and slashed at the thick wool while Peter busied himself with loading the scant amount of supplies into the rear of the wagon.

Rose entered, carrying two slices of bread and two boiled eggs. "You men need to eat something before we leave."

"What about you?" Peter asked.

"I've already had my share."

Her brother muttered a one-sentence prayer of thanks and wolfed down his portion. Nathaniel gazed at the food for a long moment. The guilt one felt for eating when so many others were starving. He ate the food but hardly tasted it, despite it being warm and fresh.

He placed the blankets next to the other supplies.

"I'm telling Agent Royer that we're leaving," Peter said. "I'll ask him if he has anything to send, messages or supplies. We'll have to leave soon if we're to make it there and back before dark."

CHAPTER 24

December 28, 1890

The sun crested over the eastern horizon, ushering in a new day. Streaks of red, pink, and gold light stretched from one end of the sky to the other. The air warmed by a few degrees, but the chill of winter still kept Rose bundled deep under her wraps, perched on the wagon seat.

Peter drove the wagon, dressed in civilian clothes that she hoped would build trust with those at the camp. Nathaniel, also dressed in civilian clothing, rode his horse alongside the wagon.

The air was cold, still, and quiet. Her mind wandered from thought to thought. She feared the army's presence would incite violence but hoped that peace had settled over the camp instead.

Hours later, the tips of tepees appeared on the horizon. Tiny specks along the banks of Wounded Knee Creek that grew larger as they rode closer. Soon, she saw people striding toward them and waving.

Peter steered the wagon to the middle of the camp, near the creek. He pulled on the reins, and the horses halted. He then set the brake and wrapped the reins around the handle. "Wait, Sister. I'll help you."

The conveyance squeaked as he hopped down. Rose grasped his shoulders, and her feet hit the frost-covered ground. Peter then led the horses to the water and set the picket lines so they could graze and drink while they were there.

At a shout, she pivoted in time to see Little Hawk and his mother running toward her. Rose stooped and lifted the boy into the air. He threw his head back and laughed. His parents approached and welcomed her to the camp.

Rose asked, "Is everyone well here? Does anyone need medical attention?"

Spring Bird replied, "No one in my family is sick or hurt, but I don't know about the rest of the camp."

Little Hawk's father reached for his son and hugged him close. "The last of the antelope has been eaten, and we're boiling the bones for broth."

Sensing the question, Rose swallowed.

"Did you bring food?" he asked.

She pointed to the rear of the wagon. "My brother is unloading what we're able to spare."

"The supply wagons are late again, so there isn't much to be had, but we brought what we could." Peter unhitched the wagon's tailgate and hefted two burlap bags onto his shoulders.

Rose reached for her medical bag.

Nathaniel said, "I brought a few blankets and what food I could buy from the mercantile. A bag of beans, two bags of flour, and a package of lard."

Rose was glad she'd thought to bring a basket of food for herself, Peter, and Nathaniel, but decided to wait until they left before eating. Three slices of cheese and bread wouldn't do much to ease their hunger, but it would suffice for the ride home. She refused to partake of a meal in front of people who had nothing to eat, and she couldn't imagine her brothers or Nathaniel doing so either.

Before long, the aromas of frying fish, caught from the nearby White River, and baking bread filled the air. The mood in the camp seemed as dreary as a lingering cold but was interspersed with bursts of laughter from the children as they played.

She once again scrutinized the church on the hill, contemplating whether or not she wanted to speak with the priest.

"Spring Bird, what can you tell me about the father who runs the church up there?" Rose pointed to the building.

"Some from camp say he's a good man," Spring Bird said. "I do not know him well, but he seems nice."

Little Hawk let out a whoop that drew her from her musings. He ran to Nathaniel, holding up his wooden toy.

"See this bird?" he said. "My father made it for me. He said it's a hawk, like my name."

Nathaniel dropped to one knee and examined the toy. "That's a fine carving. Your father did great work." He ruffled the boy's hair and stood.

"*Philamayaya*," Little Hawk said.

"You're welcome," Nathaniel replied.

Little Hawk ran to his parents. They hugged the child, their love for him evident in the way they beamed at him.

Peter tapped her shoulder. "Start saying your goodbyes. We need to leave shortly. You should make your rounds and do what you can for anyone who's sick."

"You're right. Spring Bird said she didn't know of anyone who is sick, but I should see for myself." She hitched up her skirts and proceeded to the nearest tepee. There, she dosed an elderly man with cough syrup. Everyone in the next two dwellings she visited was in fine health. In the next tepee, she used her Pinard horn to listen to a pregnant woman's heartbeat and that of her unborn babe. As she gathered her things, the woman emitted a long, low moan and clutched her rounded abdomen.

"When is your baby to be born?" Rose asked.

"Last moon," the woman said.

Tension skittered up Rose's spine. This baby was well overdue and had a very slow heartbeat. Though she longed for the warmth and comfort of her bed, every instinct within her told her to stay for the sake of this woman and her child.

Peter and Nathaniel would be upset when she told them she wasn't returning with them. But under no circumstances would she leave this vulnerable pregnant woman who was likely in the throes of labor. If anything happened to her or her baby, it would haunt Rose for the rest of her life.

She took the woman's hand, hoping the gesture comforted her. "How far apart are your pains? And is this your first child?"

The woman cried. "My first two babies died of the white man's sickness, and my husband was killed two months ago." Tears streamed down her cheeks as she squeezed Rose's hand. "Please, help me. Help my baby."

Rose gently pried her fingers from the woman's grasp. "I promise I'll do everything I can to save you and your child."

After standing to her feet, she emerged from the tepee and was surprised to see daylight fading fast. Granted, it had taken them hours to reach the camp, and she'd taken longer with her patients than she expected, but stay she must.

Rose plodded to where her brother and Nathaniel had already prepared to leave. They stood by the wagon, immersed in what appeared to be a serious conversation. Six people filled the back of wagon, sick and elderly who needed Dr. Eastman's care. Kaneenawup leaned against the wagon, his head hanging low, looking defeated.

She folded her hands in front of her, hoping she wouldn't have to go into detail about the pregnant woman in the throes of labor. "Peter, Nathaniel, please don't be angry, but I've chosen to stay. There's a vulnerable patient here who needs me, and my mind is made up."

Peter grimaced and yanked his hat from his head. He twisted it in his hands and glared. "I don't like it, Rose. I'm tempted to tell you no, but you wouldn't listen, would you?"

Nathaniel stepped between them. "If the patient is that ill, why can't we just take them with us into town?"

Rose chewed her lower lip, searching for a delicate way to describe the situation. She lowered her voice to a whisper. "Because she's having her baby right now and doesn't want to give birth in the back of a wagon with a bunch of tribal police within earshot."

The woman's pain-filled moans echoed from the tepee.

"Fine." Peter shoved his hat in place. "I would stay, but one of the men here says he found the body of Coyote Who Sneaks, shot in the head. We have to take the body back to town, and I need to file a report on the incident."

Rose gulped. She'd heard terrible things about the man, but there was no joy in his death.

Peter said, "It shouldn't take long to investigate his murder, so I'll return tomorrow to bring you home. In the meantime, Kaneenawup can stay here with you. He will come home with us tomorrow."

Nathaniel added, "We need to get these sick and elderly people to town where they'll have a warm place to stay. I'll return tomorrow as well with any food I can find. Maybe supplies came in today. Wouldn't that be nice?"

"Yes, it would be. Divide the basket of food between those in the wagon. Nathaniel, will you please check on my chickens? You can eat any eggs you find."

Distress emanated from his eyes. "All right. I'll see you then." He pulled her aside, cupped her cheeks in his hands, and gazed into her eyes. Her knees seemed to have turned to jelly and threatened to buckle. He ran the pad of his thumb across her cheek and kissed her on the forehead. "Take care of yourself."

Rose watched the men quickly climb into the wagon and drive away. The spot on her forehead, where Nathaniel had kissed her, remained warm as the wagon faded in the distance.

Another round of pain-filled groans filled the air. She sprinted to the tepee, where it was warmer, but only by a few degrees. The expectant mother heaved a few deep breaths and laid back, her eyes closed.

Birthing could take hours, sometimes days. Rose would be hungry by morning, but that couldn't be helped. She smiled, anticipating Peter and Nathaniel's return. She, as well as others, hoped they would bring food.

She checked her timepiece and noted that thirty minutes had passed since the expectant mother's last birth pain, and still, she slept. Rose sat against the wall of the tepee and wished she'd thought to bring a book. She leaned back and closed her eyes, but only for a minute.

The pounding of horse's hooves, jangling spurs, and the clanking of metal jolted her from slumber. How long had she napped? She jumped to her feet. "I'll be right back," she assured the expectant mother.

Rose stepped from the tepee and squinted into the waning twilight.

In the distance, a band of ragged Indians trudged toward them. Could this be Spotted Elk and his band of followers? She assumed they were.

A troop of military soldiers and conveyances followed close behind the weary and defeated-looking Indians. What looked like an entire regiment of soldiers sat atop sleek, well-fed horses. Their sabers bumped against their sides as they rode into camp. Several teams of horses pulled what looked like four small cannons.

She couldn't help but notice that the carts the cannons were mounted to, the wagons hauling extra weapons, the crates filled with ammunitions. . .they were made of wood.

December 29, 1890
Hours Before Dawn

Nathaniel snuggled under his blanket, but sleep proved as elusive as a cloud of pollen seeds blowing across the vast prairie. The only food he'd been able to procure was a loaf of bread from Agent Royer and the remnants of his own small bag of flour. That wouldn't even feed one family.

He was willing to spend every cent of his own money for provisions but wondered how helpful that would be. Most of this month's wages had gone for Christmas presents for his family and Rose. Besides, Dawson's shelves were bare. If the store was out of food, there wasn't much he could do about that.

He prayed, asking God for provision like fishes and loaves and that He would guide the shipment of supplies to the reservation. If it didn't happen soon, his people would starve. Sleep finally claimed him as prayers escaped his lips.

The crowing rooster jerked him from his slumber. The sky was just beginning to lighten, though the sun hadn't peeked over the horizon yet. Cold morning air nipped at him, but he threw off his blanket, stood, and shivered. There was no sense feeding the woodstove. He and Peter wouldn't be there much longer.

Nathaniel dressed quickly and read through Proverbs 29. Verse ten leaped out at him. "The bloodthirsty hate the upright." Chills swept the length of his spine. He voiced Romans chapter eight, verse twenty-eight. "And we know that all things work together for good to them that love God, to them who are the called according to his purpose."

The verse helped him feel a little better as he counted what few coins remained from his pay. Then he marched to the deputy's office and roused his friend. Peter counted what was left of his wages. Together they had enough to buy a bag of cornmeal.

"I doubt Dawson's is open this early in the morning. I know folks at the camp are hungry, but I can't see waking the man for a bag of cornmeal." Nathaniel pitched hay into his horse's manger. "Still, it won't hurt to check."

Peter filled the water trough. "I'd like to go as soon as possible. You check the store. I'll let Agent Royer know we're going and tell him we'll return as soon as we can."

Nathaniel tried to focus on the more optimistic verses of Proverbs, but his mind was unable to grasp much in his befuddled state. He was hitching his horses to the wagon when Peter entered, his face as dark as a tornado.

His friend leaned against the table, shaking, his head hanging low.

Nathaniel dropped his hands to his side. This didn't look good.

Peter spoke. "Half the tribal police force is sick, and Agent Royer has asked to speak with one of the military commanders who arrived last night."

"About what?" Nathaniel raked his hands through his hair.

"He didn't say. I bet it's about Coyote Who Sneaks, but it doesn't matter. I need to stay in town. I wish the man would have been a better deputy and not gotten himself killed. Then we wouldn't be short of deputies and I could go with you."

"Don't worry. I can take care of things." Nathaniel believed his friend had good cause to worry and wanted nothing more than to bring his siblings home.

"When you see my sister and brother, will you please persuade them to come home?"

"You know I will." Nathaniel stuffed the coins into his pocket. After Sitting Bull's death, Coyote Who Sneaks was the only tribal police officer who'd refused to wear civilian clothing. He suspected the man had met his untimely demise at the hands of a disgruntled Lakota warrior.

Nathaniel steered his thoughts to the moment. "If it's late when I get there, I might just stay the night."

"Fine with me. We have Ezra here, and another possible recruit. We'll manage. I hope the soldiers will help keep the peace rather than cause discord."

Nathaniel said goodbye to his friend and hurried to Dawson's store. He was relieved to see it was open for business, with several soldiers milling about the entrance. Weariness washed over him, but it wasn't from sleeplessness. His soul was tired of seeing his people struggle to survive.

When Rose and Kane returned to Pine Ridge, he'd sleep better. He remembered that she'd asked him to check her chicken coop. That was the next stop after the general store.

Inside Dawson's the shelves were indeed still bare. The owner complained that the shipment was late, likely due to bad weather. Hauling freight was hard enough when roads and railroad tracks were clear. It was next to impossible when several feet of snow covered the ground.

Nathaniel left with the last box of crackers and a small bag of cornmeal. He also acquired four eggs, courtesy of Rose's chickens, and voiced a prayer of thanks.

In the barn, he took a few minutes to boil the eggs to keep them from breaking during the bumpy trip to the camp. Finally, he packed the foodstuffs into the wagon along with a blanket from Miss Goodale.

He'd have to leave soon if he was going to arrive at the camp by afternoon. He thought of Rose and the new life he hoped she'd delivered by now. If anyone at camp was sick, it would be difficult to persuade her to leave, but leave she must, if the army was confiscating weapons.

Wearily, he traipsed to the clinic to ask the doctor for any medicine he could spare. The bell above the clinic door jangled when he entered.

Dr. Eastman emerged from his living quarters. "Morning, Nathaniel. Are you headed to the camp? I hope you can bring Rose back. I'll feel better once she's in town."

"I thought I'd stop here before I left and see if you have any supplies I can take to her. I think there's a much better chance of her returning if everyone there is in good health. Having medicine she could leave with people would help with that endeavor."

The doctor sighed. "I don't have anything to send with you. My supplies are nearly depleted. I can give you a bottle of German bitters. It's all I can spare."

"Thank you, that's better than nothing." Nathaniel took the bottle and trudged to the barn. He tucked it into the blanket Miss Goodale had donated, then led the team outside, climbed onto the wagon seat, and drove the animals toward the camp.

Two miles from town, Nathaniel heard someone behind him. He swiveled around.

Peter approached, his horse's hooves chewing up the dirt as it galloped. A tendril of fear gripped Nathaniel.

Something was wrong.

"Whoa." Nathaniel called to his team and pulled on the reins.

"Seems like there's trouble brewing everywhere," Peter gasped. "A family of settlers rode into town. They saw a band of Indians somewhere near Fort Robinson and feared a skirmish was imminent. They panicked and rode hard for Pine Ridge."

Nathaniel blew out a sigh. "There's always rumors of skirmishes."

"Apparently there's some truth to this one. Agent Royer has ordered you to hurry to the camp and return to town as fast as you can."

"That was already my plan."

Peter swiveled his horse around and galloped toward Pine Ridge. Nathaniel wasn't sure what kind of trouble brewed in town, and he wasn't looking forward to finding out.

CHAPTER 25

December 29, early morning

Dawn broke just as Rose swaddled the newborn girl in a wisp of a blanket. The thin cloth wouldn't do much to keep the child from freezing, so Rose pulled off her shawl and wrapped it around the infant. The baby's wails cut through the cold, predawn air, and Rose handed the tiny girl to her mother, Bright Star.

"Thank you," Bright Star whispered. Her eyes shone in the dim firelight, and a smile spread across her face as she removed her cotton blouse and held her baby to her breast. She whispered sweet words to her child and then closed her eyes.

The girl was small but otherwise appeared healthy and would survive, providing she had enough nourishment. Rose hoped she would, and her mother too.

Rose's own eyelids grew heavy. She yawned, lay down, and prayed that sleep would come. The early-morning air was bitterly cold. Without her shawl, goose bumps formed on her arms, and she shivered. Exhaustion overtook her in spite of the chill. Sleep beckoned, and she succumbed to it.

Rose dreamed of the warm barn where she and Nathaniel had practiced the Lakota language, of her house in Pine Ridge where her chickens laid eggs and the potbellied stove kept her warm when she read, of the vegetable garden she'd till, of her brothers, wrestling in the dirt outside as they used to do before their parents died.

Shouting outside dragged her from slumber. She slowly eased herself into a sitting position and stretched her aching, tired muscles. How long had she slept? It couldn't have been long. Her eyes burned, and she rubbed them to clear her vision.

She opened the tepee's flap and popped her head outside. Though daylight had broken, the morning was still young. She'd slept longer than she'd thought but still didn't feel completely rested.

Had Nathaniel returned?

With renewed vigor, she ran her fingers through her hair, swiftly plaited it, and then stood on shaky legs. Bright Star clutched her sleeping child to her chest, fear etched in her features. The child woke and fussed. Bright Star kissed her tiny head and then held her to her other breast.

Rose was affronted at such an awakening for a new mother and her baby. She patted Bright Star's shoulder, hoping the gesture conveyed assurance. "Continue nursing your baby and try to sleep. I'll return in a moment."

The baby suckled noisily and seemed to settle. Bright Star's eyes remained open, likely to be ready if danger threatened.

Rose tried to reassure her. "I'll see what's going on. Don't worry. I'll be right back."

Stepping from the tepee, she bumped into someone tall and then looked up to stare into the eyes of a white man dressed in army blue. Her heart skipped a beat.

Mustering her courage, she straightened her spine and squared her shoulders. "Excuse me, sir, but what's going on here?"

The man spit a wad of tobacco at her feet. "We're upholding the law. Confiscating all weapons."

The word *why* sailed into her mind. Not wanting to risk a confrontation, she clamped her lips closed. Arguing wouldn't help.

Rose yelped when he moved to enter the tepee. "You can't go in there. A woman has just given birth, and she needs her rest and privacy."

"I need to check for weapons," he growled.

She placed her body at the entrance and held her arms out to block him. He shoved her aside and poked his head into the structure.

Bright Star screamed.

The baby cried.

The soldier yanked his head back and glared at Rose, his cheeks the color of ripe tomatoes.

"I told you so," she muttered.

He scowled, turned the air blue with profanity, and stomped away.

"Serves him right," she muttered.

She exhaled and ducked back into the tepee. If she and Kaneenawup were returning to Pine Ridge with Nathaniel later today, she needed to sleep. She thought of Ellie Gardner and wondered how well she was doing with her new bundle of joy. It saddened her that, due to circumstances of birth, the Gardner child had a better chance of survival than the newborn girl she'd just delivered. Didn't all children deserve the same chance to live?

For the umpteenth time since coming to Pine Ridge, she contemplated the thought of having children of her own someday. Though she'd vowed to remain single so she could continue to practice nursing, she'd spent a lot of time with Nathaniel lately and had grown quite fond of him. She questioned her resolve to remain single and the logic of such a notion.

Images of Nathaniel floated into her mind. How could a relationship between them work when they didn't share the same faith? Well, she did believe in God, but trusting Him was something altogether different.

Nathaniel should be here soon. She reclined next to Bright Star and felt a smile spread across her face.

Her eyes hadn't been closed for more than a few seconds when another outburst roused her.

From outside the tepee, someone shouted, "He can't hear you. He's deaf."

A loud boom cut through the shouting.

Screams rent the air.

Rounds of gunfire seemed to go off at the same time.

All of it—the screams, the shouts, the sounds of guns rapidly firing—reached an unholy crescendo.

Rose got to her feet and peeked outside the tepee to see what was happening.

The Lakota people, mostly women and children, ran toward a ravine in the distance, crying, screaming, and tumbling to the ground as they were shot down by soldiers who seemed rabid with emotion.

The small cannons on the hill by the church launched rounds into the camp with little regard to where they fell or who they landed on.

Soldiers from the cavalry mounted their horses and chased the women and children, firing at them as if they were ducks in a shooting gallery.

The need to protect herself collided with her desire to reach the wounded, and then she saw a sobbing tot about two years old toddling through the melee.

Rose launched herself from the dwelling, scrambled over fallen bodies, and grabbed the child. She managed to scramble to the tepee with the terrified boy without being shot. She ducked inside, unharmed.

To Bright Star, she said, "Stay inside with this child, and lay low."

Rose yanked her medical bag off the ground and rushed outside. The first body she reached was that of a little girl, not more than six, clutching a doll. Blood soaked the girl's chest, but Rose checked for a pulse anyway.

She found none.

She clambered to the next body, a young woman, possibly the girl's mother. She reached to check for a pulse but noted a gaping hole above the woman's ear.

Resisting the urge to empty her stomach, she crawled to the next body.

Found a pulse.

Tied a bandage around the compound-fractured wrist of a teenage boy.

Boom!

A cannon's shell landed about twenty feet away from her. She fell to the ground as dirt and shards of metal rained down on her.

Pieces of hot metal cascaded onto her legs.

Screaming, she brushed them off.

"Mama! Papa!" A boy lay a few feet away.

Blood pumped from his midsection.

Rose crawled to the medical bag she'd dropped when the shell landed, retrieved it, and then crawled to the squalling boy. She pulled him into her arms and shielded him the best she could with her own body as another round of shells exploded around them. She yanked a bandage from her bag and placed it over his abdomen.

Smoke hung in the air.

"Mama?" he cried.

Rose gazed into the child's dirty, tear-streaked face. "Little Hawk!"

Tears poured from her eyes. Where were Spring Bird and her husband? Possibly lying dead somewhere nearby? Rose's gaze traveled until she spotted them a few feet away, blown to pieces.

Her stomach revolted, but there was nothing to expel.

So many dead.

She couldn't think about that now.

Though Little Hawk's wounds appeared fatal, she had to try to staunch the blood pumping from his torso.

In the chaos, she uttered a few words of prayer, begging God to spare the life of this small boy. She worked feverishly to save him.

The crack of gunfire continued to echo around her.

An eerie zipping sound whizzed in her ears. Simultaneously, a sharp, hot pain streaked across the top of her head. An unseen force knocked her forward.

She screamed and hit the dirt, face first. She reached for the painful spot on her head.

Her hand came away sticky with blood.

She groaned and raised herself up on her elbows.

"Little Hawk," her dry throat croaked. He stared at her, his lower lip trembling. In his tiny hand, he clutched his toy bird.

Fighting pain and dizziness, she wrapped him in an embrace and rocked him in the chaos, whimpering the words of a Lakota lullaby, trying to ease his last moments on earth.

His eyelids fixed themselves open, eyes staring at the heavens, vacant and unseeing.

Life slipped from his little body, and her guttural cry of anguish tore through the icy air.

Her ears rang, and with every shot and boom of the Hotchkiss guns, her head seemed to explode like the shell fragments raining down on her people.

Another bout of dizziness.

Darkness enveloped her.

The sense of foreboding inundated Nathaniel as he rode to check on those at the camp. He gripped the reins so tight his fingers ached. He paused for a moment to seek the Almighty. "What are You trying to tell me, God?"

Hurry!

What seemed like seconds later, loud booms rattled the air and shook the ground. Horror skittered the length of his body. His middle convulsed. If he wasn't mistaken, it sounded like cannon fire coming from the camp.

"God, have mercy."

Desperate to reach camp, he slapped the reins on the horses' rumps and urged them into a gallop.

The sky was the color of gunpowder from one end of the horizon to the other. Clouds amassed overhead. The sun seemed unable to shine on whatever trouble brewed on the earth below.

There was a frigid bite in the air that seeped into his bones. Though he'd dressed appropriately, he continued to shiver, and his teeth chattered.

He sensed a snowstorm on its way.

"I don't like how the sky looks, God. Help me find Rose and Kane and get them safely to Pine Ridge before snow flies."

Nathaniel clicked his tongue, urging the horses along. He tried to tell himself that if the worst happened, and a blizzard struck, he could hunker down in a tepee with Kane until the storm passed. Then he could gather Kane and Rose into the wagon and ride home. He would be missed in town, but if a blizzard struck, it couldn't be helped.

His prediction proved correct when a flurry of flakes descended from the sky and whirled around him like autumn leaves caught up in a gusty wind. The air grew colder. Two miles from camp, the wind blew across the prairie with enough force that he fought to stay seated on the wagon.

Ahead, a company of wagons, horses, and military conveyances approached. Perplexed and frightened, his mind tried to process the scene, but couldn't. Nathaniel nudged his horses into a gallop until he met the party.

"Can't stop but a minute," the driver of the first wagon called to him. "I've got wounded that need a doctor."

"A doctor?" Nathaniel bellowed. "What happened?"

"The army had orders to confiscate the Indians' weapons this morning. A gun went off, and a battle ensued. There's hundreds of dead and wounded."

"But not the women and children?" Nathaniel asked, hoped, prayed.

The driver scrubbed his face with his beefy hand. "Mostly women and children. Loaded as many as I could into the back of my wagon."

Nathaniel felt the blood drain from his face, and he sank against the wagon seat. He swayed before finding the strength to right himself and scream, "Rose! Kane!"

Nathaniel leaped from the wagon seat, screaming their names again. His feet unsteady, he stumbled and grabbed the side of the driver's wagon and peered inside. To the driver he said, "They're not here. Where are the rest of the people?"

"Nobody by those names in my wagon, but you can check the others." The man pointed at two wagons hurtling across the snowy landscape.

"My friends are at that camp!" Nathaniel cried.

Moans wafted up to greet his ears.

"I gotta get these people to the doctor in Pine Ridge!" The driver slapped the reins on the horses' backs and rode away.

Nathaniel jumped onto his wagon seat and snapped the reins. The horses squealed and took off at a gallop. Later, he'd ask God to forgive him for treating them so harshly, but he had to find Kane and Rose.

He babbled hasty prayers as his vision was clouded by the falling snow. He was afraid of what he'd find in the back of the approaching wagons and at camp, if he made it that far.

Two more wagons stopped. Nathaniel checked them, but Rose and Kane weren't among the survivors. Once again, he bolted toward the camp. What would he find when he reached it?

He believed his horses could pull a wagon full of wounded people, but he feared it would overexert the team. It would tear his heart in two to do that, but if lives were at stake, what choice did he have? Much as he loved his horses, people were a priority.

Would he find anyone alive at the camp? *No!* He couldn't think that way. He had to find them. He had to!

If only his horses could run faster, but he had to use caution so as not to exhaust them too soon. It wouldn't do the wounded any good if the horses gave out before they could get back to town.

The camp lay just ahead.

Bodies littered the ground.

His chest constricted, and fear smacked him in the face.

Would he find Rose and Kane among the dead?

Nathaniel sprang from the wagon seat and shouted their names over and over. The snow cascaded in great flurries now. He had to find them fast and return to town, or they would freeze on the prairie.

He found Kane, wounded, shot through the leg, but alive and awake. Nathaniel helped him stand, and slowly they ambled to the wagon. Kane emitted an agony-filled groan as Nathaniel hefted him into the rear of the wagon. Then he searched frantically for Rose.

He stumbled over a woman, shot through the shoulder, but alive. She wailed for her lost children. Nathaniel scanned the ground around her but saw no little ones. Torn between searching for the woman's children and getting the wounded to Pine Ridge, he chose the latter and hefted the woman into the wagon.

If he spotted any wounded youngsters, he'd place them in the wagon too and hope they belonged to the sobbing woman.

Ahead were two females face down on the ground, unmoving. Either one could be Rose. He lurched forward, his chest heaving, and turned one over, then the other. He was relieved they weren't the woman he loved, and yet a pang shot through him for their families.

Then he saw her.

Sprawled on the ground.

Her white nursing apron drenched in blood.

"No! No!" Nathaniel released piercing screams. "Rose!" He knelt beside her body. The air went out of his lungs in a whoosh. With trembling fingers, he rolled her over.

A small child lay beneath her.

Tears smarted in his eyes. It was just like Rose to use her body to shield a child, but at the cost of her own life?

Blood seeped from her head.

His trembling fingers fumbled around her neck, desperate to find a pulse.

"Praise God," he cried. She had a pulse. It was weak, but her heart still beat. There was hope that she'd live.

Nathaniel wrapped her in his arms and lifted her from the freezing ground. He rasped, "Let's get you to town where Dr. Eastman can make you right as rain."

Blood continued to flow from her wound and soak her long hair, even as he laid her beside Kane in the back of the wagon. "She's alive, thank God."

Kane mumbled something and reached for his sister.

Nathaniel whipped off his new scarf and told Kane to press it over the spot where a bullet had cut a groove along the top of her scalp.

With Rose nestled beside her brother, he searched for any other survivors among the carnage. None of the bodies moved or showed any signs of life. Unable to take it all in, he turned his focus on the child who had been beneath Rose. He rolled the small, cold body over and stared into the lifeless eyes of a little boy who clutched a carved bird in his tiny hand.

"Little Hawk," he cried, but the child's lifeless eyes were fixed in place. Nathaniel gulped. Had it been only yesterday that this boy had proudly shown him his toy bird?

Unable to dwell on the heartbreak, he stood and scanned the area. Bodies covered the ground, and helplessness washed over him in great waves. He could give but three wounded people a chance at life. Kane, Rose, and the woman sobbing for her children.

A soldier appeared and pointed at a tepee.

The thirst for vengeance engulfed him. He marched toward the man. "What happened here?" Nathaniel swung his arms wide. "What have you done?"

His lungs burned as he sucked cold air into his lungs, and his hands clenched into fists.

The soldier wisely retreated two steps and motioned to a tepee. "There's a mother and a new baby in there, and she's determined to stay. I need any food and blankets you brought."

Reason slowly seeped into his mind. "I'll get them." He hurried to the wagon and retrieved the items.

After giving them to the soldier, he said, "I should go now. I don't want my friends in the back of the wagon to freeze."

"All right." The soldier waved him off.

He returned to the wagon and hopped onto the seat and prayed the horses knew the way to town, because he couldn't see anything in front of him.

The snow and wind increased. Rose moaned as the wagon lurched forward. Nathaniel knew that Kane would try to reassure her, but there was little her brother could say that was encouraging, considering the death scene they'd just left.

Nathaniel prayed, "Please, God, help me make it to town."

The horses trotted along as if they knew the way. Eventually, the lights from Pine Ridge came into view through the dusky twilight. A crowd was gathered outside the Holy Cross Episcopal Church, where lanterns lit the interior of the building.

When they reached the church, Nathaniel pulled on the reins and hopped down. With Rose in his arms, he entered the church. The scene shocked him. The pews had been hastily torn from the floor and cast aside and replaced with a blanket of fresh hay. People lay in rows like sardines in a tin.

So many wounded.

In juxtaposition, the Christmas garlands and wreaths still adorned the walls.

Dr. Eastman moved with lightning speed, tending to one patient then another. Miss Goodale followed close behind. Both of their aprons were slick with blood. The woman handed instruments to the doctor and helped him bandage wounds.

"Doctor," Nathaniel cried above the noise.

The doctor looked up, and his shoulders slumped. He heaved a deep sigh. "Rose."

"Where do you want me to put her?"

"Over here." The doctor led him to a spot in a corner where Nathaniel laid her onto a pile of soft hay. He hurried to Kane and brought him inside, where he lay beside his sister.

The doctor examined the gash on her head. "I have to stitch the wound closed, but I don't have any morphine to give her."

Rose's eyes popped open and locked on Nathaniel. "Where are my brothers? Where are Little Hawk and his parents?"

CHAPTER 26

December 30, 1890

Rose tried to sit up, but the fiery pain slashing across her scalp stopped her. Head throbbing, she fell backward. She reached for her hairline and winced.

She yanked her fingers away until the pain dissipated. More slowly, she gently explored the top of her scalp and discovered a bandage covering a tender spot there. How much time had passed since the shootings at Wounded Knee Creek?

Her brothers!

Where were Peter and Kaneenawup?

She tried to sit up again, but strong hands pressed on her shoulders, and she reclined against what felt like hay. Smelled like hay too. Where was she?

Light pierced her eyes as she opened them. She winced and immediately closed them. When the pain subsided, she opened them again. Her bed consisted of scattered hay inside the church. Had the clinic been so full of wounded people that they had to be moved to the church?

She scanned the room and saw that the pews had been torn out and the floor covered with hay for the wounded to rest upon. Her mind struggled to reconcile the comforting sanctuary where she'd worshiped on Christmas Eve with the morbid scene before her. The church had become a house of suffering and death.

Nathaniel sat by her side, his hand in hers. "You're safe now, Rose."

"Where are my brothers?" Kaneenawup had been at Wounded Knee Creek. Was he injured? Had he survived unscathed? A cry escaped her lips at the thought of anything happening to him.

Nathaniel, as if he'd read her mind, reassured her. "I found Kane and brought him home. He's wounded, but he will live."

"Thank God," she muttered.

He squeezed her hand. "I'm glad I went out there when I did. Any earlier and I might have been caught up in the massacre myself. Any later, and the snowstorm would have kept me from reaching the scene, and you and Kane might not have survived. Reverend Cook says God's timing is perfect, and he's right."

Rose remembered being introduced to the reverend on Christmas Eve and remembered his kindness. Such kindness was evidenced by how he opened his church to those in need and tended to the wounded in his care.

While Rose was thankful to be alive, curiosity churned within her. "What happened out there? Why were those soldiers shooting at us?"

"I'm not sure what started things. Rumors are flying like snow flurries. Agent Royer might want to talk to you, ask questions about what you saw, what you heard, and what you remember."

"It was chaos." She turned her head away, not wanting to remember, but flashes of memories inserted themselves into her consciousness. Bright Star and her new baby. "I delivered a baby not long before the shooting began. A tiny baby girl."

"They were found by a soldier, and despite the mother's objections, he brought them into town. They're staying at the clinic for now, so they can have privacy."

"What about the little boy I left with her?" She hoped no harm had come to him and was heartsick at the possibility.

"He was separated from his parents in the chaos. We reunited them and they chose to stay at the camp to search for the rest of their family."

Rose closed her eyes, thankful for three miracles: A family safe and reunited, Bright Star and her child escaping unscathed, and a soldier enduring the elements to bring them to safety.

"The snowstorm is beginning to let up, and we can search for survivors," Nathaniel said. "I hear there's going to be a military investigation. General Nelson Miles is demanding an explanation."

"I saw soldiers shooting women and children." The image of Little Hawk and his parents, dead on the prairie, floated to the surface of her mind. The entire family, gone. Her heart seized with agony, and for a moment her breath froze in her lungs.

Sobs bubbled in her middle and demanded release. "Where are my brothers?"

He patted her hand. "Peter has been working overtime at the deputy's office. Kane is recovering from his wounds."

The church door opened and closed.

Peter came into her field of vision. "Hey, Sis, glad to see you awake. You gave us quite a scare. Kane is over there, resting. He got shot in the leg. Thankfully, Dr. Eastman didn't have to amputate."

Nathaniel lifted her gently to a seated position, and she spied Kaneenawup sitting up against the wall, not far away. Her emotions were a strange mix of gratitude and guilt; she was thankful her brothers were alive, but sorry for those who'd died and their loved ones.

Kaneenawup waved to her, and Rose exhaled with relief. Both her brothers were alive and whole. Not everyone was so lucky. How many dead and dying friends had she seen on the field?

"I saw Little Hawk and his parents. They're all dead, aren't they? It wasn't a bad dream?" she whispered.

Peter and Nathaniel exchanged glances. Her brother knelt beside her and took her other hand. "Yes. When we found you, Little Hawk and his parents were already dead."

Tears slid from Rose's eyes and along her cheeks. An entire family killed by soldiers who were not supposed to harm Indians, especially women and children. Nathaniel held her close and let her cry.

"Many of our people died yesterday, Rose," Nathaniel said. "There is some good news, however. Photographers are out there recording the scene. There will forever be a record of what happened at Wounded Knee Creek."

"I hope those pictures are used to convict the soldiers. It seemed as though they went wild and shot at anything that moved." Rose's mind flitted back to the scene. The soldiers seemed exhilarated as they shot children in the head. How could she face the future with such horrid memories clouding her mind?

Nathaniel squeezed her hand, bringing her back to the present.

"Dr. Eastman, Miss Goodale, and others are heading to the site to search for survivors. We'll have to put them in the barn, because the clinic and the church are full."

"Help me up, please," Rose said. "I'd like to go see Bright Star and her new baby." She stood on shaky legs and leaned against Nathaniel for a moment. Then he helped her into a nearby chair.

"You need to take it slow, Rose. You're injured, remember?"

She tenderly touched her bandaged scalp and winced as hot pain knifed through her. "Yes, I remember."

Rose ate a bowl of broth and an hour later trudged through the snow and into the clinic. Nathaniel guided her to the spot where Bright Star and her new babe rested.

"Dr. Eastman looked them over and pronounced them healthy. He said you did good work." Nathaniel beamed, as if he was proud of her.

Rose squatted until she could meet Bright Star's gaze. "How are you feeling? Is your baby nursing all right?"

The woman rubbed her baby's back. "Yes, we are well. Thank you for staying and helping me with my baby."

"Does she have a name yet?" Rose asked.

Bright Star ran her fingers through the child's thick black hair. "It's *Piya Wiconi*."

The Lakota words meant "miraculous new life." Rose thought that a fitting name. After a few minutes of polite conversation, she excused herself so they could rest. "I'm ready to go home now," she said.

Nathaniel offered his hand and helped her to her feet.

Rose leaned against him. "I need to check on my chickens. Nathaniel, will you please ask Peter to bring Kaneenawup to my house, if he's willing to recuperate there."

"I'm sure he will be." He helped her walk outside. Snowflakes continued to drift lazily to earth. Nathaniel wrapped a protective arm around her and assisted her across the street to her home. She checked the chickens and found six eggs. If she had enough flour for bread, she and Kaneenawup would eat that night and maybe in the morning as well.

Later, after Peter had brought their brother over, she scrambled the eggs and cut a slice of the bread she'd made. She handed Kaneenawup his plate, and he devoured the food, but he still clung to his buffalo hide. It helped keep him warm, so what was the harm?

The snow was deep outside, and it was cold in her house. Nathaniel carried in an armload of wood, and she fed a few pieces into the stove and reached for a blanket. She plopped into her rocking chair and gazed at her bookshelf, wondering if things would ever be the same again.

Nathaniel woke early on New Year's Day. The storm had abated. If there were survivors at Wounded Knee Creek, they had to be reached soon. Members of his tribe could have died a slow death out there in the blizzard. They could have bled to death or frozen before help could arrive. That thought had haunted him for the past two days.

"C'mon, Peter, get up." With his toe, he nudged his friend, who slept wrapped in a wool blanket on the barn floor.

Peter yawned and stretched. "I hope we find survivors at Wounded Knee Creek, but it's not very likely. I'm not looking forward to helping identify the dead."

Nathaniel wouldn't take pleasure in the task either, but he had hope. Even if they didn't discover survivors, at least the dead could be accounted for and put to rest.

Impatient to reach the site as soon as possible, he quickly worked through his morning ablutions. Next, he saddled the horses and hitched them to the wagon. "You mind the horses, please. I'll ask Dr. Eastman if he's going with us."

"All right." Peter threw off his blanket and scrubbed his hands down his face. "I'll see if I can find us some grub."

Nathaniel stepped from the barn and out into darkness. Streaks of light had just begun to illuminate the eastern horizon. Already groups of people were readying themselves for a trip to what was left of the camp. Dr. Eastman and Miss Goodale were piling blankets and medical supplies into the rear of the doctor's wagon.

Nearby, a photographer loaded equipment into his conveyance.

The doctor waved and tramped through the snow to reach him. "Elaine and I are going to the site. I hope we find—" He paused, sighed, and shook his head. "I don't know what we'll find. You'll help us out there, won't you?"

"Peter and I won't be far behind you. I hope we find survivors." Nathaniel finished the man's sentence and then trudged back into the barn.

Peter had already piled blankets into the wagon. He was perched on the seat and ready to go. Nathaniel opened the barn doors and drove the team outside, then closed the doors and climbed onto the seat beside his friend.

Two to three inches of snow prevented a speedy trip to the camp, or rather, what was left of it. Three miles from the site they pulled alongside Dr. Eastman's wagon. He'd stopped to check the body of a woman who'd been shot in the back. Looking very distraught, the doctor declared her dead, then climbed onto his wagon seat and urged the horses on.

Later, when they reached the site of the massacre, Nathaniel had to swallow the bile climbing up his throat.

Dead bodies lay everywhere. He jumped from the wagon seat and spun a slow circle, gazing at the carnage that looked so much more horrific in the daylight.

The doctor stepped over bodies, checking each one for a pulse. The man's shoulders slumped every time he stood and moved to the next frozen body.

The photographer had mounted his camera on a tripod and was taking pictures of a corpse half buried in the snow. He kept busy sliding negatives into and out of his device. Then he turned over the body, and Nathaniel recognized Spotted Elk, the man soldiers called Big Foot.

Would the nightmare of witnessing such a scene ever go away?

CHAPTER 27

Early January 1891

Rose borrowed a buggy normally used by the tribal police and rode out to the mass grave site of most of the victims of the massacre at Wounded Knee Creek. Because it was the middle of winter, there were no wildflowers or any other flowers to put on the grave. With Reverend Cook's permission, she'd taken a Christmas garland from the church and fashioned it into a wreath to represent her respect for the fallen.

Little Hawk and his parents. When she closed her eyes at night to sleep, she could still hear the little boy bragging about the toy bird his father had carved for him. Had he been buried with his precious treasure, or had it been heartlessly stolen by greedy relic hunters?

Pain sliced through her, like the bullet that had carved a groove across her scalp.

The victims were buried in a mass grave. The so-called undertakers had counted the bodies, but many bodies had been removed, likely by family members, prior to the burial. Calculating how many of her people had actually died was near impossible.

The victims hadn't even received the decency of being buried in coffins. When she thought of poor Little Hawk, how his small body had been tossed into a hastily dug pit like trash, her heart wrenched in two.

She'd heard rumors that the grave hadn't been dug big enough and that the diggers had used shovels to break the bones of the dead to compact them all into the trench.

One more reason for her to be angry at the government. She could have easily been one of the victims, but thanks to Nathaniel, she'd miraculously survived. This fact both solaced and haunted her. Part of her craved more information about the tragedy. The scores of newspaper articles she'd gotten ahold of held little truth. She'd read the blistering things columnists had to say about her people, namely L. Frank Baum of *The Aberdeen Saturday Pioneer*, who called for their total extermination. She wished she'd never bothered to investigate the matter.

When she reached the site, she was stunned at how serene the place looked. The wind blew gently, and the prairie stretched for miles. The sun cast its rays across a cloudless azure sky. There seemed to be a sense of peace around her, as if the victims had found a rest in the afterlife that they had been unjustly denied while on earth.

The large mound of turned earth drew her attention. It was the only clue to the location of the mass grave. There was no marker of any sort, nothing to indicate that the bodies of more than one hundred souls lay buried beneath it.

Rose reached for the wreath and climbed down from the buggy. Tears blurred her vision as she approached the grave site. Dropping to her knees, she placed the wreath atop the mound. It was an eerie feeling, knowing that she could have been one of the many who lay here.

Why had *Wakan Tanka* spared her? For what purpose?

She pulled a handkerchief from her coat pocket and mopped the tears that freely streamed down her cheeks. She cried for Little Hawk and his family. She cried for the loss of Sitting Bull. She cried for the loss of her people's way of life. It seemed that everything about her people was being yanked from them and vanishing in the air like the vapor her breath left behind on this bitterly cold winter day.

Hadn't Peter and Nathaniel told her they needed to adapt if they were to survive? Hadn't Kaneenawup told her that the whites wouldn't be satisfied until every Lakota custom and tradition was eradicated?

Oh, how she'd hoped they were both wrong, but after the events of last month, the realization had sunk in, like a heavy anchor dropping into the depths of her soul. She became cognizant of the fact that she'd never be the same again.

None of them would.

She patted and smoothed a rough patch of earth. Her tears dripped from her chin and left wet spots on the dirt. Numb, she stood and walked what she thought was the length of the grave. Though the burial hadn't occurred that long ago, she had difficulty discerning where it began and ended. A testament to how little care the site had been given.

The sound of a horse's bridle jingling drew her from her musings. She swiped the handkerchief across her face once again and turned to see who approached. The rider was too far away for her to distinguish his identity. She shielded her eyes with her hand and walked toward him.

Peter.

"Hey, Sis." He dismounted but hung on to the reins, as there was nothing to tie them to. "I heard you were out here, so I came to keep you company. That is, if you want company."

"I don't mind you being here."

He exhaled a guttural sigh and cleared his throat. "Truth is, I'm worried about you. I'm your big brother, and after Ma and Pa died, the job of taking care of you and Kaneenawup fell on my shoulders."

Rose shook her head. "You were a kid yourself at sixteen years old." It pleased her to hear him use their younger brother's Lakota name. The government had taken enough from her people, and she'd be tortured before allowing them to take Kaneenawup's name from him too.

"I keep telling myself that," he mumbled. "But the truth is, I feel like a failure."

"What? Why?" This news stunned Rose. She'd always believed he'd done a good job of being there for her and their baby brother. Yes, they had been torn apart, but that was through no fault of his.

"Kaneenawup won't give up our native customs, ever, even if he has to perform them in secret. When I saw you on the ground, bleeding from the head, I felt like it was my fault. I should have protected you both from the carnage."

She cupped his face in her hands. "You hear me, Peter, you are a good big brother. You did everything you could to keep us together. We're together now because of you. Do you know how many Indian siblings"—her voice cracked—"will never see each other again?"

She watched his Adam's apple bob, and her heart swelled with love. Though she and her brothers had lost their parents, at least they were allowed to remain in contact with each other. How many Indian orphans had been torn from every blood relative they had and were left with no sense of family?

Peter stepped back, cleared his throat, and muttered something indistinguishable under his breath. It wasn't often her stoic brother displayed emotion, but then, tragedy had just befallen their people, and displays of emotion were happening all over the reservation.

Her brother placed his hat on his head and tightened the string under his chin. "We need to get back to town."

Rose hopped into the borrowed buggy and reached for the reins. Peter mounted his horse and stayed alongside as they made their way to Pine Ridge.

Thankfully, the supply wagons had finally arrived. When she and Peter reached her house, they ate dinner there with Nathaniel.

Rose said, "I'd like to go over the testimony I plan to give to General Miles."

Nathaniel twirled his fork between bites. "I'll find a few sheets of paper for you in the office so you can write everything down before you forget it."

"I'd like a few pages too, if you wouldn't mind," Kaneenawup said.

"How do you think the inquiry will go?" Peter asked. "I hear that Forsyth's men are loath to testify against him."

Nathaniel shrugged. "I don't know. I hope they tell the truth and allow the victims to tell their side of things too."

Rose nearly choked on her food. She swallowed and harrumphed. "They better listen to what I have to say. I was there!"

"I've got a bad feeling about this." Peter shook his head.

"Me too," Kaneenawup groaned.

When the meal was finished, the men excused themselves. Rose brought the dishes to the kitchen and dunked them in a sink of sudsy water. She hummed a tune and tried not to focus on her brothers' misgivings.

Though the men seemed to feel uneasy about the hearing, Rose was full of hope. She was sure the military officials in command would want justice. The army was supposed to be a disciplined bunch, not full of soldiers who went around shooting women and children with reckless abandon!

From her spot at the sink, she called over her shoulder to Nathaniel and her brothers, "I believe General Miles will listen to me or at least read my statement when I present it to him. He owes our people that much, at least. Don't you think?"

The silence permeating her home threatened to deafen her.

Nathaniel trudged from the deputy's office to the barn that night. Uneasiness churned deep in his stomach. Dinner had smelled heavenly, but he'd hardly tasted it. Rose's sunny predictions were naive at best. She failed to see how uncaring and unsympathetic military officers and soldiers could be.

That worried him. News of the Sand Creek Massacre had reached the Pine Ridge Reservation years ago. They'd heard how the men who'd perpetuated such horrific crimes hadn't been held accountable. It was likely the soldiers who'd participated in this massacre wouldn't be either. He didn't want to see her heartbroken, but he also sensed that heartbreak barreled toward her like a runaway locomotive.

He entered the stalls and checked the horses. They rested on beds of fresh hay and had enough feed and water to keep them until morning. He fed the woodstove in the corner and dropped onto the cot in the tack room.

The barn door squeaked open and closed.

"That you, Peter?" Nathaniel called.

"Yeah," his friend replied. "Mind if I talk to you about my sister?"

Nathaniel sat up and rubbed his eyes and temples. "Nah, I don't care. What's on your mind?"

Peter appeared before him and removed his hat. "I want you to make me a promise."

Nathaniel's curiosity was piqued. Peter had asked for many favors in the past, all of which Nathaniel had happily done for his friend. Peter had gladly repaid them, but none of the previous favors had sounded this serious. "C'mon, pal, you know there's nothing I wouldn't do for you."

"If anything happens to me, promise me you'll look after my sister and brother."

His stomach turned a somersault as he stood. "You know I would, but I'll promise it anyway."

Peter met his gaze. "Thank you."

"C'mon, Peter, you don't have anything to worry about. You're young and healthy." His attempt at humor fell flat in light of recent events.

Silence stretched taut between them.

A myriad of thoughts and emotions swirled in Nathaniel. He couldn't imagine what he'd do without his best friend, but the massacre had driven home the reality that God could call them home at any time. That left him feeling small and vulnerable. He imagined Peter and the rest of the Lakota felt the same way.

Peter retreated a few steps. "I'm the on-duty deputy tonight, so I'll be sleeping in the office. Holler if you need anything. Otherwise, I'll see you in the morning."

"Sleep well." Nathaniel dropped onto the cot. He heard the barn door creak open and closed again. Though his mind was full, he was exhausted and quickly nodded off to sleep.

When he woke, sunlight streamed through the cracks in the barn. Today would be a good day to patch them. Dr. Eastman had a few outdated catalogs for medical supplies that he'd offered him. They could be used to cover the cracks, just like in so many cabins across the reservation.

A grin stretched across his face. This was a perfect excuse to visit the clinic and see Rose. As if he needed an excuse to see her. He had dinner with her almost every night.

Which reminded him, he needed to stop at Dawson's for groceries. He hated arriving at her house every night empty-handed. It wasn't her job to feed the entire tribal police force. He crawled out of bed, splashed water on his face, and dressed.

A few minutes later he stepped into the lobby of the tribal police office.

"Hey, Peter," he called.

"I'm in the office, filling out the ledger. You wouldn't believe how illegible some of our deputies' handwriting is."

Nathaniel chuckled. "Yeah, I believe it."

"Maybe we should ask Miss Goodale to teach them proper penmanship," Peter groaned as he shuffled through a stack of loose papers.

"I think Dr. Eastman would have something to say about that. You know how sweet he is on the woman. Judging from her comments, I'd say she feels the same about him."

With their clerical duties completed, they left the office and strode along the street to see Agent Royer. They entered the administration building and were greeted kindly by the front desk clerk.

They exchanged pleasantries before the clerk ushered them into Royer's office.

Peter began. "Has anything been decided regarding the shooting last month? What kind of trial will there be, and when is it taking place?"

Agent Royer sighed. "I want to see things cleared up as much as you do, but I haven't heard anything yet. How are the survivors doing?"

"I think most of them are healed up on the outside, but I fear their hearts will be forever wounded."

The agent grunted and shrugged. He shuffled papers on his desk, appearing as though he'd rather have dental surgery than be there conversing with them.

Was the man afraid the Indians would testify against him? Already, the government was looking to replace this unqualified official.

Nathaniel choked on the words he wished to say at the man's indifference. "It doesn't help that the supply wagons are usually late or don't arrive at all. If the people didn't trust the government before, they sure don't now."

Agent Royer wrinkled his nose as if he agreed but didn't want to admit the truth. Then he muttered, "There are rumors that some twenty soldiers might be receiving Medals of Honor for their actions that day."

The air whooshed out of Nathaniel's lungs. "What kind of government gives medals to soldiers who shoot women and children in the back? How are the people supposed to trust the tribal police when the government does such things?"

"We have a hard enough time getting the people to speak to us," Peter added. "This will make our jobs much more difficult."

Agent Royer raked his fingers through his oil-slicked hair and then reached for his pen. "I'll let you know as soon as I hear something. I need to get to work now."

They left the building and headed for the clinic. Nathaniel hoped to see Rose there, but he couldn't tell her about the Medals of Honor, especially when it was almost impossible for him to believe such a thing could be true.

CHAPTER 28

Nathaniel wanted to talk to Rose about faith. She had said she had questions about it. The conversation might determine where their relationship went.

He pushed open the clinic door and listened to the bell jangle.

Dr. Eastman looked up from his medical book. "Morning, Nathaniel. If you're looking for Rose, she isn't here."

"Do you know where she is or when she'll return?"

The doctor nodded. "A young man's wife and two young sons were killed at Wounded Knee. Rose has gone to visit the grief-stricken father, whose remaining child, his three-year-old daughter, is suffering from influenza."

This tragic news hit Nathaniel like a stampeding buffalo. He rocked back on his heels. "I'm sorry to hear about this child and her father. I'll pray that she survives."

"As we will also," Dr. Eastman said. "If you'd like to see Rose, you can check in tomorrow."

Nathaniel left the clinic, wondering if the doctor could read his emotions like the book in his lap. Rose filled his every thought, and the desire to protect her, to be with her, kept him awake at night. With a sigh, he realized his sister was right. He was sweet on the woman.

The next morning, Nathaniel stopped by the clinic and discovered Rose was still gone. Frustrated, he asked the doctor, "Where is she today?"

"She and Peter rode out to see the Gardner family. Rose wanted to make sure they were all right, and she wanted to see the new baby."

"So they probably won't be back until after sundown."

Dr. Eastman shrugged. "I couldn't say for sure, but I *did* tell her that you stopped by yesterday, looking for her."

Nathaniel sighed. "All right. Thanks, Doc. I'll see you later."

He left the clinic. It was January, and the cold on the reservation had deepened, as it always did, but this year felt different. Despondency seemed to have frozen the hearts of his people like the icy puddles on Main Street.

He shivered on his way to the deputy's office. As soon as he stepped inside, he fed an armload of wood into the stove. Ezra sat behind a desk, filling out paperwork. The kid looked up, offered a wan grin, and continued writing.

The Ghost Dance had screeched to a halt after the massacre, as well as every form of mischief. Defeat emanated from his people's eyes as they moved about the town and the reservation. It hurt to watch.

Since the massacre, tensions had settled considerably. For that he was relieved, but he was bored during the long days with nothing to do.

He should probably ride out to see Sarah, Joshua, and the children. Though the family wasn't stricken with illness, they were likely hungry. January had always been a hard month to survive. Too much cold and too little food didn't bode well for the elders, the sick, and the children. The past few months he'd seen enough sickness and death to last a lifetime.

"I'm headed out to see my sister. Send a rider for me if I'm needed." Nathaniel wound his freshly washed scarf around his neck, donned his hat, and pulled it low to cover his ears.

"All right. Hey, do you think Miss Rushing Water would allow me to borrow one of her books? I'm told she has quite a collection."

"I'm sure she'd be fine with that."

Outside, he mounted his horse and wished he had food to take to his sister and her family.

When the horse drew near the homestead, he saw puffs of smoke wafting from the chimney and easing into the brisk blue sky. Dismay washed over him to see part of the fence had once again blown over, the rails scattered across the wind-whipped prairie. Probably the result of the last blizzard. Thank the Lord the fence posts were still standing. A lowing cow was tied to a picket line not far away.

Though the sun shone high overhead, it did nothing to warm the air. An icy wind blew across the land, and he was glad his niece and nephew weren't outside playing. They could so easily become sick again.

He reached the cabin, dismounted, and tied the reins to a post. Before he could knock, Joshua pulled the door open and ushered him inside. In the dimly lit interior, he noted very little firewood and almost nothing to eat.

Joshua interrupted his reverie.

"Can you help me with the fence in exchange for a meal?"

Guilt nibbled at Nathaniel, and he almost wished he hadn't come. He gulped. "I'm happy to help with the fence, but Peter's checking on settlers and the deputy on duty is a young kid, and he's green at that. I'll need to return to town as soon as the job is done."

Joshua seemed to understand. They left the cabin and trudged to the gaping hole in the fence. Though what Nathaniel had said was the truth, it wasn't the whole truth. He didn't want to wrestle with the guilt of eating their food. Starving would hurt less.

"I know it looks like we don't have much," Joshua said. "But I've almost saved enough money for a new mule, maybe two."

"That's good news. Spring is a good time to buy livestock. Let me know if I can help with the endeavor." Nathaniel was even more determined to help his sister and her family.

Joshua lifted his head. "I appreciate that, Nathaniel."

They nailed the stray rails into place for the next hour. When the fence was complete and sturdy, he shook his brother-in-law's hand and rode toward town.

Darkness had enveloped the world by the time he steered his horse down Main Street. No lights shone from Rose's house. If she was home, she was likely in bed. That was fine with him. She was still recovering and needed her rest.

By lantern light he saw Ezra conversing with Agent Royer. Neither of them looked happy. Nathaniel dismounted and, with reins in hand, walked toward the pair.

"What's going on?" he asked, glancing from one man to the other.

The young deputy wrung his hands and seemed to study the snow-covered ground. "I just heard one of Forsyth's men bragging about lying to General Miles about the fight the other day. He's from the Seventh Cavalry."

Nathaniel's shoulders drooped along with his spirits. This couldn't be good. "Go on," he mumbled to the deputy.

"He called us Indians a few names I don't dare repeat in church and said Wounded Knee was revenge for the Little Bighorn."

Rose handed the healthy baby boy to Ellie Gardner so she could nurse him. Much as she hated to admit, a twinge of yearning rooted in her heart. She wasn't jealous of the woman—quite the opposite, she delighted to see this family—but since the massacre, she found herself longing more and more for a family of her own.

"He really is beautiful, isn't he?" Ellie beamed. "And healthy too."

"Yes, he's adorable and the very picture of health. You and your husband must be so proud."

The baby released a cry and fisted the front of Ellie's nightgown.

"We are." Tears wet the woman's cheeks as she untied the strings holding her shift closed. The baby nursed with vigor, judging from the sounds he made.

Rose turned away to offer Ellie privacy to feed her new babe. She remembered her friend Bridget and how much she had looked forward to being a mother. Perhaps marriage and children would still be possible if any potential husband allowed her to continue to practice medicine. An image of Nathaniel popped into her mind, as it had more often since the tragedy. She couldn't picture him relegating her to caring for the house if they married.

She shifted in her seat, determined to speak with him soon about the matter.

Where had these thoughts originated? She chased them away as she stuffed her instruments into her medical bag. "I'll ask Peter how much longer he's going to be. We should go now if we're to reach town before nightfall. Good to see you again. I'll return when I can."

Ellie said her goodbyes, and Rose hurried out the door.

Moments later, she found her brother helping Mr. Gardner repair a fence around an area that would become the garden. She stamped her feet and shivered from the cold.

"All done inside, Sis?" Peter asked.

"Yes, I'm ready to leave when you are." She faced Mr. Gardner. "Sir, your son is beautiful and as healthy as can be. Congratulations."

"Thank you, ma'am. Thank you for coming out." He clapped Peter on the shoulder. "With another mouth to feed, I need to make sure this garden is protected from deer and wild rabbits. Thanks for your help."

Her brother handed the man his tools. "Until next time."

Rose and Peter hustled to the wagon. He helped her up onto the seat, and they were on their way. She wanted to broach the subject of families but didn't know where to start. How would her brother feel if she and Nathaniel became a family? The two men were best friends, and she certainly didn't want to interfere with that.

"Penny for your thoughts?"

Rose stammered, "Wh–what? I mean, what did you say?"

He nudged her with his elbow. "You're usually like a little magpie, chattering about everything. But since the massacre, you hardly say anything at all. Are you all right?"

She scoffed. "Well, nearly being killed, I suspect, changes a lot of people." The faces of many of the Lakota people who were slaughtered flashed through her mind, first and foremost Little Hawk and his parents. Those lucky enough to survive were doing their best to recover, physically and emotionally. She still had trouble sleeping at night.

"I'm sorry. It's just that Kaneenawup and I are worried about you."

Rose snapped to the present. "Did you just call our brother by his given name? It's not the first time I've heard you do it."

Peter chuckled. "Yeah, I did. You're right. Tragedies like what happened at Wounded Knee Creek change people. I'm so thankful the both of you are still alive, it no longer matters what names you go by."

Rose wrapped her brother in a side hug. "Thank you."

They rode for a while, chatting about what herbs and vegetables to plant in the spring and whether or not to purchase more chickens from the East. She laughed at one of his jokes, and he beamed when she told him she'd ordered fabric to sew him a new shirt. During those few precious hours, Rose felt as if she'd regained a bit of her old life.

Pine Ridge soon appeared in the twilight. Everything looked well as half of the sun dipped below the horizon. She longed for warmer weather and planting season.

"Before we reach town," she said, "there's something I need to ask you."

"What is it?"

She drew in a breath for courage. "How would you feel if Nathaniel and I courted? Not that he's asked me. Oh, I'm being too forward, but I do care for him. I just don't know if he feels the same way about me. Well, I think he does."

She clamped down on her lips to cease her ramblings.

Peter released a deep belly laugh. "I'd say it's about time. I've long suspected you already are, and so does half the town." He playfully wagged a finger at her. "But that doesn't mean I like you two keeping secrets from me. And I don't want to see you kissing in the middle of Main Street."

Heat crept into Rose's cheeks. She ducked her head but was unable to contain her joy at her brother's change of heart.

Eventually, she found her voice. "Nathaniel and I are only speaking Lakota in private, and if a word or two slips out, we'll face any consequences head-on."

"Most of us are so upset at the massacre, we don't give much thought to the language rules doled out by the government now," Peter said.

He stopped the wagon in front of her home. "I'll put up the horses and wagon and be over in a bit."

"Very well. I'll find something to fix for dinner." She waved him off and stepped indoors. The house was chilly but not too horribly cold. She fed wood into the stove and rubbed her arms as she hurried into the kitchen and stuffed the cookstove with wood and lit the burner.

She pulled a kettle of beef bone broth from the icebox and placed it on the stove. Then she retrieved the bread she'd baked the previous night. She sliced it and covered the slices with a towel to keep them from drying out.

Then she stepped into the lean-to, reached for the washtub, and focused on washing her apron again. Her hands were chapped from the many times she'd scrubbed the garment across the washboard, the hot water, and the amount of strong soap she'd used. Would the bloodstains ever come out?

The aroma of beef broth wafted from the kitchen. After wringing the water from her apron, she went to check on it.

When her brothers and Nathaniel arrived, Peter had a small sack of potatoes with him.

"Thank you." She gave him a hug and returned to the kitchen. There, she chopped the tubers into small pieces and dumped them into the warming beef broth. Peter and Nathaniel brought in firewood, and Kaneenawup kept the stove fed.

When the meal was ready, Nathaniel blessed it, and they ate. Rose was fine with the prayer, but how did Kane feel? She opened one eye and looked at him. He seemed all right with it. She grinned.

Conversation turned to the ongoing government inquiry about the events at Wounded Knee Creek.

Rose said, "I hope General Miles will have a change of heart and request an audience with me and other survivors to ask for our version of events."

Kaneenawup shrugged. "I doubt we'll be allowed to."

Rose bristled. "I don't see why not."

"I'll ask Agent Royer about it next time I see him," Nathaniel said.

"When will that be?" Rose asked.

"I've still got a bad feeling about this," Kaneenawup said in a low voice.

"It'll be Monday before I can speak with the agent. Not sure if he'll know anything by then." Nathaniel finished his meal and shoved back from the table. "I've got to go. I'm on duty tonight."

Rose stood and walked him to the door. "I'd like to speak to you more about this government inquiry."

He sighed. "I think it's a farce."

She shook her head. "Let's wait and see how things play out."

"Okay. I'll pick you up in the morning and take you for a ride. Remember the picnics we had, out by the trees near White Clay Creek?"

"Of course I remember. Especially that first one." Except for the soldiers' presence. She wasn't comfortable divulging that his words that day had seeped deeper into her soul. The way he explained how God could allow evil in the world had made sense, and she wanted to explore it further. Questions ran through her mind at night when she tried to sleep. She hoped he had answers. Tomorrow would be the perfect time and opportunity to find out.

They stared deep into each other's eyes for a long moment. Then he leaned in, wrapped her in an embrace, and squeezed her tight. She placed her head against his chest and was comforted by the sound of his heartbeat. Her own pulse thrummed like a steaming locomotive at full speed.

After a moment he abruptly let go and dashed out into the night. Rose closed the door and leaned against it. Being with Nathaniel felt right. He'd only just left, and already she longed to see him again.

The discussion between her brothers sounded blessedly civilized. She smiled and strode into the sitting room to join the conversation.

CHAPTER 29

Nathaniel awoke to Peter informing him that Rose had been called away to tend to a sick family. Their picnic to White Clay Creek would have to wait. At least he'd see her at dinner that night.

After tending to the stock, he paid a visit to Agent Royer that ended sourly. He left the man's office, slamming the door behind him. Anger boiled hot in him. Sweat beaded on his forehead, though the temperatures were near freezing. The inquiry was taking place, and considering the circumstances, he didn't know what he should tell Rose.

Due to testimony exclusion laws, Indians weren't allowed to testify, not even in their own defense. One soldier declared that since Indians weren't part of the military, they had no cause to testify.

Rose wasn't going to like this one bit.

They had been spending a lot more time together. He'd taught her more of the Lakota language, but they didn't hold regular lessons like they used to. He guessed they needed time to heal, but how could one heal from such a tragedy without Jesus?

He stopped in at the deputy's office to say hello to Peter. "Will you be at Rose's house again tonight for dinner?"

"Yes, and I'm bringing more potatoes, as many as I can procure." His friend stopped filling out reports and reclined in the chair, twirling the quill between his fingers. "You have something else on your mind?" Peter asked.

"Nothing I want to talk about right now."

Ezra entered the building and struggled with the wind to close the door.

Peter replied, "I'll talk to you later. I gotta show this youngster how we record the goings-on here in the office, in these ledgers." He gave the boy a playful jab on the arm.

The wind had picked up when Nathaniel stepped outside. He held his hat to his head to keep it from flying across the prairie. He needed to find food to take to Rose's house tonight. He couldn't expect her to feed him without contributing to the meal in some way.

He entered Dawson's and left minutes later with two bags of cornmeal, one for Sarah and one for Rose. It was time to pay his sister a visit, but he wouldn't be staying for dinner. He hoped Rose would forgive him for showing up with so little. He stuffed the cornmeal into his saddlebag and mounted his horse.

When he arrived at Sarah and Joshua's house, the children came outside and ran to him. After dismounting and hugging them tightly, he drew the cornmeal from his bag and knocked. Sarah called for him to enter. Why didn't she open the door herself?

He turned the knob and stepped inside.

Sarah sat up in bed.

He stopped short. "What are you doing in bed? You're not sick, are you? Should I go for the doctor or Rose?"

"Sorry, Brother. I'm more tired than usual lately." Dark half-moons rimmed the underside of her eyes.

Joshua stepped inside, whistling a lively tune. "Hello, Nathaniel. What brings you out this way?"

The grin on his brother-in-law's face stretched nearly to his ears. How could he smile when his wife was obviously sick? Nathaniel wanted to shake some sense into him.

Cooling his reaction, he said, "You're whistling and smiling like it's Christmas. Can't you see your wife"—he waved his arm in her direction—"my sister, is sick?"

Sarah interrupted. "Don't be angry, Nathaniel. There's a happy reason why I'm not feeling well."

"Now, what does *that* mean?" Nathaniel remembered when he'd been sick a few months ago. The raging fever, his raw, parched throat, the weakness, pain thundering in his head. It had been anything but a happy occasion.

Joshua wrapped an arm around him in a side hug. "Nothing another six or seven months won't fix."

Six or seven months! He couldn't imagine being sick for six or seven. . . Wait a minute. Realization dawned on him. He whipped his gaze to his sister.

"Sarah, you're going to have another baby?"

Her blushing cheeks and light chuckle told him it was true. He was going to be an uncle again. Releasing an Indian whoop that would have made Kaneenawup Rushing Water proud, he scrambled to his sister's side and took her hands in his. There was no way he'd ask her to cook corn bread for him now.

He said, "I brought something for dinner. I'd like to use your kitchen to make a pan of corn bread and leave the rest of the meal for you and the family."

Sarah pushed herself up off the bed. "I'm actually feeling all right now. I can make it."

"She's been napping all day," Joshua said. "If she says she's all right, she's all right. I could use your help outside."

"All right then." Nathaniel followed his brother-in-law to the barn.

"Can you help me with some repairs? It's been so cold I had to use three fence posts for firewood. I've only recently been able to visit the creek for more logs."

For the next hour, Nathaniel helped Joshua repair stalls for the cow and the new mule he'd recently purchased.

Joshua whistled while he worked and paused long enough to add, "I put our milk cow in with a friend's bull last September, right before the accident. I've been so busy trying to catch up with all the chores, I just found out she will calf in the summer."

"That's good. I hope it helps improve your finances after the loss of both your mules and your produce last fall." Nathaniel grinned at him. "You'll need it with another mouth to feed."

When the repairs were finished, Nathaniel went inside and said goodbye to his sister, niece, and nephew. Sarah handed him a square of corn bread. He promised to return when he could. "I'll bring any extra food I can find."

Then he left and rode toward town.

Rose finished her letter to her friend in Boston, stuffed it into an envelope, and licked it shut. Bridget's husband's business was investment banking.

Bridget also had a new baby, a little boy who, at two months old, looked just like his father. The proud new mother said she and her family wished to come for a visit. Rose penned a reply to let her know they were welcome but that supplies were scarce on the reservation and to bring enough food to feed themselves. Rose could hardly wait for a response.

She pushed herself away from her desk and donned her coat, along with a new scarf and hat she'd ordered. She'd also ordered a new medical book on nursing. She had debated between buying food or the medical book and came to the conclusion that the book had the potential to save more lives.

After mailing her letter to Bridget, she left the post office and strode toward the agency's administration building. She breezed past the startled desk clerk and marched into Agent Royer's office.

"Sir," she began, "I must impress upon you my desire to speak with General Miles. My testimony has worth." She crossed her arms over her chest. To her way of thinking, after the army had nearly blown her head off, the least they could do was to sit and listen to her testimony.

The agent blew out a deep sigh and turned his face to the ceiling. "Writing a statement is the only thing you can do. I'm happy to give it to the general, but I can't guarantee he'll read it, much less give it any credence."

Stunned, she dropped her arms to her sides. How could this be? Her breath hitched, and her hands trembled. She clasped them together in front of her. Did the army agree with newspapermen like L. Frank Baum, who called for the Indians' extermination?

Someone knocked on the agent's door and then burst into the room.

"Peter," she exclaimed.

"You're needed at the clinic."

Uneasiness settled over her. Was it due to the agent's declaration about her testimony or the threat of more sickness descending on the reservation? She'd hoped they were past the worst of the illnesses plaguing the tribe.

Peter said, "An injured man has arrived at the clinic, and the doctor is out visiting a sick elderly woman."

"Give me a moment to collect my things." Assuming her conversation with the agent had ended, she bolted from the building and raced home.

There, she reached for her bag and hurried to the clinic, hoping the injury wasn't too severe.

Clear skies and a bright sun created a picturesque landscape fit for a postcard but did little to warm the winter air. Rose stepped carefully to navigate around the slippery puddles. She longed for rain that would water edible plants and vegetables. Crops that would grow enough produce to feed her family at least.

When she entered the clinic, she eyed a man sitting on a cot, holding a bloody bandage to his left forearm.

"Hello, my name is Miss Rushing Water." She placed her bag on a table and drew out a clean cloth and a bottle of antiseptic. She doused the cloth and stepped to his side. "Can you tell me your name and what happened?"

"I'm Timothy." He winced as she applied the antiseptic to the wound. "I was digging a hole for a fence post. I plan to have stock come spring. Anyhow, I slipped, and the shovel got in my way as I fell."

"That doesn't sound like any fun at all." She smiled at him, hoping to put him at ease with her ministrations. She pulled the cloth away and examined the wound. It appeared that only the skin and a bit of muscle were sliced open. Thankfully, his other muscles seemed to have escaped injury.

"If you don't mind, Timothy, it would be best if I sutured your wound closed. Infection is a nasty thing to contend with, and I don't want this to get worse."

The man shrugged. "Whatever you think is best."

"Unfortunately..." She cringed. "I don't have anything to give you for the pain, but I'll suture as fast and safely as I can."

Peter, who had been standing in the door, asked, "Should I get him a stick to bite down on?"

Timothy looked indignant. "What kind of a yellowbelly do you think I am?"

Rose glared at her brother. "I don't think that will be necessary."

"Suit yourself." Peter shrugged and stepped outside.

In almost no time, she had sutured Timothy's wound and tied a clean bandage around his forearm. She handed him two additional dressings. "Keep the wound clean, and change the bandage twice a day. If the pain worsens or if it becomes red and tender to the touch, that means infection has set in. Come back to the clinic immediately. It could save your life."

"Thank you." He handed her a small, shriveled potato with a few sprouts. "You can cut this up and plant it and grow more," he said.

She declined the payment but said if he helped her start a garden once she got the supplies, she would call it a deal. He left as she gathered her things and stuffed them into her bag. Then she left a note for Dr. Eastman and exited the clinic. From there, she darted around mud puddles and past the post office on her way back to the agency administration building.

She entered then shrugged out of her coat and hung it on the coat-tree.

"Good afternoon, sir," she addressed the clerk. "I hope to finish my conversation with Agent Royer if he's not busy."

The man looked up from his typewriter and stared directly at her. He was silent for a moment, as if he fought an internal battle, and then he scooted his chair back and stood. "Right this way, Miss Rushing Water."

She followed him down the hallway, wondering what had caused the change in his demeanor. Compared to when they first met, he now acted much kinder and more thoughtful and patient with her. Had the massacre opened his eyes to the plight of her people? Regardless of the reason, he seemed more empathetic, and that brought a smile to her face.

The clerk ushered her into the agent's office. She thanked him, and he took his leave.

Agent Royer looked up from his desk and rolled his eyes. "What is it this time, Miss Rushing Water?"

Before she could reply, she heard the front door open and close with a loud bang. The noise of heavy boots thumping against the hardwood floor filled the air.

"What the devil?" Agent Royer stood and threw his quill pen onto the desk.

Several men in military uniform entered the room.

Rose's mouth went dry, and she gulped. What had she walked into? "If you'll excuse me, please," she croaked, then bolted from the room.

In the front lobby, she stared at the wide-eyed clerk.

A loud voice resounded from the agent's office. "Agent Daniel Royer, you are hereby relieved of your duties at Pine Ridge."

CHAPTER 30

January 10, 1891

Rose gulped, staring at the temporary agent, who was filling in until a new one could arrive and take over.

She watched the muscles of his jaw working and the hard glint in his eyes. She squirmed under his scrutiny.

"Royer was afraid something like this would happen. He tried to warn you people to abandon your ghost dancing, and now look what happened," he growled.

Rose stepped back as if he'd thrown scalding water at her. "Sir, all they did was dance. There's no harm in dancing. I understand the settlers and Mr. Royer were alarmed because they didn't understand it, but they meant no harm."

He reclined in his chair and folded his arms across his chest. "And how were the settlers to know? How were any of us to know that the dancers weren't preparing for war?"

She straightened her spine and lifted her chin. "Sir, since when has anyone been killed by dancing? Besides, it's not fair that the soldiers get to tell their side of the incident but the Indians don't get the same courtesy."

The agent shot to his feet, leaned forward, and placed his fists on the desk. "Miss Rushing Water, I'm sorry so many of your people were killed, but as I said earlier, you brought this on yourselves because of the dancing that was *strictly* forbidden."

The acid in his tone could have pickled fresh cucumbers.

"That doesn't excuse the soldiers chasing women and children across the prairie and shooting them in the back!" Her hands clenched into fists, her frustration boiling over.

When he stepped around the desk and stormed toward her, she withdrew until her back bumped against the closed door. She scooted aside and was rendered mute as he reached for the knob and flung the door open.

"I have it on good authority that none of you Indians will be testifying before General Miles, and there will be no arguing over the matter. I spoke with M. Gray Cloud about this two days ago, when I was relieving Agent Royer of his duties, and I don't care to reiterate the facts. That will be all, Miss Rushing Water."

Tears smarted in her eyes, but she refused to cry in his presence. Instead, she turned and bolted from the room, colliding with the desk clerk at the end of the long hallway.

He reached to steady her. "Are you all right, Miss Rushing Water? Do you need anything?" The compassion in his eyes was a nice change and one she appreciated, but what could he do to help?

"Thank you, but I'm needed at the clinic." She rushed outside, where an icy gust blew over her, nearly whipping the shawl from her shoulders. What had the agent meant when he said he'd already spoken with Nathaniel? She was determined to find out.

She stormed through the front door of the deputy's office. Ezra, the youngest and newest member of the force, jumped up from his seat and dropped his magazine onto the desk. "You're Peter's sister, right? He's not here."

"I'm not looking for him. I'm here to see Nathaniel."

The kid shrugged. "He ain't here either. He's at his sister's house and said he won't be back until after dark."

Rose sighed, her shoulders sagging along with her spirit. "Will you please tell him I'd like to speak with him as soon as he has time?"

"Sure thing." The young man nodded, dropped onto his chair, and picked the magazine back up.

Rose left and dodged puddles on the way to her house. Once inside, she lit the lamp, fed the stove, and sat in her rocker with a Jane Austen novel.

Questions rolled in her mind like tumbleweeds, hindering her ability to focus on the dilemma between Marianne and the unscrupulous Mr. Willoughby. The words blurred on the page, and before she reached the end of the chapter, she closed the book.

Her mind kept repeating what the new, temporary agent said about the Indian survivors not being allowed to speak with General Miles. The man claimed to have told Nathaniel, but Rose was hesitant to believe him. Curiosity mixed with dread pushed at the door to her heart. What exactly did Nathaniel know? How long had he known this information? And most importantly, why hadn't he spoken with her about it?

She wished she could confront him with the knowledge, but he would be gone until after dark, so it would be a while before she had the opportunity. Stewing over the matter would do nothing except swirl the uneasiness in her soul. While dressing for bed that night, she did her best to set the matter aside until she could speak with him.

But feelings of betrayal pricked her being like a thousand needles. No matter how many times she turned over in her bed, no matter how much she tried to focus on happier times, the issue relentlessly bored into her thoughts.

Nathaniel crawled out of bed and stretched his tired muscles. The entire previous day he'd spent working with Joshua, constructing a new corral for the mule his brother-in-law had recently purchased. Joshua's leg was not completely healed, and Nathaniel feared he might always walk with a limp. He hated to injure Joshua's pride, but the man had needed help with the corral.

Nathaniel had just finished dressing when Peter entered the barn.

"Hey, would you mind helping me settle a dispute at the Gardners'?" Peter asked.

The boot Nathaniel had meant to put on his foot dropped to the ground. Hoping his friend didn't notice his frustration, he picked it back up and shoved his foot into it. He'd hoped to see Rose. He needed to tell her what the new, temporary agent had said about Indians not being allowed to testify before General Miles. Though he detested keeping the news from her, he knew how upset she'd be and wanted to break the news to her as gently as possible.

"I suppose I can go to the Gardners', if you need me to." He didn't know the family well, but he knew they were hardworking, upstanding citizens. With an acquiescing sigh, he tied his bootlaces. He had a job to do. His conversation with Rose would have to wait.

As Peter saddled his horse, he muttered, "Someone has accused Matthew of stealing, but the troublemakers are telling a flimsy story, likely a ruse to get him arrested so they can steal his land. Local law enforcement wants our assistance."

"I'm happy to vouch for Mr. Gardner and be a character witness, if necessary." Nathaniel saddled his horse, mounted, and followed his friend to the homestead. By the time they arrived, Mr. Gardner had produced the proper paperwork. The local authorities had read the documents and then run off the unscrupulous claim jumpers.

Peter spoke to the authority in charge. "Nathaniel and I can stay the night in case the jumpers come back. You don't mind, do you, Nate?"

Much as Nathaniel itched to speak with Rose, he couldn't leave his friend alone to defend an innocent family, especially a woman with a baby. He stifled a groan. "Sure, I can stay."

"Thanks," Mr. Gardner said. "I'll see if Ellie can rustle up something to eat for you."

After a bowl of thin bean soup, Nathaniel bedded down next to his horse in the Gardners' barn, worrying about Rose. By now, she may have found out that the Indians wouldn't be allowed to testify. Prayers for her spilled from his lips as he drifted to sleep.

The next morning, with no sign of claim jumpers, he and Peter headed back to town. Nathaniel had been away from home for two days now, and he longed to see Rose. By now he'd had enough time to rehearse the impending conversation in his mind.

The clinic was the first place he stopped.

"Rose isn't here, but she'll return shortly," Dr. Eastman told him. "You're welcome to wait."

"Nah." He reached for the doorknob. "Just tell her to meet me in the barn when she has a chance."

Resuming his duties, he received a message from Dawson's General Store. The plow he'd ordered for the community had arrived. He'd envisioned the families taking turns using it, because none of them could afford one on their own. Not that he believed farming would pull his people from poverty, but having prosperous vegetable gardens would certainly help keep them fed, at least for a little while.

After he finished repairing and oiling the tack and hanging it on the wall, he trudged to the deputy's office. "Morning, Ezra. How did things go in my absence?"

"That nice nurse from the clinic has been asking about you. She told me to tell you she wants to talk to you right away and that it's important."

Heaviness settled over Nathaniel. He feared somebody had told her she wasn't testifying. He still couldn't believe it himself, that none of his people would be allowed to tell their version of the events at Wounded Knee Creek.

Nathaniel reached for a pencil and a scrap of paper and scribbled a note. He handed it to the boy. "I'm on duty now, so you can go, but will you deliver a message to Miss Rushing Water for me? She should be at the clinic by now. If not, can you please deliver it to her house?"

"Sure." The kid took the note and ducked out the door.

Nathaniel sighed, leaned against the counter, and braced himself for the whirlwind that was sure to blow into the office at any moment.

After stoking wood into the stove, he poured grounds into the coffeepot. He had a feeling he and Rose would need it. He placed the pot on the stove. Plunking into a chair in front of the desk, he opened the ledger book and reclined in his chair to read the reports for the past two days.

As he knew she would, Rose stormed into the office. Anguish radiated from her eyes. Her hair hung lifeless about her face. There was more to this than him being gone for two days. The ledger slipped from his hands and slapped onto the desk. She must know about not testifying.

"How long have you known, and why didn't you tell me?" she fumed.

"I found out just as the new agent was arriving, right before I rode out to Sarah's house to help Joshua with chores. By the time I returned to town, it was dark and not a light was to be seen anywhere. I meant to tell you first thing the next morning, but Peter said he needed my help at the Gardners' residence."

She squared her shoulders. "Kaneenawup is going to be really upset about this. Please tell me the military has so much evidence against those killers that our testimonies aren't needed. Please tell me General Miles has every intention of seeking justice for us."

"I hope that's the case." Nathaniel stood and strode to her side. He pulled her close and held her tight. "We have to have faith that justice will prevail. One officer I spoke with said the men went berserk instead of following their orders. Let's hope the soldiers tell the truth about what happened."

"I have hope." Rose snuggled against him.

He loved how perfectly she fit in his arms.

"But I'm going to insist that we be allowed to submit written statements. They owe us at least that much."

The coffee percolated, and the aroma filled the room. Nathaniel poured cups for both of them, then joined her at a small table.

"Guess what, Rose?" Nathaniel slapped his knee. "Sarah is expecting another baby. I'm going to be an uncle again this summer."

A smile spread across her face. "That's wonderful. Congratulations. I'll ride out to see her as soon as I'm able."

Though he was as happy as a fish in a stream, he worried about having another mouth to help feed. Rose had grown quiet. He wondered if she dreamed of having her own children someday. He did, and part of him dreamed of having them with her, but he didn't dare say it. Come to think of it, Rose had never mentioned wanting to have children. Did she? He hoped so.

He drank the last dregs of his coffee. "Rose, let's head to your house, and you can show me where you want your garden. The plow I ordered has arrived, and I can hardly wait to try it out."

"That sounds great, but what if someone needs you for something?"

"You live close enough to where they can find me, and it won't take long, but I'll leave a note in case someone needs me.

He stood, scribbled a note, and reached for her hand as they exited the building. Hope for a better future burned a little brighter in his heart, and he hoped that future included Rose. But as much as he wanted to tell her so, he thought it prudent to wait until the military inquiry was over.

CHAPTER 31

The day dawned bright and sunshiny, offering Rose glimmers of hope. The postmaster had sent word that she'd received a package and a letter from Bridget. Rose believed her friend had sent a book, but the letter, she hoped, contained news that Mr. Leon had received justice.

Nathaniel was so busy with his deputy duties since the massacre, she didn't wish to bother him with her questions about his faith. So she'd asked Reverend Cook from the Holy Cross Church to meet with her.

Perhaps he could answer the questions she had. She understood free will, that people had the choice to follow Jesus, but why did God allow people to abuse others in His name?

If someone used one of her medical instruments to harm a child, she'd want them hog-tied and thrown to the wolves! Some said one could not earn God's love, but others said that if she committed the slightest sin, God would send a lightning bolt to earth with her name on it. Who was right, or could they both be right? Was the truth somewhere in the middle? Oh, how these things vexed her.

Anticipating good news from Bridget and her meeting with the reverend, she believed the day would be a good one. She'd bathed the previous night and washed her hair. As she donned her best set of clothes, she had a spring in her step and a lightness to her mood that could only be attributed to her belief that justice would be done and that she'd have a clearer understanding of God.

Someone's knocking resounded through the house. She bounded to the door and flung it open. Her breath caught in her throat. Nathaniel stood there in his best suit, sporting a nice new haircut. His lopsided grin sent her pulse racing.

Overcome by his handsomeness, she temporarily lost her ability to form words.

He tugged at his collar. "Rose, you're beautiful. I better keep you on my arm, because I don't want any other man stealing you away."

"But what are you doing here?" Not that she wasn't happy to see him.

"I got the day off, so I stopped to see Reverend Cook. He said he was expecting you. I thought I'd come over and escort you there." His eyes darkened. "Plus, there are a lot of soldiers and military officials in town, and I don't want you harmed." She'd forgotten about General Miles' inquiry. Her shoulders drooped at the reminder. She ducked her head and drew circles in the dirt with the tip of her shoe.

"I hear a verdict, if one could call it that, will be announced soon." His tall frame leaned against the doorjamb.

"Thank you for the escort. I'm happy to be seen with you, but I need to stop by the post office first. There's a letter and a package for me from a friend in Boston."

"We can stop on the way."

She placed her hand into the crook of his elbow and strolled beside him.

Before they reached the post office, they met Peter.

Her brother said, "We've heard that General Miles is making an announcement today. The new agent wants a strong tribal police presence in town in case it doesn't go our way. He fears there'll be bad news and that the Indians won't take it well and will revolt."

Nathaniel squeezed her arm. "I don't think the news will be good," he said.

Silence stretched between the three as they walked. Rose believed Nathaniel and her brother were wrong. She believed justice would prevail, but she thought it best to remain silent. At least until they had cause to celebrate.

At the post office, she entered and signed for her package, then untied the string and tore off the brown paper. Just as she had predicted, it was another book. She ran her fingers over the detailed cover of *Treasure Island*, by Robert Louis Stevenson. She placed the book under her arm and tore open her friend's letter.

After reading the first two paragraphs, Rose wanted to crumple the pages and toss them into the nearest fire! If three women reported unscrupulous behavior on Mr. Leon's part, one would think the university would take notice. But such was not the case.

> *I'm so sorry to inform you, my dear Rose, that the university professors believe the three of you, but they are reluctant to reprimand, and thereby humiliate, Mr. Leon. So he's being transferred to another university, one in New York.*
>
> *Given the glowing recommendations the professors have given him, his reputation likely won't follow him. This grieves me, my friend, because I doubt Mr. Leon will mend his ways, and this leaves more innocent women vulnerable to his advances.*

Rose stuffed the letter back into the envelope. It had to be a mistake. First, she'd write Bridget and ask for the name of the university in New York. Then she'd write to the headmaster and every professor there and enlighten them regarding Mr. Leon.

"Rose?" Nathaniel stood just outside the post office door.

"Yes, I'm fine. Let's head to the church."

"All right," he said. "But stay close. We have to pass the military camp to get there."

They dodged around the muddy sections of the street on the way to their destination.

At the camp, they passed military conveyances and a few horses tied to hitching posts. The sun cast a warm glow over the tents. Rose held her hat to her head as she pivoted in a slow circle to take in the scene.

A number of men dressed in military uniforms milled about. Rose watched them snap to attention and salute a gentleman whose army uniform was covered in medals. The stern-faced officer returned the gesture and paraded into the nearest tent.

Rose kept her distance but still managed to peek into the tent the officer had entered. She observed the polished wood desks and a table strewn with papers. Her heart squeezed at the knowledge of not being allowed to testify. Mr. Leon might have evaded justice for the time being, but, for the most part, the military were an honorable and disciplined group of men. She had expected more from them.

Not a single military officer had spoken to Rose, Nathaniel, or her brothers about the events of that terrible day, and that didn't sit well with her.

Prickles raced along Nathaniel's spine. He bit back an angry comment as he and Rose stood outside the tent, listening to soldiers testify about what the Indians called a massacre. Exaggerations were one thing, outright lies were inexcusable.

He had personally seen many women and children shot in the back, miles from where the so-called battle took place. With commanding officers like Chivington, of the Sand Creek Massacre, and others calling for the complete extermination of his people, he believed the soldiers lacked credibility.

After listening for a few minutes, Rose wavered on her feet. Nathaniel caught her elbow and helped steady her. "Are you all right?" he asked.

Her sharp nod belied the pain in her eyes. "I can't listen to this anymore." Her voice cracked. "I want to go home."

The meeting with Reverend Cook would have to wait. Nathaniel placed a hand at the small of her back and hurried her toward her house.

They were still within hearing distance when a soldier emerged from the tent. "Colonel Forsyth is found innocent of wrongdoing and reinstated! Twenty of us will be receiving Medals of Honor!"

Whoops and hollers resounded from the military encampment.

Foreboding rolled across the plains like dark storm clouds. Nathaniel didn't want to be caught in the midst of it but feared he would be.

CHAPTER 32

Rose screamed and beat her fists against Nathaniel's chest. This was the proverbial straw that broke the camel's back. Her hair came loose from its pins and tumbled over her shoulders as she sobbed and wailed out her anger and frustration.

Innocent of wrongdoing.

Reinstated.

Medals of Honor.

Not only had Mr. Leon evaded any repercussions for his actions, but so would the soldiers who'd murdered her people. Nathaniel tried to calm her, but she wrenched loose from his grasp and bolted toward the barn.

Once there, and desperate to leave Pine Ridge, she wept with frustration as she saddled a horse. Despite wearing a skirt, she mounted and rode hard for the prairie, her destination unknown.

Many had hoped for justice, but instead, the soldiers who committed the terrible atrocities would face no consequences, while her people lay cold and dead in a mass grave. If that wasn't enough, twenty of the soldiers would be awarded Medals of Honor.

What, pray tell, was so honorable about shooting terrified children as they ran for their lives?

Tears streamed down her cheeks, and her hair flew in the wind behind her. A myriad of emotions collided in her and swirled in her stomach like a witch's brew. She breathed in deep, raspy gasps that left her lungs burning from the exertion.

The horse slowed its pace, and only then did guilt sweep over her for exerting the poor beast. She slackened the reins and spoke quietly to the animal as she rubbed its neck. The horse took deep, harsh breaths and then whinnied and shook its head.

Rose jumped to the ground, praying she hadn't driven the poor thing to its death. After a few moments, it was breathing more normally, and she exhaled with relief.

Only then did she realize where she'd ridden to. The banks of White Clay Creek, where she and Nathaniel had spent hours talking and getting to know one another. She dropped the horse's reins near the water so it could drink its fill. The way she'd ridden the winded creature, it was likely thirsty.

She craned her neck upward to view the branches that had once held leaves in shades of red, orange, and brown. How beautiful the scene had been then, before the terrible massacre that killed so many of her people.

Pangs of agony pierced her heart. She dropped to the ground, curled into a ball, and wept.

She cried for the children who were killed, for the parents and families who'd survived to face the losses. She cried for the children who were left orphans like her. She cried for the lost hopes and dreams she'd had of living as a traditional Lakota. She cried for the old ways that had been shot to pieces that terrible day.

Many times in Boston she had yearned to return to her people, to live as her elders once did, before white settlers arrived. Now it seemed those days were gone forever. Peter and Nathaniel were right. That painful reality, that loss, cut through her like a thousand knives.

Her gaze landed on the tree with branches that were shaped like a cross.

"Where were You?" Her scream, so filled with agony, left her throat raw. She picked up a rock and hurled it at the tree. A loud cracking noise pierced the air as the rock smacked against the trunk, right in the middle where the two branches stuck out, right where she imagined Jesus' heart would have been.

A chunk of bark broke off, leaving a bare spot that resembled a wound.

She screamed again. "Where were You when Mr. Leon attacked me? Where were You when my people were being shot to bits? Where were You?"

When her eyes and lungs burned from racking sobs, she sat up and fought to regain her composure. She mopped her cheeks with the hem of her skirt and tried to smooth the tangles from her hair. How wild she must look. She was glad Nathaniel couldn't see her now. Rising to her knees, she contemplated, did she have the strength to stand?

Hoofbeats resounded from somewhere.

She scanned the vast prairie and saw a rider approaching.

When the person drew closer, she saw it was Nathaniel. She groaned. The last thing she needed to hear was a sermon about how everything was in God's hands and that everything would be all right.

Things weren't all right! In her eyes, if this was how God handled things, He had forfeited His right to complain if she never set foot in a church again.

Nathaniel dismounted near her horse. Only then did she realize she hadn't tethered the animal to something. It was a wonder the creature hadn't run off. Nathaniel added her horse's reins to those from his mount and tied them to a nearby tree trunk, close enough that they could still drink from the creek if they desired.

Rather than approach her and fill her with trite Bible verses, he remained by the horses. That wasn't what she expected. She noted his haunted expression.

He took a deep breath and then another. "Rose," he said, "I don't blame you for being upset. We all are."

She jumped to her feet. Apparently, she did have the strength to stand. "I suppose now you're going to tell me that God works all things together for the good of those who serve Him, that He is close to the brokenhearted, that He will make everything right in His own time." She added a fiery bite to her tone. "I don't need trite platitudes. I want justice!"

He stepped back as if she'd tossed a bucket of scalding acid at him. "I wasn't going to say that."

She swiped a shirtsleeve across her nose, not caring that it was unladylike.

He held his hands up, palms facing her. "You feel what you feel, Rose, and there's no wrong in that. Look, I'm just as infuriated as the next Lakota. It's all right to be angry. Even Jesus was angry at the Pharisees."

Anger boiled hot in her veins. "How could God let this happen?"

"It's a fallen world, Rose, full of liars, thieves, and plenty of people who commit horrible sins against their fellow man."

Tears streamed from her eyes again. "Where was He? Where was God when men mowed children down like ducks in a shooting gallery? Our people are being decimated, and He's doing nothing to stop it!"

"You're furious with God right now, but you can't believe He's all fine and dandy with what happened. He isn't!" His hands clenched into fists. "It's all right to be angry, even enraged. I have big shoulders, Rose. It's all right if you want to cry on them. I'm right here."

She fell into his embrace and clung to him as sobs poured from the depths of her soul, wounds so deep and painful she wondered if she'd ever be whole again.

He wrapped his strong arms around her and ran his fingers through her tangled hair. His anguished cries mingled with hers, and she ached for him as much as for her entire tribe.

Dare she tell him about Mr. Leon? Would it tarnish his view of her? The way she viewed herself as tarnished?

"Nathaniel," she began, "while I was at the university hospital, I was tending to three sick children. The anatomy professor, Mr. Leon, stopped by to check on them. He asked me to get him a bottle of medicine."

Memories of that terrible night assailed her, but desperation to lance those painful recollections like a pus-filled boil overwhelmed her.

"I hurried to the dispensary to retrieve the bottle. When I turned to leave, he—Mr. Leon—grabbed me." Her anguished words erupted from the depth of her soul. "I screamed and fought."

His eyes widened, and she saw something dangerous enter his gaze. "What happened?" he asked in a low voice.

She took a deep breath. "I was able to get away before he could hurt me."

The air whooshed out of him in one long exhale, and he held her more tightly. "Thank God," he whispered.

His affirmation infused her with courage. She blurted more of the story. "In the scuffle, several bottles of expensive medicine were broken. Finally, I was able to kick him and run from the room. I thought that would be the end of it."

"But it wasn't?" Nathaniel rubbed the spot between her shoulder blades.

Rose chewed the inside of her cheek. She wanted to be honest with him. She didn't think he'd react the same way the nasty headmistress had, but what if he did?

He stooped to meet her gaze. "Rose, you're safe with me. I promise."

She drew in another deep breath. "Mr. Leon was questioned about the scratches on his face. He told everyone that I lured him into the dispensary for carnal purposes. People already think we're savages, so he easily convinced the university board of his version of the events." Sobs tore through her. She covered her face with her hands as if to hide her eyes from the ugly accusations.

He lowered her hands and cupped her cheeks. "I'm so sorry, Rose."

"What's worse, without that medicine, the children got sicker, and one of them nearly died. The cruel headmistress at the dormitory where I was staying beat me with a paddle and told me I wasn't fit to be around children."

"Oh, Rose." He wiped her tears with his thumbs.

Rose hugged herself and murmured, "She said I needed to confess my sins to God and beg His forgiveness. She made me memorize the Lord's Prayer, Psalm 23, and other scriptures. If I made a mistake in reciting them, I went without dinner."

"And you reached the point where you despised God and blamed Him for allowing these abuses to happen."

She lifted her head and stared into his eyes. "Yes. The university handed me my nursing certificate and sent me on my merry way."

"Rose," he said, "what that woman did—and said—was wrong. You are justified in your anger."

"Justified?" She stepped back, and his hands fell to his sides. It was the first time she'd heard someone say that.

"Yes, justified. But no matter how infuriated we are at these people, we can't allow these crimes—yes, Rose, what that man did to you was a crime—we can't allow them to stain our view of the world. We can't let our righteous anger fester into rage, bitterness, and a thirst for vengeance, no matter how much it hurts."

She shook her head, not wanting to believe it. "I'm sorry, Nathaniel, but I *want* to hate Mr. Leon, the headmistress, and those soldiers. I *want* to hate people who prey on the vulnerable. I *want* to hate everyone who thinks we ought to be exterminated. We're made in God's image too, aren't we? And they still want us wiped from the face of the earth. Wouldn't that be like wiping out a piece of God's creation?"

"Yes." His raspy reply was hardly louder than a whisper.

Her frustration bubbled again. "So how can I not be angry and bitter and scream for vengeance?"

He cupped her face in his hands again and stared deep into her eyes. "Rose, don't say that. The thirst for vengeance is what caused this tragedy.

Bitterness will do nothing but inflame the conflict and bring about the end of us. Hatred is a hungry monster that is never satisfied. It will chew your heart to pieces and render it unable to love. Is that what you want?"

He took a handkerchief from his pocket and handed it to her. She wiped her cheeks and nose.

"Rose, look." He pointed to the copse of trees. "Do you see the green sprouts budding on those tree limbs? Life continues even in the face of adversity."

She pulled from his arms and spun until she viewed the cross-shaped tree. The center was scarred from where her thrown rock had hit it. But bright green shoots were budding on the branches and on almost every tree there. How had she not seen that? And how was it possible at the end of January?

He continued, "We will remember these dark days and pass the stories along to our children and grandchildren, but we won't let this darkness define us. We will survive this, Rose, because we are a strong and resilient people."

"Yes, we are," she said. "No matter what evil people have done to us, we're still here. We always will be, because we're made in God's image."

Nathaniel was right.

Hatred, rage, bitterness, and the need for vengeance would destroy her, and then she'd be of no use to her people. If she was going to help the Lakota survive, she must find the strength within herself to rise from the ashes of this terrible injustice.

Memories of their picnic together filtered into her mind. Nathaniel had said that it would be silly to not use wood products just because some people chose to use wood for evil. Turning away from God for what those men had done was like vowing to never read a book again because evil men chose to use wooden carts to haul the cannons that killed her people.

She could almost hear Jesus knocking on the door of her heart.

"Nathaniel," she croaked, "help me choose love instead. Help me choose Jesus."

He pulled her close again and brushed the locks of hair from her face. "I'm so glad to hear you say that."

Together they knelt in front of the cross-shaped tree.

It was nearly dark when Nathaniel rode into town. Rose followed not far behind. He dismounted, opened the barn doors, led the horses inside, and then helped her dismount. Quietly, he stoked the embers in the potbellied stove.

Rose stood next to it, rubbing her hands together. "When I rode off this afternoon, I didn't think to take a coat."

"You weren't thinking much of anything, I bet, except finding a safe place to vent your feelings." Nathaniel removed the bridles and saddles from the horses.

"Let me put these away, and I'll be right back." He carted the items into the tack room and hung them in their places. His emotions were in a tangle, but he was glad that General Miles' military inquiry was over. Though it wasn't the verdict he'd hoped for, he hadn't expected anything different. His thoughts wandered to what Rose had told him about this Leon fellow and the headmistress's reaction to the situation. Righteous indignation coursed through him, followed by sadness and the desire to help Rose heal from the ordeal. She'd healed enough people; it was time someone helped her restore her broken heart.

"Nathaniel," Rose called.

"Yes?" He banished his thoughts to the recesses of his mind and strode to her side.

She didn't say anything, so he said, "Rose, will you be all right tonight? Would you like me to send Peter or Kaneenawup over to stay with you?"

She bobbed her head. "Yes, that would be fine. I'm tired, and I'm expected at the clinic in the morning. I'd be happy to bring you lunch tomorrow, if you'd like."

He pulled her into a close embrace and nuzzled the top of her head with his chin. "I'd like that. Thank you."

She merely hummed a short response, one he believed was due to her overwrought state of mind. "Let me walk you home," he said. "I won't stay, because I need to finish tending the horses."

They held hands for the short walk along the street. He hugged her again and then hurriedly returned to the barn. After he fed, watered, and combed the horses, he walked to the deputy's office.

"Hey, what's up?" Peter asked. "Is my sister all right?"

"She's fine, but a bit overwhelmed. I think she'd like you to stay with her tonight."

"Sure, I can do that." He called to Ezra, and the boy appeared from the rear of the building.

Nathaniel and Peter explained the situation and asked if he'd be all right for the evening.

Ezra straightened his spine and lifted his chin. "Take care of your sister, Peter. I can handle things here for the night."

"Thanks." Peter reached for a bag and stuffed a few items in it.

The boy disappeared into the stockroom.

Peter said, "It's hard to admit this, but I'm glad I didn't go with you to find her today."

Nathaniel scratched his chin. "Why is that?"

His friend ambled to the door and placed his hand on the knob. "She trusts you more than she does me. As much as that smarts, I'm glad she has someone to confide in. Someone I trust."

"Thanks, that means a lot."

"I gotta go." Peter turned the knob and disappeared into the night.

Nathaniel reflected in the quiet moment. It had been an overwhelming day. Though there was heartache, Rose had chosen to give God a chance. He imagined that, in the privacy of her own home, she was praying and working through things with the Almighty. And that brought a smile to his face.

"Ezra," he called to the boy, who was still rummaging around in the stockroom, "I'm in the barn if you need me. Have a good night."

"All right. I'll send for you if I need anything." He waved him off.

A minute later Nathaniel entered the barn. He rubbed the horses down again, then changed out of his day clothes while chewing on a few bites of jerky and a piece of dry bread.

Then he collapsed onto his cot. A wide yawn threatened to unhinge his jaw. Weariness washed over him, but he needed to settle his mind before he could sleep.

While lying in the dark, he recited his favorite scriptures and prayed for peace between the Indians and the whites. Though it lodged in his throat like a fish bone, he prayed for the umpteenth time for those who'd perpetrated the massacre and those who'd declared the guilty to be innocent. If they ever asked God's forgiveness and truly repented for what they'd done, he believed their sins, though forgiven, would haunt them for their entire lives. What a sad pickle they'd gotten themselves into. In that moment, a drop of pity seeped into his soul and brought a tiny measure of peace and something he hoped was healing.

The barn door creaked open, and only then did he realize morning had arrived.

CHAPTER 33

Months had passed since the massacre at Wounded Knee Creek. Spring budded on the reservation, covering the rolling hills with a carpet of green grass. Rose spent her days keeping busy at the clinic, planting her new garden, and tending to her chickens. A few months ago, she'd purchased a rooster and three more hens. Eight eggs had hatched, and she now had more than a dozen of the feathery creatures.

Dusk settled over the prairie. Rose scattered the chicken scratch on the ground and watched the birds scurry to gobble it up. "Hey, chickens, I'm marrying Nathaniel tomorrow, and he'll be helping me take care of you."

Her heart thrummed with anticipation, and contentment settled over her. After watching the chickens for a few more minutes, she lifted her chin and walked into the house.

She spent the evening perusing the scriptures. Tonight, the words leaped off the page and sprang to life before her eyes.

"And we know that all things work together for good to them that love God, to them who are the called according to his purpose."

When her clock chimed ten, she closed the book and mulled over what she'd read. There was much truth and hope tucked within those thin pages. She climbed into bed and drifted into peaceful slumber.

Just as the sun began to color the sky, her chickens woke her with a series of clucks and a crow or two. Excitement seemed to electrify the atmosphere.

A knock resounded on her front door, and Sarah's voice called from outside.

She leaped from her bed and rushed to invite her soon-to-be sister-in-law inside.

"I'm here to help, and don't worry." Sarah placed her hands over her pregnant belly. "I won't overdo it."

Rose started a pot of coffee and hurried to prepare dozens of pieces of fry bread.

Sarah brushed flour from her hands. "Our brothers have been busy making jerky from the wild antelope they shot and butchered."

"I'm happy to hear that." Rose placed the pieces of fry bread on a cooling rack. They would be her offering to the guests who attended the ceremony.

While the bread cooled, she slipped into the dress Sarah had helped her sew. Her friend fastened the row of buttons down the back of the garment. Rose considered silk a frivolity and had forgone the use of it. Pale pink flowers adorned the white cotton fabric she'd chosen. Its softness caressed her skin.

"Joshua is here. I have to go." Sarah pecked her on the cheek and rushed out the door.

Rose laid her fingertips on her cheek and smiled, thankful to have a sister.

Next, Rose wove a pale pink ribbon into her hair as she braided it. Necklaces, fashioned from beads sewn onto strips of leather, completed her ensemble.

Minutes later, her brothers arrived at her front door in a new buggy. Peter, dressed in a new suit, stood next to Kaneenawup, who wore traditional buckskin that looked new. Rather than bicker about their differences, her brothers had learned to accept each other as they were.

She placed her basket of fry bread next to the box of antelope jerky. Kaneenawup helped her into the buggy. Peter drove them toward White Clay Creek, to her and Nathaniel's special picnic area, where the ceremony would take place.

The copse of trees came into view, as did the cross-shaped tree, now wearing a cloak of green leaves. Rose was pleased to see the crowd of guests who'd gathered for the occasion.

Sarah held her hands to her rounded abdomen and greeted Rose with a hug. "After today, we'll truly be sisters."

Joshua kept Chaske and Winuna busy at the creek. Peter and Kaneenawup helped unload the food, then joined Nathaniel by the tree.

Rose paused to admire the man she loved. His long hair was slicked back, and he wore a headband embellished with a feather and many beads. His smile, as bright as the morning sun, nearly undid her senses.

"Welcome to the family." Peter beamed and clapped his friend on the shoulder.

Dr. Eastman and Elaine Goodale strode forward to congratulate them, as did Ezra.

The Gardner family arrived next. Matthew held their son in his arms as he helped Ellie from their wagon.

Reverend Cook announced it was time for the ceremony to begin. Nathaniel and Rose stood before him, and Peter and Sarah took their places alongside them. Reverend Cook hadn't said more than two sentences when the rattling of horse hooves echoed in the distance.

"What on earth?" Rose used her hand to shield her eyes from the sun.

A fancy buggy crested a hill, the kind that wasn't often seen on the Pine Ridge Reservation. Murmurs swept through the crowd as it moved toward them. Who could the occupants be?

The conveyance lurched to a halt at the top of the creek bank. The door popped open, and a woman in fancy clothes emerged.

"Bridget!" Rose hiked up the hem of her dress and sprinted to meet her friend and to pull her into a hug.

"Your last letter said you were getting married," Bridget gushed. "I wanted so badly to be by your side, I told my husband it was time for a visit. We boarded the train, and here we are."

Bridget wrapped Rose in another warm hug. When she released her, she said, "This is my husband, John." Bridget placed her hand in the crook of his elbow. "Sweetheart, you remember my friend, Rose Rushing Water, from the university."

The man extended his hand. "I believe we met briefly at graduation. It's a pleasure to see you again. And this is our daughter, Rosy. We named her after you. Would you like to hold her?"

Rose was touched by their trust in her. "No, I, uh—" Before she could protest further, John deposited the baby in her arms. Rosy smiled at her, babbled two nonsensical words, and reached for her necklace.

Warmth flowed in Rose's heart. Babies were wonderful indeed.

Bridget said, "I've acted as a nurse midwife to two of my friends. Seems I have a knack for it, and John approves."

This was a relief to Rose. Though Nathaniel had said he'd support her nursing endeavors, Bridget's situation gave her hope that she would be able to continue nursing even after children arrived.

Rose proceeded to introduce her friends to each other.

For the second time, Reverend Cook announced it was time for the ceremony. Peter wrapped a ragged blue blanket around Nathaniel's shoulders, and Kaneenawup placed one around hers.

Reverend Cook said, "These tattered blankets represent your past life as a single man and woman. Now is the time to shed them and leave your old life, and its tribulations, behind you."

Rose and Nathaniel shrugged off the blankets.

"Now." The reverend nodded to both of them. "Step into your new life with each other."

Nathaniel grasped her hand, and together they stepped forward. Peter and Kaneenawup draped a brand-new white blanket around them.

Reverend Cook continued. "Let this blanket represent your new life together and the love of Jesus. By staying close together, under His care, He will keep you warm and safe from the enemy."

The reverend added traditional wedding vows and finally pronounced, "Nathaniel Gray Cloud, you may kiss your bride."

Nathaniel swept Rose into his arms and kissed her soundly to the cheers and applause of their guests.

He released his grip, and her eyes focused on him, and then on the cross-shaped tree. She inspected the spot that had been damaged by the rock she'd thrown all those months ago. The area was marked by a scar. Though the scar would always be there, it hadn't stopped the tree from growing bigger and stronger, from branching out, from sprouting a multitude of leaves.

Rose believed her people were a lot like that tree. The atrocities committed against the Lakota tribe had scarred the hearts of many, but those scars could not stop them from growing mightier and bonding closer together.

They were a resilient people, with the will to survive and thrive. That tree, with its scarred bark and green leaves, planted its message deep in her soul, a gift for her and her family of an enduring hope in Jesus for a brighter future.

AUTHOR'S NOTE

Dear Reader,

I'm almost loath to say this, but to date, *The Caregiver of Wounded Knee* is the hardest book I've ever written. In researching Rose and Nathaniel's story, I read every book about the massacre that I could get my hands on. I found the *Eyewitness at Wounded Knee* by Richard E. Jensen, R. Eli Paul, and John E. Carter and *"All Guns Fired at One Time" Native Voices of Wounded Knee, 1890*, compiled and edited by Jerome A. Greene, to be the most beneficial.

Helpful documentaries and movies I watched included, but were not limited to, episode eight of *The West*, a PBS documentary series by Ken Burns, and *Bury My Heart at Wounded Knee*, based on the book by Dee Brown.

I visited the South Dakota history museum in Rapid City, South Dakota, where I sat in a tepee, a replica of the ones used in the time before whites came to America. *Tepee*, by the way, is the Lakota word for "dwelling." I was surprised at how big those structures were. I spoke with the curators there, who referred me to a bookstore that sold many good books about the massacre.

I also ventured to Pine Ridge, South Dakota, and stayed on the reservation for a few days. It's a beautiful part of the country, with rolling hills that stretch for miles and a plethora of trees that lined the creeks I saw. While there, I spoke with as many people as I could who were willing to talk to me about that terrible day. The stories I heard were so tragic, they literally kept me up at night.

I owe a debt of gratitude to the Re-Creation Center, an Assembly of God church in the community of Oglala, whose members welcomed me with open arms and a delicious hot meal. They answered my questions and kindly invited me to return. I hope to do so someday.

I took flowers to the Wounded Knee Massacre Memorial to pay my respects and placed them on the mass grave. The bodies of more than 140 men, women, and children are buried in what was a rectangular-shaped pit, many of them having been robbed by relic hunters. As I walked the length of the grave, I couldn't help but think of the countless victims throughout history who have been buried like this.

I trudged along the fields where the massacre took place and beside the Wounded Knee Creek. The creek was surprisingly small. I could have hopped across it in three steps, and the banks were steeper than I thought they'd be. I tried to imagine the terror those poor victims faced that horrific morning and in the hours that ensued, lying on the cold snowy ground, helpless, afraid, dying with no one there to comfort them.

I literally wept over these pages as I wrote and I begged God for the strength to keep writing, which He supplied, as evidenced by the book you're holding.

To Him be all the glory.
Debby

Debby Lee was raised in the cozy little town of Toledo, Washington. She has been writing since she was a small child, and has written several novels—but never forgets home. The Northwest Christian Writers Association and Romance Writers of America are two organizations that Debby enjoys being a part of. As a self-professed nature lover, and an avid listener of 1960s folk music, Debby can't help but feel like a hippie child who wasn't born soon enough to attend Woodstock. She wishes she could run barefoot all year long, but often does anyway in the grass and on the beaches in her hamlet that is the cold and rainy southwest Washington. During football season, Debby cheers on the Seattle Seahawks along with legions of other devoted fans. She's also filled with wanderlust and dreams of visiting Denmark, Italy, and Morocco someday. Debby loves connecting with her readers through her website at www.booksbydebbylee.com

MORE FROM THE ENDURING HOPE SERIES

When life seems weighed down by challenges, there are always pillars of enduring hope and love to be discovered.

The Angel of Second Street
By Barbara Tifft Blakey

Ida Dempsey tries to keep secret her efforts to help prostitutes on Second Street and share Jesus with the Chinese immigrants, but her kind-hearted efforts get her into deep trouble.

Paperback / 979-8-89151-112-5

The Undercover Heiress of Brockton
By Kelly J. Goshorn
A socialite working as a journalist and a compassionate firefighter unite to investigate the aftermath of the 1905 Brockton, Massachusetts, shoe factory explosion.

Paperback / 979-8-89151-177-4

The Daughter of Shiloh
By Terri J. Haynes
A celebratory convention turns into a tragic stampede on September 19, 1902. When Lealia Bevard is caught in the fray, will her injuries steal all hope for her future?

Paperback / 979-8-89151-199-6